HANDS
OF AN
ANGRY GOD

HANDS

OF AN

ANGRY GOD

a novel

Douglas Martin

Published by P.E. Nowell
Advance, N.C., U.S.A.

ISBN 978-1-7324792-0-3

Belief wisps fragile, unsure.
Doubt waits sturdy, certain.

CHAPTER ONE

Wilderness, Upstate New York
Early Winter 1776

Barren tree limbs overhead angled dark against empty gray sky. Winter scythes, bitter blades poised angry.

The young farm boy glanced away uneasy. Eager cold nettled his hands and face, wiled his throat and wormed his spine. Its harsh edge ran jagged, hungry this day. Hide coat collar upturned, he shivered deep.

A mountain creek rippled alongside, spare sound against the thick brood of surrounding vale. Squat knees to chin at the water's edge, he prodded loose rocks with a stick in search of small stones to skim or use as marbles. Remembered smells from the family meal kettle the night before mocked his nose and empty belly.

Wind carried the anxious bark of his dog from beyond the woods, vague alarm, but the insistent push of water and dried forest rustle muted further worry. He thumbed grit from an uncovered flat black stone on his open palm.

Across the creek the presence of a boy like him peeked from behind a tree. Part real and part made up, the wisp and sometimes companion always stirred dim memory, pained pieces of a shadowed other life.

"Saw you first," the farm boy lied.

He extended the stone in pretend gift and offer of play. The presence approached to the edge of the far creek bank.

"Last time you took my skip. Cheat." The farm boy shifted the stone back and forth between hands, sibling guile learned early.

He offered the rock again but the presence faded among the trees. Ire soured the farm boy's throat. He disliked being alone and wanted his play.

So he chirped. Soft at first then louder and more insistent, the distressed call of a young bird for its mother. A cruel tease. The ploy often drew the presence back.

Stubborn, the farm boy waited sure but impatient cold again crept inside his coat and he threw the stone into the dark creek current. Neither would have the prize. His revenge.

Eyes closed, he surrendered deep within the easy swirl of water sound. Numb quiet, his shell, and the place he hid. Soft pops, muffled noise and the dog's continued bark carried past without his heed.

The boy's head cocked, eyes wide. Gunshots and angry shouts burst, jarring and clear beyond the woods behind. He hurried to the edge of the tree line beside a small fir.

In the clearing dense black smoke roiled off the thatched roof of his family cabin and flames crackled inside its windows. Sharp burn smells pinched the boy's breaths and frightful war whoops ravaged his ears.

Indian warriors in the yard shot the plow ox, torched crop sheds and chased scurried chickens. His father defended with a field rake but fell under an attacker's tomahawk and the dog, struck repeatedly by arrows and clubs, yelped and died nearby.

At the cabin steps his mother wrested a younger sister's limp body from an Indian and cradled it to her chest. Arm raised against a looming death blow, she saw her son at the tree and reached outstretched fingers toward him in final desperate plea.

"Run!" she screamed. "Run!"

Instinct to flee pounded the boy's heart and limbs. Instead he quivered, wide eyes full and unblinking, rooted and overwhelmed by the sudden destruction of everything he knew.

Face and shaved head painted red and black, a fierce Mohawk held his grisly war club over the dog's body. Eyes rose to the boy, he charged forward and shrieked a frenzied prey beast cry of ancient menace and blood hate.

Pierced by the awful scream, the farm boy stumbled backward and fled into the vale. Harsh tree limbs poked his cheeks and briars slit his hands. He knew not where or how to hide.

Hope. Mercy. Escape. The boy pleaded and promised as he ran, scared incoherent sounds from a dark nameless inner place. Violent snaps of sticks and limbs and gaining footfalls by his enemy taunted in cruel answer.

The boy churned into the waist deep creek, struggled and stalled. Cleaved by frigid water his life warmth bled into the dark stream and he dwindled, almost ceased. The presence of the other boy pulled him forward.

The farm boy clambered and scraped over rough-edged rocks at the bank and lunged uneven among desolate trees, breaths strained and frantic. Splashes and guttural grunts closed behind and he dared not look back.

A second piercing shriek, savage and immediate, staggered the farm boy to his knees. The presence looked back, sorrowed and afraid, hands outstretched but too far.

Terrified deep in his being the farm boy crawled desperate, helpless against suffocating mounds of dead leaves and unforgiving fate, bewildered by the abrupt end to his short unlived life.

◑

Dead autumn leaves.

All around Dayne mounds of dead leaves hid the ground. The world robbed of color, life. Winter's cruel, unwanted end.

His young fingers traced the leaves' brittle veins and edges, felt their sadness and pain. Another loss, another burden he did not understand. Hope of spring seemed too long, too far.

Dayne turned back through empty woods. Wide eyes up he squatted knees to chin beside a bouldered pool. High overhead a rain swollen stream surged off a rock ledge and thundered down. Dayne drifted within the cocoon of unending sound and fury, safe from further emotions.

Behind rankled veils of spray mist layered crags in the rock formed the solemn face of an old Indian. The sunken eyes never moved yet always watched, an unwelcome follow. Inside the mouth crease animal bones and strange wall markings guarded a small cave. Dayne thought the den a hiding place for unsettled spirits and entered only with his brother. Several times he offered the Indian bits of crops or colored crystals from his father's fields to make peace. None worked. Like him the stone chose stubborn silence.

Resentment bubbled Dayne's throat. He wanted someone to share his struggles to speak and know his fears. Stood, he screamed loud and long until his breath ended, a release of bitter torment and frustration. The face gave no sign it cared and the waterfall's stark roar drowned his anger, swept it away unheard. Thwarted, Dayne dwindled and closed his eyes.

Tugs on his loose shoe tie ended the wallow. A black and white kitten rolled playful and pawed Dayne's muddied breeches, lost interest and moved away along the stream.

Dayne followed. Burrowed deep within his coat he rummaged hazelnuts from a pocket, meager breakfast the price of his early morning flight from the farm.

Stubborn frost crusted rocks in damp recesses and long puddles marred the flood ravaged lower stream bank. With a stick Dayne prodded tadpoles, curious how such small toil and squirm changed into large nimble frogs. The lonely call of an unseen bird drifted past.

Small hot springs steamed the air downstream. Colored mineral deposits pitted exposed rock and Dayne's fingers briefly chased rising vapors. Along the upper bank he searched small clefts and crevices for trinkets or marks of passage sometimes left by Indians or hunters.

Between root bumps at a tree he uncovered his secret buried cloth of prized possessions gathered on prior walks across the farm. Small pine cones, animal teeth, charcoaled wood and deer hooves hinted the past. His favorite, a shattered young turtle shell missing its corner, spoke grim fate and violence yet always soothed his anxious thoughts. Dayne wanted such a shield and place to hide behind.

An unexpected object at the bottom of the hole surprised his hand. Grit scraped clear, the black flint arrowhead glistened cold and hard on his open palm, chiseled edges jagged and sharp. Whether weapon or tool he could not tell, only that it was meant for him. Ancient menace seeped Dayne's fingers, blunt reminder and promise. The back of his head pinched and swirled, snared by cruel fears, hurts and angers from dark dreams which often haunted his sleeps.

Threat and betrayal surged. Only the old Indian knew his secret spot and he whirled to confront the waterfall, a voiceless demand. The stone face stared unmoved.

Dayne rocked back and forth, arms closed tight to his body. The water and woods carried unspoken rhythms, life as it came, yet also unseen spirits, omens and unkind nature. Over recent months ill change crept close along edges of the forest and into his father's fields. Disturbance, violent upheaval would follow. The arrowhead proved it.

The lonely bird called again and an answer came from dense laurel thickets on the slope across the stream.

Alarmed, Dayne glanced up. His father said Indians sometimes made such sounds and often he ran afraid through fields and forest to escape unseen enemies. He peered uneasy, unsure among barren woods. Only the waterfall, the push of the creek and scratch of windblown leaves on the ground disturbed the quiet.

Dayne placed the arrowhead in his coat pocket. He would hide it in the fields far away from his eyes and thoughts. Cloth and hole covered over he gathered the kitten, turned along the path and crested the upper bank to overlook a narrow knobbed valley.

Scattered crop remnants poked uneven farm fields and a distant road creased wilderness beyond. Forbidding mountains loomed over all, stark and unforgiving, giant bony beasts buried restless and angry in the earth.

A large snowflake settled on Dayne's nose. He wiped away the blur and started forward reluctant. Dips and rises changed his direction and sodden ground clutched his shoes. In the middle of the field he clawed under an exposed rock sheath to bury the flint but it pulsed his hand with curiosity and guiled his ears with unclear whispers. He returned it to his pocket.

Tired and cold, on the far side of the fields he ducked between rails on the last fence and led the kitten along the bordering road. The stone inn, large barn and rear pastures of his father's farm waited ahead.

Isolation. Confusion. Secrets. Home.

He stopped. Hated stench came on chill wind. Dayne shuttered too late.

Killing day on the farm.

CHAPTER TWO

WHITE VAPORS CURLED from a roiling cauldron in the barn yard.

Thick forearms bared defiant against the cold the Innkeeper hoisted a scalded hog carcass by its hind legs from the water with rope and pulley set over a tree limb. Line anchored to the trunk he gutted the hog, scraped entrails down slanted planks into a large pot and wiped the long killing knife on his smithy apron. Hogs in an adjacent pen jostled and snorted, agitated by sight and scent of the slaughter.

With a block scraper the Innkeeper scoured the reddened hide to remove grit and leftover tufts of hair. Memories of hog killings in his youth drifted, twisted echoes and images. During gatherings of neighbors over several days at the end of autumn his father and other men killed a dozen or more hogs for winter meat. The women made lye soap, linens and harvest pies and the children played games and avoided work until forced to join. Death and butchery, seasonal realities on a farm, became welcome social ritual.

As a boy the curious white sticks of an animal's bones and dense coils and viscous ooze of its organs fascinated and repelled, mysteries and life lessons most blunt. As an adult he still dreaded the long day of grisly work but always counted the meat.

He learned to kill by doing. His father made sure he knew the cold hard of the blade, raw shudder in his arm as he slit the hog's throat and surprised squeals as blood gushed pools on the ground. Forced to stoke the horrid boil of the cauldron he often flinched at the black glisten of the hogs' scalded unseeing eyes yet seldom turned away. Taint from the awful, overpowering stench never left. His sons would know the same.

The Innkeeper lowered the carcass to a work bench, untied the pulley and retrieved his knife. "Dayne! Dayne! Is time. No more hiding."

He crossed the yard to the corner of the open barn door. "You are eleven. Old enough for this. Come, help me and learn the ways of the farm."

The kitten meandered forward and flopped at his feet.

"I know you watch," the Innkeeper said. "A hard chore but needed. Meat for winter and lard for cooking. You will eat the hams and loins soon enough. Earn the right."

Stubborn silence. Unhealed wounds and constant festers stayed between them once more. The Innkeeper frowned and turned back across the yard.

Inside the barn Dayne emerged from a stall and peeked through gaps and knot holes in sideboards. His father entered the hog pen, knife hid but poised at his side.

Dayne moved to the edge of the barn door, upset he could not see the hog with dark face spots and an ear gnawed soft by a sibling. The former piglet often followed him over farm fields.

Scared squeals and frantic snorts from the hogs rippled the air. Afraid, Dayne covered his ears and shut tight his eyes but could not escape the sounds. Kitten clutched tight to his throat he stepped stiff and awkward, lured into the yard by grim urge.

His father dragged the new hog kill from the pen. Its gnawed ear flopped as always.

Tears welled Dayne's eyes. Half formed words, anguished utterances and angry bursts of rage and shame seared his throat but no sounds came. He heaved, strangled by violent silence.

Hog bled into a bucket, his father gutted the carcass on the pulley and lowered it to the cauldron.

The iron monster's cruel boil fouled Dayne's nose and he glanced away, drifted back and dropped his eyes a final time. A quick goodbye to the hog girded his confused heart.

His father stepped in front. "Like you, my first killings I saw only the hogs. Animals are part of the farm as any harvest. One day you will see it different, if not better."

Bloodied knife open in hand his father knelt. Imposing strength, full dark beard and hard reluctant face made a difficult mask Dayne struggled to see himself within.

"Killing is survival," said his father. "You must learn how. Here, for the kitten too."

Offered crackling from a small kettle, Dayne shook his head. His father forced his chin up and the grip smudged blood across Dayne's cheek.

Jaw clenched, Dayne resisted the touch and wiped at the taint.

His father withdrew the crackling. "Speak to me, son. The stubborn silence of these years must end."

Dayne shook his head. He placed two fingers from the tip of his nose across his mouth and extended his hand out, silent words trailed from an unseen string. His father reached for the fingers but Dayne moved away. His father's frown deepened, cold displeasure.

Crackling tossed back into the kettle, his father turned toward the fire. "A poor choice. Yet your own."

Afraid of further temper Dayne's mind raced, wavered and emptied. He escaped across the yard to the inn's rear cellar door.

The Innkeeper set aside the knife, rinsed his arms over a bucket and brooded. The water's slow drip summed his dismay and ire. Neither he nor his son reached the other. No cause. No reason. No answer.

He turned back, another try. Too late. Weary, resentful he roughly stoked the fire, hoisted the hog from the cauldron and scraped hard with the block.

Finished with the carcass, the Innkeeper crossed to the barn. An empty milk pail left by Dayne in the main corridor annoyed and he stubbornly yelled for his son, aware a reply would not come. In the cow's stall he uprighted a stool with his boot and began his son's chore.

Garnet-colored with distinct black flank stripe the Welsh Red cow thrived on the farm's rough pasturage, doubled as a draft animal and produced enough milk for butter and cheese. His favorite, he saved over three years to buy her from a farm fifty miles distant and endured several long return trips before she bred with the seller's bull.

The cow munched dried cornstalks and her bell rolled soft, content.

"The old Dutchman along the river wants you back," the Innkeeper said. "I will not let that happen. Not now. His need is not my bargain."

Pinched through his hands into the pail the warm rush of pungent raw milk soothed and reassured. Eyes closed and head rested against the Red's sturdy side, he listened to inner sounds of her spring calf, nature's affirmation of new life on killing day.

The Innkeeper lingered longer than needed before he stroked the cow's broad forehead and left the stall. Arthritic hands briefly limbered by the udder, he flexed free but knew age and the day's use would again swell and pain his bones. Often he wished away such unfair hurts and reminders, visible and not, a guilty man's hope his past might fade and cease.

It never did.

◐

In the broad pasture behind the barn the Innkeeper dragged an empty wood sled up the steep slope of an old apple orchard. Planted in the farm's early years the trees declined, worn by exposure and blight, and repeat spring seedlings never survived the harsh ground.

Lifeless fields and the forbidding surround of wilderness stirred chronic melancholy and a hard frown. Ragged mist straggled from mountain tree lines and deep cold and snow weighted brooding overcast beyond, another storm in an already too wet season. Winter came early.

Lungs and legs daunted by the climb, the Innkeeper paused to gather. His cautious eyes roamed ridges and likely hiding places among lower woods and creeks. Too often neighbors lost lives or animals to marauders, unprepared or unarmed on their own lands. Several times in recent months an old blanketed Indian stood watchful high among the stark woods, an unwelcome sentinel and harbinger. The Innkeeper kept a long rifle constant and ready at his side.

With an ax he felled a tree split by summer lightning, chopped the wood into lengths and stacked the sled. Rifle placed on top he looped the tie rope twice around his chest, grunted and pulled the load beast-like back down soft cloying ground of the slope.

Fields and pastures stretched before him. His life carved among rocky hillsides, creeks and stands of stubborn timber. Across the narrow valley the land leaked through a gap toward the distant curl of a broad river. Beyond rose mountains and the ominous forests of Iroquois lands.

Farm buildings occupied a small flat. Dug into the side of a rise the stone inn's two upper stories fronted the road and the basement cellar and tavern accessed the rear yard. An oversized five-sided barn dominated, his testament of persistence, pride and hard won survival.

The Innkeeper pulled the sled into the yard through the barn gate. The harsh stench of hog entrails remained on the breeze.

He stopped. Across the yard the saddled massive black draft horse of Thaler, a local militia enforcer and instigator, stood the post rail outside the basement tavern. Four prisoners filled a slatted iron cage on back of a wagon. Tied behind the wagon an aged, overloaded ox carried sacks of apples, gourds, seed corn, bundled tools and house items.

The Innkeeper rolled stiff shoulders and tightly exhaled. Spawn from the taint of politics and war, the jail wagon's increasing visits nettled his stubborn, careful neutrality.

Quayland rode into the yard past the wagon and dismounted at the well. Awkward and gaunt, he resembled a muddied wayward heron. Mismatched kerchiefs secured an oversized red tricorn hat and concealed his long neck.

"The weather turns ill," said Quayland. "I should not have ridden."

The Innkeeper unloaded wood at the cauldron. "You look a man with the toothache."

Quayland touched his hat and kerchiefs. "A windy day but undaring, I admit."

"How goes the river?"

"Still swollen from the rains, the ford impassable. But the creeks run strong with good drops and flows. A mill owner would do well here."

"Some have," said the Innkeeper. "My father was one until fire took the site."

Quayland unstrapped a surveyor's tripod and compass box from behind his saddle. "Most of the original names on the land patents in the valley are Rhinelanders, not English."

"Palatines, religious outcasts. The first here. Also Welsh, Dutch, some Scots. Only the stiff-backed survived."

"And you?"

The Innkeeper pulled the sled toward the basement. "Mostly Welsh. Some other."

Quayland followed, bow-legged undulations of fits and stops like a poorly jointed marionette. He removed a gnawed lemon peel from his mouth.

"Such bitter fruit are scarce here," said the Innkeeper.

The surveyor pried a seed from his teeth and spit. "A small indulgence which succors my throat."

Wood from the sled stacked atop head high piles at the tavern door the Innkeeper paused beside the black draft horse tied to the rail. Long coarse hair draped its lower legs, cruel quills.

"The animal daunts more than the wagon." Quayland said.

"Is meant to."

A Scottish farmer who once helped repair the barn reached out between cage slats. "Do you remember me work? Will you not help a neighbor?"

The Innkeeper did not approach. "Why this wagon?"

"These robbers plundered along the river," the Scot said. "Rude brash boatmen they be. Miscr'ants, crim'nals. I gave mats and a meal, only that."

A prisoner behind the Scot snickered. "Don't be a drum, Keeper. The highland shite was thick with us from the up."

"Knew naught of any of it, on me oath," said the Scot. "Still they took me cottage, me ox, me tools. 'Specially me tools. Spouted a new law about treason. But lawless is what I say. Bold tyr'nny."

"Any who side publicly with the Crown are subject to property forfeit," said Quayland. "That is the new law. The sad way of things now."

Manacled hands pleaded the Scot's innocence. "But I didna do it."

"So say all accused." The surveyor resumed his peel.

"Words are one matter," said the Innkeeper. "Thievery another. Should know better."

"Will you not help an inn'cent man?" The Scot pressed against the slats.

Jerky removed from his pocket the Innkeeper placed a hand against the cage.

The Scot took the meat and chewed greedily. "Make me a rotter, they will. Do you hear, Keeper. A rotter. Rotter."

The Innkeeper turned and pulled the sled toward the barn.

Quayland followed. "A poor tale if true. Regrettably the common good does not always run fair."

"Fair means little on a farm."

The surveyor gestured at the iron silhouette of an Indian head on the corner of the barn roof. "An odd ornament."

"Says this land is mine, bought from an Iroquois sachem. The Nations know I am not a squatter."

"A slender shield." Quayland said. "Why not to take from the sovereign? Royal grants hold sway over Indian titles."

Sled tilted upright against the barn, the Innkeeper turned. "The king is across an ocean and his governor thrown from office. The tribes are close. So are their tomahawks."

"Wilderness sense. Yet you are fortunate the fighting does not reach here. Soon it will."

The Innkeeper crossed the yard and dropped a roped bucket down the well. "The locals talk war and take sides upon the other. Much of it greed, grudge. The jail wagon shows it. No reason. Life here is strain enough."

"At least this valley holds more Rebels than Tories. A hopeful sign."

The Innkeeper hauled the full bucket from the well. "Be careful. Many here fought for Britain against France in the last war. Old notions and loyalties die hard."

"And you?"

"Ran messages for the King's militia. Never enlisted."

"Not a fighter?"

"Not a fool." The Innkeeper emptied the bucket into the simmering kettle and with a board stirred the hog entrails.

"The war will not let loose a sturdy man so easy," said the surveyor. "Both sides seek influence and the means to fight. So what say you? The Crown or independence?"

"Words come cheap, false. Same as too many questions."

"Yet I remain dogged. Which is it? Rebel or Tory? Patriot or Loyalist?"

Annoyed, the Innkeeper turned. "I favor no cause but my own. I work this land and tend what travellers come. The rest does not concern me."

Quayland stepped closer. "Even an innkeeper must make a choice."

"Poor business if I do. And I'll not be bullied by either side."

Board set aside the Innkeeper took up the bucket and started toward the barn but stopped, head ticked to one side. The cow's insistent bell in the rear pasture alarmed and he pivoted.

A Peddler in frayed Indian buckskins, worn black frock coat and dented gentleman's hat fed dried stalk to the Welsh Red past the barn gate.

"Back away," the Innkeeper said.

The Peddler fed the last piece, opened the gate and entered the yard. A large pack made of sticks, sinew and mixed hides bent his back and dangled feathers, animal claws and trinkets.

"Fair greeting," said the Peddler. "How far to the crossing?"

Quayland stepped beside the Innkeeper. "The river floods. And you'll not make the ford by dark. No doubt you are welcome to some corner straw in the barn."

"You have no business here, tinker," the Innkeeper said. "Be off."

Hat removed, the Peddler lifted a squaw strap over long strings of filthy hair and eased his pack to the ground.

Swirled Indian sign marked the right side of his face and his tongue sifted the air. Intense eyes, one brown and the other green, bluntly assessed the Innkeeper.

"A fine big house and barn," he said. "Full of proud spirits to be reckoned."

"You come cross country," Quayland said. "Why avoid the road?"

The Peddler returned the top hat on his head, slowly blinked and looked at the surveyor. "I am of the deep forest. The trodden path is not mine."

"Be off, gypsy," the Innkeeper said.

"Perhaps first a small exchange. My burdens run heavy, the prices light."

The Innkeeper picked up a blacksmith hammer and stepped forward. "I said be off."

Rag covered hands spread palms open the Peddler's half grin bared rotten teeth. "You drive a harsh point. Know I am not always this easy."

He hefted the pack, touched his hat brim and shuffled further across the yard. Near the cauldron he paused and deep inhaled, eyes closed.

"Killing time," he said. "Blood is life. Life is blood. There is much here."

At the tavern hitch the Peddler lightly danced fingers across sacks and bundles on the ox.

"Watch him quick," said the prisoner beside the Scot. "He's a knuckler, sure."

The Peddler dribbled a handful of seed corn from a sack to the ground. "I am a thief. A taker of the worst sort. You must stop me."

Slid close against the cage the Scot stretched a hand between the slats. "Duhna do that."

Seed emptied, the Peddler bit an apple from a basket. "Worm food. All of you."

The Scot's enraged swipe fell just short and he futilely rattled and kicked at the cage. "Shoulda be you in here, canter. Shoulda be you."

The Peddler spit chewed apple into the air. "Sing ye, caged bird. Sing ye."

Hammer poised, the Innkeeper strode toward the jail wagon.

The Peddler continued up the front rise to the road. He glanced back with raised hand, crossed a downed fence rail and entered a thicket in the far field.

The Innkeeper pursued to the road edge and waited several minutes before he returned past the wagon and along the basement.

"I spoke out of place for him to stay," Quayland said. "You did right to refuse yet I hold no envy. Will be a cold night."

"Gypsies are liars, thieves and worse," the Innkeeper said. "I have no place for them."

He roughly tapped the hammer against the wheel edge of a freight flatbed at the rear cellar entrance.

"One son ignores me and cannot stomach the hogs," he said. "The other is lazy and leaves goods unloaded at the door. Yet you pester me with questions of tinkers and rebellion. This is a farm. There is work for doing."

He tossed the hammer to the ground and opened the cellar door.

CHAPTER THREE

Trapped.

Dayne crouched beside a besom and bucket on the narrow floor behind the bar counter at the rear of the drink room. Armed men at a table near the outside door blocked his escape.

He rocked on knees, arms wrapped tight to his body, unsure what to do. Earlier he hid in different spots in the cellar afraid his father would find and make him return outside to the hog slaughter. Scared squeals and images of his father's bloodied knife, furious boiling water and scalded carcasses ravaged his thoughts. He hated the cauldron. It dominated the yard with awful smells of death, lard, sinew and lye. He never walked near it and never let it take his eyes.

Of age, the gnawed ear hog would be killed. It was the way of the farm and why Dayne fled early that morning to safe haven at the waterfall. Yet he did not forgive his father's delay of its butcher until his return. Hard punishment, cruel and undeserved.

He wanted to speak and save his pet. Bitter rawness scourged the back of his throat. Weakness and shame chided his heart.

Dayne slid to the bar corner to peek out. Three men in muddied boots and great coats spoke over tankards at the table with his older brother Lauch. Still gangly and soft at nineteen, his brother sat uneasy, awkward and out of place. Dayne sensed no friendship from the men, only discord and distrust. Two long guns spiked upright against nearby chairs.

The large third man kept his rifle across the table like a wicked club. Shadowed beneath the tilt of a broad brim hat his face held stern menace.

Dayne recognized the man from prior visits of the jail wagon and a town trip with his father for supplies. Atop the huge black plow horse, grim rifle across its saddle, the man forced a family from land near the river. Tarred, feathered and tied to a wheel cart piled with possessions the farmer looked an animal, snared and helpless.

Sobbing and frantic his wife ran between the cart, the man and his father's wagon and pleaded for mercy but his father drove on. Scared, confused faces of small children peeking wide-eyed from the cart still haunted Dayne.

The man drank and eased back in his chair. "We've rid the valley of most Tories. A few skunks still crawl back from Canada and raid, thieve. Four sit outside. We got their wares and will see 'em hanged."

A squat thick-jowled companion nodded. "Coomittee of Vig'loonce. We gut, sehr gut."

Dayne shifted and inadvertently knocked over the besom. Its loud whack on the floor crackled the air.

The man's other companion rose but stopped when Lauch grasped his coat sleeve.

"Come out, Dayne," Lauch said. "Take the broom and do the hearth."

Dayne retreated behind the bar. Able to hide no longer he stood with the besom and bucket and crossed stiff, timid toward the large stone fireplace at the far end of the room.

The squat man's stubby finger followed him. "A ruunt. Not a mensch, strong and gross vike his Vater."

The other companion resumed his chair. "More of the Keeper's weak spit."

The large man's rifle captured Dayne's eyes. Its easy glint, the flintlock's sharp angry curve and deadly barrel bored the same rage and violence as his father's long gun.

"My brother does not speak," said Lauch. "He will not repeat our words."

Dayne swept ash from the grate into piles, filled the bucket with his hands and gathered residue with a wet rag. Ill at ease he glanced behind. The large man's harsh stare squeezed him like a field mouse.

The man shifted his peer to Lauch. "I bring news. Renegades from the Nations gather near Unadilla. Last week two families to the south were butchered by an Iroquois half breed called the Beast. Men skinned alive and boiled is what they say. Worse for the women."

"Murder outright," said the other companion. "Lawless. Vicious."

Leaned forward, the man rested his hand on the rifle. "Rumors are the Beast comes this way, again and soon. Let me hear that rag, boy."

With both hands Dayne scoured the stone harder.

"Spies for the British work the valley, here to do devilry with the Beast," said the man. "Guns and powder for more killing and torture, ale and whiskey to goad his hate. If we don't stop him the Tories and savages will have us all."

"What of the militia?" Lauch nervously fingered his tankard.

"They patrol but not enough," the man said. "The Continentals are holed at Fort Stanwix across the river and too far. It may be we, we ourselves who need rise up and see it done."

Lauch gnawed his lip. Tankard moved in tight circles, he pushed it aside but returned and lifted to drink. Only air.

The other companion smirked. "Empty-assed like his noggin. No spine, plain. Told ya."

"A coo-ward," said the squat man.

Lauch slumped and shifted in his chair. "I will not fight unless forced. The war is still off, away, not here."

"The Keeper's own true son," said the man. "Afraid of the stand, scared of the choice."

"No, the words are my own," Lauch said. "I will not hunt neighbors and friends based on rumor and guess."

The man stiffened. "What I say is not mere gabble."

"Ja, my faamilie'll not be bootchered," said the squat man. "Help us now, you shood. We caatch and haang whoever."

Lauch twitched and shook his head. "I want no violence but can watch the road. How will I know these spies?"

"This be the last wayside before the wilderness and the Nations," said the man. "Suspect anyone, everyone. And especially your neighbors. Do it or you'll burn by the Beast."

Dayne carried the besom and bucket past the table to the bar. He knelt and peeked around its corner, upset by the men's words and his brother's distress.

The man stared hard at Lauch. "We need know which you are. One of us or—"

The cellar door opened and Dayne jerked stiff.

His father loomed overhead, angry and annoyed. The surveyor pressed the doorway behind, hand on the peel at his mouth.

The Innkeeper strode around the bar. "Enough. My sons have work for doing without such flummery. Lauch, you left freight at the rear door. Dayne, milk is in the barn."

Lauch rose off balance and scraped his chair on the floor. "Only simple talk."

"War always is," the Innkeeper said. "I will have none of it. Not here, not in my house. Go as I ask."

Embarrassed and resentful Lauch swayed unsure but frowned and meekly moved past to the cellar door. Hand on the jamb he glanced back and left. Dayne followed.

The Innkeeper approached the table. The squat man and other companion rose tense, uncertain and stepped back.

"Lauch is my son, mine alone," the Innkeeper said. "Not fodder for the likes of you, Thaler."

"Can't hide from the war, Keeper. Is here and all around. Soon it may be on your very farm." Thaler did not move his hand from the rifle.

The Innkeeper angled slightly, voice taut. "You will not have my sons. Out of my tavern. Now."

Thaler slowly drained his ale. "You're white-livered and scared. Saw it at McKillop's farm. A neighbor yet you drove past."

"McKillop was not my fight."

"What is? Not the Scot dung outside."

"He lived near. I heard no treason."

"His pub talk was different. Witnesses. Papers."

"You cage a man for drunk words."

Thaler stood brazen, defiant. "The law is the law. So is the Committee of Vigilance and Safety."

"Vigilante's excuse. You come a foul parasite."

"Found plunder in the Scot's cottage," said the other companion. "Guilt."

The Innkeeper stepped closer, eyes firm on Thaler. "He says other."

Unhurried, Thaler dropped small coins on the table, nails loud into a board. "Then the thief is both liar and traitor."

He passed his rifle in an admonishing arc across the Innkeeper's face. "We'll remember today. You're isolated here, Keeper. When the time comes expect no aid."

Rifle crooked across his elbow Thaler fingered ale from his lip and turned toward the outside door. The squat man and other companion followed him from the tavern.

Quayland stepped forward past the bar. "You are a formidable man, Keeper. Principled and keen, forceful. Either side would do well to have you."

Kerchief untied from his hat brim the surveyor wiped at his neck. "A brisk encounter. I shall quietly tend my horse and compass."

He returned to the cellar. The squat man's call to the hitch team and heavy rattle of the jail wagon filtered from the yard.

The Innkeeper paced angry, tight beside the table. He pushed aside the tankards of the men but lingered over Lauch's empty mug.

His fist slammed into the table top.

◑

Dowd descended the tavern steps, heavy footfall punctuated by the metallic tap of a nail tip in his walking stick. He squeezed hard between his eyes at sharp head spasms and blinked. The pinch did not work.

In simple black attire and round brimmed hat a man scraped muddy brogans at the hearth beside an animal girth belt and cargo saddle sprawled the floor. He did not look up.

Annoyed by the disregard Dowd rumbled his throat. "You are bespattered. Mud, muck."

"Such is the road."

"Stout boots would serve better."

The man continued to scrape. "Humility and plain shoes hold a man closer to his path."

Dowd pointed his stick at the man's worn cloak and leggings. "You are indeed humble. Also new."

"This morning. My sole companion is a contrarian old mule. Sometimes Jerusalem lets me ride, sometimes not. I am grateful for shelter ahead of the weather."

"Only a fool or vagabond walks country roads alone. On what business?"

The man finished his shoes and looked up. "You are a stranger and rude early. Why such questions?"

"A prudent man determines with whom he lodges."

"A wiser man knows not to pry."

"You have the heft and hands of the trades. A working man."

The man rose and gathered the girth and saddle. "I have been many things. Now a simple traveller, contrite in spirit, who trembles at the word of God."

Dowd pursed. "A damn Quaker."

The man gathered the girth and saddle and stepped past. "If you say."

"And proud too, by your air. Quakers are no different than Papists and rare here. As for friends, you will find precious few in this valley."

"I am told otherwise." The man smiled and went up the steps.

Dowd plodded to the outside door. Shoulder cape on his great coat uplifted he left the tavern. In the barn yard mud and chill wind curdled his mood and he caned slow and stiff. Stench from the simmering hog cauldron forced a kerchief across his face.

Puffed by exertion, inside the barn doorway he settled unsteady on a barrel and scraped yard residue from his gentleman's boots against a hoe. Strong dung and livestock smells further burdened his nose and peeved his mouth. The kerchief stayed poised.

The Innkeeper emerged from a stall and emptied a pitchfork of soiled straw to the manure sled.

"You raised a pretentious shed, Keeper," Dowd said. "Big beyond need. No doubt on purpose."

"The barn is the center of a farm. Not the house."

"Vainglory is a sin. As is a barn odorous and wretched with dung and piss. Do you not find the smells repugnant, the routine tedious?"

The Innkeeper pulled the sled to the next stall. "Nature and necessity. The smells ease with time."

"Not the cauldron. Stink unlike any other."

"A harsh chore. Yet all eat the meat."

Dowd stood and adjusted his great coat. "A wandering Quaker arrived. He seemed dull, without repute. Likely another sluggard who refuses the rebellion. Is he a Tory? Many Quakers are in private."

The Innkeeper entered the stall. "He works for his board."

"More prudence is required. Vermin and opportunists frequent the road."

Dowd crossed the corridor and inspected tight canvas coverings and nailed leather straps on two large deep bellied freight tandems. So far his hidden cargo stirred no undue curiosity yet he worried constant. All eyes pried and he trusted no one.

"What of the Iroquois?" he asked. "Have you much contact?"

The Innkeeper emerged and emptied the pitchfork. "Only at distance. Their paths west to Oswego and Niagara are not far. Some are shades who pass quiet, others bring presence. Often the woods have too many eyes. They want me to know they watch close at hand."

"Most will war for the Crown. That be sure of."

"Both sides bribe for loyalty. Neither will likely get it."

"Yet you carry no arms."

The Innkeeper gestured at his powder horn and long rifle leaned against a corridor post.

"My weapon is never far."

"Still no word on my freight," Dowd said. "The bateaux sent for are delayed while the river floods."

Sled pulled toward the barn door the Innkeeper turned. "The tandem drivers said they abandoned because you would not pay."

"Rude tavern gossip, insult," said Dowd. "Untrue. The cowards demanded double wages after departure, rank highwaymen. I had no option but to strand here. Better than the wilderness."

He rested his walking stick on top of a tandem wheel. "Are my wagons safe?"

"I brook no thievery or mischief but make no promise. Your property is your own."

Dowd sniffed petulant. "Do you always so easily evade your obligations?"

The Innkeeper dragged the sled to the barn door. "A gypsy tinker passed earlier. Watch the wagons close."

"Gypsy?" Mouth open to inquire further, Dowd started forward but the Innkeeper pulled the large door closed.

Dowd rapped his stick insistent against the wood. "You do little to instill confidence, sir. I shall remember the affront."

The Innkeeper escaped across the yard to the rear pasture and forked manure across the fence. He held no patience for boors. Cold wind gained his face and rankled swirl of overcast deepened overhead. Worried, restive eyes found no figure or portent along the far ridgelines but instinct did not lie. Tumult came with the weather.

He put out the cauldron fire with water from the well bucket and emptied the kettle of stewed entrails into a large tub he carried into the smokehouse behind the cellar.

Cured hams and shoulders hung from hooks tied around low ceiling beams. Strong scents of raw meat and charcoal smoke thickened the air.

Gray haired and gnarled, Gert dropped corn to the dirt floor to bait chickens in a corner. She cooed soft, a knotted wood cane hid behind her back and slashed sudden, smiled and stepped over the victim to coo again.

"The chickens should know you by now," the Innkeeper said.

"They know I feed them, that be all. An old guile."

He appreciated Gert's leathered bluntness. She carried ill moods and ways but demanded little and ran a good house.

"The kettle meat is done." The Innkeeper set the tub on the ground.

"The hogs proved fat and will cure well," Gert said. "Fresh lard and grease for the hearth.

One hog was Dayne's favorite. A pet."

"A hard lesson to learn. He hid the barn and cellar. I almost went to find him."

The Innkeeper chopped fresh hams, loins and quarters of meat on a work bench and rough kneaded coarse salt and saltpeter into the meat. Stiff hands ached, balked.

"You work grim," said Gert.

He nodded. "Last week's rains brought no favor and delayed the slaughter. Now cold comes early and with it storm. I like not the brew of things."

Gert tossed two disabled chickens beside a stool and plucked the third in her lap.

The Innkeeper lined in-ground half barrels with salt, set the rubbed meat inside beneath cover boards and mounded dirt and straw over top. Pinch-backed, he paused on the shovel.

"Your rheumatoid worsens," Gert said. "Plain in your walk, your face, your hands. Some Indian tobacco would aid."

"Save your hemp and poison leaves. More help at chores would salve my aches."

Gert's short firm twist ruptured one chicken's neck and she placed tufts of plucked feathers in a sack. "Thaler and the others scurried off."

"Agh, they muddle Lauch's mind."

She twisted the second bird and plucked again. "Choosing sides is not muddled."

The Innkeeper roughly jabbed the shovel into the ground and added more dirt over the cure barrels. "What good is a Tory or Rebel in this house? No benefit comes from either side. The war does not concern me. Only this farm."

"Perhaps. But Lauch is now a man himself. He needs the chance to act it."

"He stays soft to the voices of others and knows not his own mind. I will not have my son stray, youth or no."

Gert wrenched the last chicken. "You treat him too severe. You know that."

The Innkeeper set aside the shovel, placed chunks of fat from cut meat into the tub and emptied a water bucket across the tainted bench.

"Smelled ale heavy on his breath these past weeks, just as before," he said. "And drink was in his eyes with Thaler. Will lash it out of him if I see it again."

"He drinks as a sign."

"He drinks because he is weak."

Gert shook her head. "You see him not, Keeper. The same with Dayne."

Chickens pecked the ground around Gert's shoes and long wool skirt hem. "You were my sister's husband and I tend this house as my own but this I say. A choice must be made and Lauch will make his as you and I did ours. We each bear what follows."

She stood and displayed the dead chickens by their feet.

"Weather always brings a full house."

CHAPTER FOUR

THE FOUR HORSE COACH jolted down a narrow rutted wagon path in a steep gorge.

Leg strained stiff against the wheel brake, Jacks shouted and pulled hard on the reins from the driver's bench but the coach swayed and below his boot the right front wheel slid precarious over the path edge.

At grade bottom the coach briefly stalled in a swollen stream and climbed the far bank. Winded horses hooved the ground and snorted, sweat-streaked and lathered despite the cold.

Jacks climbed down, slapped ride mud from his long great coat and broad hat and rapped his hand on the side of the coach as he passed to its rear.

"The brake is worn as are the horses," he said. "Best to get out. The woman, too."

Inside the coach Sybil willed herself not to retch. Arms braced stiff against the seat, she slowly opened her eyes afraid the turmoil would continue.

"Unending bumps and shakes," she said. "This cannot be a proper road."

On the seat opposite Cotswold clutched a heavy leather satchel on the floor between his legs. Annoyance seeped his sallow, pocked middle-aged face. He minced, opened the door and descended the step.

Sybil followed, burrowed inside her thick shawl and coat. Chill wind bit deep and one gloved hand absently flexed across her abdomen.

"You clutch," said Cotswold.

Sybil removed the hand. "I am surprised you noticed."

Cotswold brushed stray snowflakes from the sleeve of his heavy gentleman's coat. "Do not annoy, my dear."

Sybil waited but he offered no hand. "Perhaps I shall walk a bit. The stretch and some air apart will help both our moods."

Stepped to the muddy ground, she walked forward along the path. Lifeless undergrowth and trees pushed close just beyond and stark ridgelines topped the gorge. The cold surround of unfamiliar winter woods did little to dispel her worries.

Sybil glanced back toward Cotswold. Frayed by unexpected flight from the city and rude rigors along wilderness roads, he little resembled the successful shipping merchant she knew. Always difficult, his recent emotional withdrawals and sarcasms cut deeper, lingered more harsh.

She guessed he held similar thoughts. No longer young and energetic, her appeal also waned and the bleak prospect of abandonment loomed, trapped with or without him. Pretense she was more than his mistress seemed delusion, her grand bargain gone awry, and the new burden of her telltale stomach created a higher price. Sybil turned away.

At the rear of the coach Cotswold confronted Jacks. "Are we lost again?"

The driver re-tied a shattered wheel lashed across the baggage cover. "The weather and road worsen."

"Was your notion to take this path."

Jacks blew a nostril clear. "Was your reason."

Another snowflake irritably brushed from his coat. Cotswold looked suspicious at thick gray overcast and adjusted his shoulder cape against the chill. "How much longer?"

The driver bent to inspect the rear axle and wheels. "A day to the river, another to the town beyond. If the coach holds."

Cotswold smirked. Parasite of the city, his dependence on the driver irked and he did not trust the man. Yet he knew enough to endure the ruffian's indignities until the advantage turned his.

"Surely you can manage," said Cotswold. "I do not pay good money to end short."

He followed Jacks to the front of the coach. Nervous horses jostled, nostrils flared, and the driver rubbed the flank of the lead team.

"An ill scent on the wind," Jacks said.

Satchel set on the ground, Cotswold squinted over thick glasses along the ravine. Smoke puddled among tree-tops off the downslope ahead.

Sybil approached. "There is smoke. Perhaps a homestead is nearby, a more suitable rest and place to warm."

Jacks started forward. Cotswold hefted his satchel and with Sybil trailed behind.

Two charred overturned covered wagons smoldered at the bottom of the slope. Stark tree branches snagged colored dresses and smashed wood chests spoke sudden destruction. Scalped, splayed bodies of women and children dotted the ground among rummaged possessions. Staked and burned bodies of several men lay nearby.

Sybil averted her face. "Why must they be so inhumane?"

Cotswold wiped his glasses with a kerchief and stared curious and intent at the carnage. "Savages. Beasts. No ambiguity, only purpose."

"Surely someone will perform proper burials."

"What difference? They are dead."

Shawl pulled tighter, Sybil shivered. "You grow cold and hard. Like the weather."

"Fate without mercy. Life's answer for fools."

An arrow jutted from a red hand print painted on a tree beside the path. Jacks sneered, pulled the arrow and examined the black shaft and feathers.

"Righteous killers," he said. "Proud of their work."

The driver dropped the arrow and turned. "Your luck dims. The road is unsafe ahead and behind. Best to turn back."

Cotswold shifted the satchel between hands. "And go where? You know my need."

"You will not like what the savages do if captured," said Jacks. "Nor will she."

Sybil touched Cotswold's sleeve. "He's right. Promise me we will not end like these poor souls."

He stared at her gloved hand until she let go. "I promise nothing. You know that."

"Storm and dark also chase us," Jacks said. "Not a night to strand."

Cotswold's stare lingered over the wagons and bodies. He minced and turned impatient toward the coach. "Then why do we idle? Make for the river."

Sybil started to follow but stopped when he did not look back for her. Jacks stepped close alongside.

"Let him go," the driver said. "He and his peeved looks."

She refused the driver's blunt eyes and returned along the path. Wind rustled dried leaves and snowflakes drifted her hair and face.

Near the horses she paused. "An odd quiet. Nothing but the push of the stream, the shift of horses and renewal of a gentle snow. Nature saw this cruelty, a mute witness. Now it heals."

Cotswold glanced back and climbed the coach step. "You will not be so poetic come this night's cold. Next time cover your head. Act a lady."

Left unassisted, Sybil continued to the rear of the coach. Eyes closed, she inhaled deep and forced away anger and fear until a distinctive sound ended the moment's mend.

Across the path Jacks urinated, hefted his pants and turned.

"Men are fortunate," Sybil said. "I do not know why."

◐

Dayne hooked an oversized lantern on the road post in the front yard of the inn. Snow dusted the ground and darted past the candle flicker in dusk's early dark. Arms extended, he whirled and relished icy ticks against his up-turned face and exposed tongue.

New, deeper chill crept along his scarf. He stopped abrupt, concerned someone watched. Wind shifted shad-owed fir boughs in woods across the road and his hand rose in uncertain greeting until sharp cold curled his throat and he retreated.

An unlit coach rumbled down the mountain road, slowed at the lantern post and turned into the yard. Dayne hid beside low bushes near the inn's front door and peeked out.

The driver climbed down from the coach bench and spit stubborn grit from the edge of his mouth. He knuckled the passenger side and moved stiff-legged toward the rear.

A gentleman stepped to the ground satchel in hand, face creased by ill mood like an angry squirrel.

"We arrive after all," the gentleman said. "Undaunted and unscathed."

An unhappy woman emerged under a bonnet, blanket over her shawl and coat. "We are blessed. I feared another dreadful night outside. Or worse."

Dayne's father carried a lantern forward on the inn steps. "You cheat the storm."

The gentleman turned. "Indeed. Are you the keeper?"

"I am that."

"Two rooms. My driver needs only a floor."

"Agreed. This is an ordinary. Shelter and food at a set fare each day, nothing more. I brook no foolery on either side of the war."

"A neutral man is rare these days," the gentleman said. "Are you equally impartial about the money you accept?"

"Coin will do, royal or not. Paper I will have none of."

"A wise proprietor," the gentleman said. "Jacks will see to the trunks."

"My sons will stable the animals."

The gentleman assisted the woman from the coach step, escorted her toward the entrance and looked back at the driver.

"Fill the foot warmer," he said. "Have it in my room."

Dayne's father approached the bushes. "Come out, Dayne. Light the coach to the barn. And find Lauch. If not, do the horses yourself. You know how."

Eyes lowered, Dayne emerged and took the lantern. His father followed the gentleman and woman into the inn. The driver unloaded trunks to the stoop, looked doubtful at Dayne and carried the baggage inside.

Dayne shivered in gathering dark. Unseen watchful presence again rankled the back of his neck but the restless shift of horses and soft harness rubs and clinks took away his unease.

The driver returned and resumed the bench. "Do it, boy."

Behind the lantern's wavering puddle of light Dayne led the coach around the side of the inn past the basement tavern, across the yard and into the barn corridor. The driver set the wheel brake, climbed down and unhitched the team.

Dayne placed horses into separate stalls. He lingered with the last animal and stroked cold mud and dirt from its steaming flank and chest. Soft skin and coarse hairs on its muzzle soothed, tickled his hands and strong breaths rippled his fingers.

"You've a way with beasts," said the driver. "I like it done right. Mind, no feed till they rest."

Lantern set on the coach tongue, Dayne gathered harnesses and reins. The grizzled driver loomed in shadows at light's edge, enlarged by long great coat and large fold over knee boots. He picked his teeth with a strand of straw, a watchful field rat sizing prey.

"Your daddy's hard on you," the driver said. "Heard it in his voice. See it plain in your eyes. Mine was too. What's your name, boy?"

Dayne stiffened and looked away. He did not expect the need to speak.

The driver approached, insistent grin lopsided. "Talk to me. We both tend big smelly animals in a cold barn for someone else. No shame in it. Speak."

Dayne turned away and hung bridles on stall posts.

"Stubborn is it? Or got no manners?" The driver tossed away the straw and stepped close.

The man's size and dark manner reminded Dayne of the rider on the great black horse who brought the jail wagon. He retreated stiff, unsure.

Foot warmer retrieved from the coach, the driver tossed it on the ground near Dayne. "Fill this with fire chips from the hearth once inside and take it to his lordship's room. The fool has a wicked tongue but dainty feet."

Dayne forked hay into small feed piles in front of the stalls, confused and disturbed by the driver's unkind eyes and testing words.

"C'mon boy, tell me what you've seen," the man said. "Who else passes the road to the river? Militia? Bluecoats? Redcoats? Which?"

Dayne shook his head and forked more hay.

The driver pursued closer, more intent. "What scares you so quiet? Bold savages who haunt the woods with tomahawks? I'd be scared too, out here all alone."

Dayne eased past the man.

Climbed onto the rear axle, the driver gathered his blanket roll and kit from the top of the coach and stepped down. He crossed the corridor to the freight tandems and ran his hand along the nailed canvas cover on the back wagon.

"Fine heavy set wagons," he said. "An owner serious about his haul. What be inside?"

Dayne walked between the coach and stalls with the water bucket. The driver emerged sudden around the shadowed end of the coach and blocked his path.

"I asked what's inside the wagons. Don't refuse me. I'll have my way."

Caught between surprise and fear, Dayne clenched. Bucket held in front with both hands, anxious and unnerved eyes darted then fixed on the tip of his shoe.

"You're a skittish knob," said the driver. "Weak, wandering peekers and an empty, dumb mouth."

The man's face flared and his voice spiked. "Speak it. Speak it loud. Are you broken?"

He stepped closer but Dayne backed up.

"You can talk. I know it sure."

Dayne dropped the bucket, fled around the front of the coach and crossed to the opposite side of the corridor.

The driver grinned and churned his legs in place as if he pursued, hands slapped against his knees, heavy boots ominous thuds on the ground.

At the edge of the open barn door Dayne looked back, alarmed but defiant.

The driver lunged forward, a feint. Dayne escaped into the darkness of the barn yard.

The man's laugh and voice followed. "Run little rabbit. Run."

Dayne rushed into the cellar and peered out the side window into blackness. Ragged breaths slowly subsided and he turned only once satisfied the driver did not come.

The outside door burst open but yawned empty. Cold air and random snow rushed and Dayne lurched sideways, startled off balance. Cured hams on each shoulder, Lauch entered and piled the meat on a bench.

"Had to empty the smokehouse before the night freezes," said his brother. "Cold, thirsty work."

Lauch shut the door, blew on his hands and uncovered a small ale cask behind boards against a corner wall. "Look what I found hid in the barn. An eager surprise just for me. Already tasted it."

Cask held aloft, he gulped open-mouthed swallows and wiped spill on his coat. "Don't tell the Keeper. He'll hide me."

Dayne worried. His brother's need to drink from casks often only disquieted and angered his father. Dayne did not see its use.

Lauch's eyes questioned. "I am not a thief. Just confused, unhappy at times. Drink is my distraction. A game I play."

Cask covered, Lauch teased Dayne's hair. "Heard the new coach come in. You did the horses alone so later I'll finish the barn myself. Promise."

They crossed the cellar into the drink room and squatted stools opposite its hearth. Lauch prodded the fire and Dayne's trembled hands gradually surrendered to welcome warmth near the flames.

"You looked scared in the cellar," said Lauch. "Thaler's rough talk got us both on edge."

Dayne watched his brother, curious if he would appear and act the same when he grew older. Already they seemed different, separate. Lauch's emotions ran quick, open and unsure unlike Dayne's silent broods. Neither looked like their father or carried his strength. The deep core of blood connection Dayne expected with family never seemed true.

In recent months he spent less time with Lauch as grownup chores and bothers burdened his brother's moods. Fewer games, fewer talks. Dayne did not understand the change, only its isolation. The dwindle left Dayne lonely.

Lauch fidgeted the poker, face troubled and distracted in soft flickers of light. "Do you believe in the Beast? I do. The raids and murders make him real enough. Will he come here? What if he does?"

Dayne glanced at Lauch. At times he saw colors around people or objects, shimmers or bursts of light and emotion. Darkness creased by hints of orange surrounded his brother, faint unkind glows. Lauch's light was never strong, never sturdy. An ill omen. Dayne glanced toward shadowed steps to the main floor, disturbed by vague threat.

"Now you look sad," said Lauch.

He removed a gnarled root from his coat pocket. "Found this by a felled tree near the waterfall. I started the whittle but it's for you. Not sure why. Maybe a toy or new friend. You choose."

Coarse like a stiff bucket rag stretched over rock, the dense root pulsed Dayne's palm with ancient, unknown past. He offered the unwanted portent back but his brother turned away.

At the large wood pile along the far wall Lauch cradled a heavy load and started for the upstairs steps. "Gert will want her fire."

Dayne reached for his brother's sleeve, mouth open to speak and warn about what hid in the step shadows. No words came, only confused silence. Chance lost, he trailed behind.

On the first step Lauch nearly lost balance, grinned sheepish and passed into blackness above. Hallway door opened, he glanced back briefly surrounded and restored by faint yellow candlelight, and heeled the door shut. Darkness returned.

Cold emptiness feathered Dayne's heart, inner sadness. Once more he did not speak. Once more he failed. The root's throb pounded his hand, unyielding proof of guilt. Foot arced high across the bottom step as over an unseen object, he followed upstairs.

Past the main entrance Dayne entered the common table room and peeked around the edge of the kitchen doorway.

Gert squinted in red-orange fire glow at the blackened stone hearth, heat hardened face beaded with sweat below unruly coarse gray hair. Hands, long woolen sleeves and skirt pocked by scorch marks, she pokered open logs in a flurry of sparks, brushed stray embers from her neck and mounded fresh wood coals against a round bake oven.

Utensils and pots hung from an iron lug pole across the fire opening. Kettles, three-legged trivets, skillets, buckets and piled ash crowded the flat hearth base. The day's tread of footprints marred floor ash around stools, chairs and tables opposite.

Lauch stacked wood in the far corner and fingered cheese hunks from the table. "The cure meat is in the cellar."

"Hang it in the back by the spring," Gert said. "Will draw no nibblers there."

Warmth and comfort smells eased Dayne's brood. The kitten clawed and tumbled a sack of chicken feathers on the floor near the fire and he yielded to familiar normalcy, the basic rituals of home.

Gert ladled stew from a large pot simmering on a trammel over the fire into a tureen she carried past Dayne into the common room.

"Almost time," she said.

Dayne eagerly grabbed the large hand bell from a kitchen shelf.

Gert placed the tureen on an oblong harvest table alongside wooden knives, spoons and trenchers for six eating places. Dribbled stew overflow cleared with her apron, she arranged a salter and platters of bread, butter and cheese in uneven light of two smoky table lamps.

Satisfied with the table Gert turned to Dayne. "Work the bell."

He crossed to the bottom of the second floor stairs in the main hall and with both arms snapped three rings.

CHAPTER FIVE

GERT CARRIED A SKILLET of fried pumpkin from the kitchen into the common room. Bundled in great coats, Dowd and Quayland ate on opposite ends of a long bench beside the harvest table.

Throat rumbled clear, Dowd shifted stiff haunches. "The crude benches are a discomfort, madam. Separate chairs with backs would fare better. And the room is darker than need. I prefer to better see what I eat."

Gert set the skillet on a trivet at the table corner. "This be a work room, not just for loud gullets. Make do."

Dowd tapped his wooden spoon and knife against a square board indented by its center bowl. "You also feed us on pieces of tree, hogs at a trough. Have you no pewter or plate?"

"No need," Gert said.

"Nor forks?"

"No need."

Dowd twitched, stymied. "Such are custom in any respectable house."

"Spoons, knives and trenchers are enough," said Gert. "Wood cleans the better and is easily had. I tend the house my way."

"You and the Keeper are curious hosts," said Dowd. "Rude, stubborn."

Quayland looked up from his spoon. "But the stew is passable."

He and Dowd reached for the salter at the same time. Dowd stared, chin determined and high. The surveyor smiled polite, conceded and withdrew his hand.

Dowd waved off Gert's offer of pumpkin. "I eat no ground gourds. They yield a sour gut."

"Then you would starve on a farm," she said.

The surveyor eagerly accepted the pumpkin spoon. "I hold no such qualm."

Annoyed, Dowd glanced along the bench. "Do you always wear your hat at table, sir?"

Quayland touched his frayed oversized tricorn and mismatched neck kerchiefs. "Often when cold. And my family balds early. A small conceit."

Dowd loud-slurped stew. "More an overgrown toadstool. Vain, immodest. Poor breeding, poor manners."

"Then I ask the lady of the house to forgive me." The surveyor smiled at Gert.

She filled noggins from a cider kettle. "I care not about the big hat. A loose mouth and muddy boots are different."

Dowd extended a stiff leg beside his walking stick and soiled boots. "Mud is what is abundant here, madam. A reality of the road in season. I should think you used to its display."

Gert mumbled low. She disliked Dowd. The road brought people, news and rumors of all sorts and harsh manners ran common but she tolerated no criticism of her house or ways. Outside words and notions did no chores, cooked no meals.

With her apron Gert cleared spilled stew near Dowd's trencher. "Some mud lingers and smells hard. Unwanted dung."

The surveyor lifted his noggin. "The lady gives as good as she gets."

Brow skewed and mouth twisted, Dowd clenched as spasm slowly crossed his face and clawed fingers flexed until the fit subsided.

Gert waited. "Do you need the purge bucket? Are you sound?"

"I have certain ill humors," Dowd said. "Sudden sharp head pains. None can tell me the cause. I regret if I seem indiscriminate."

The man in black attire entered and stood across the table from the others.

"Ah, the wandering Quaker," said Dowd. "Come, sir, and sit the bench. No doubt you are used to a pew."

The man set his round hat on the floor behind the bench. "You deem me a Quaker for your own displeasure. So I will confound you further. I am not a Quaker but from the Unity of Brethren. A Moravian."

"You wear plain black dress," said Dowd.

The man sat and spooned stew to his trencher. "We share the Friends' belief against the vanities of clothing and appearance."

Dowd waggled a piece of cheese. "Charlatan. This morning you claimed Quakerism but now say you are but a cousin. Later you will tell us you are worse, a papist."

"I am only Silas," said the man. "You did not ask before because you did not care. Yet I tell you anyway."

Silas ate quickly and ladled more stew from the tureen.

"You eat hardy, with purpose," said Gert.

Mouth full, Silas slowed and swallowed. "Forgive such rudeness. My journey runs long and I covet the nourishment and joy of a well cooked meal."

"Covet is a curious word," said Dowd. "Are you also a zealot?"

"Just a wandering soul."

Quayland scratched under his neck kerchiefs. "You look a man long on the road."

"Longer than wanted."

Dowd shifted his stiff leg. "Through the valley or up from the south?"

Silas paused, spoon poised. "Does it matter?"

Dowd shifted again. "Perhaps. There is a war. Or so tis said."

Silas drank cider and wiped his chin. "An unfortunate outcome for all sides."

"Speak more about your faith," Quayland said. "I am not familiar."

"The Brethren are simple people of industry who work the land and pray only for its welfare. Our mission to the world is through congregational settlements."

Dowd spit stew back into his spoon. "Dear God, a Jesuit. Do you also draw lots?"

The Moravian resumed his food. "An ancient custom well known in the Bible."

"So you are a zealot. A lotter. Admit it."

Silas considered his answer. "At times for community decisions, yes."

Dowd sniffed disdain and pushed aside his trencher. "Fraud, heretic. True faith is bedrock and comes from a protestant God, not the vagaries of random chance and blind lots."

Noggin filled, Silas drank. "Lots are a sign of trust. Man's willingness to yield to God's will."

"Parson's poop," Dowd said. "You are a damn Jesuit."

Quayland sneezed and pried his nose with a kerchief. "Perhaps. But he speaks it right. Fate and faith are absolute."

Gert reached sliced fried pumpkin to Silas' trencher. "Whom do you seek to minister?"

The Moravian ate. "I come to master a Christian school among the Iroquois. Proper education is crucial for the Nations. What is learned early is oft what is later done."

Gert refilled his noggin. "Why make religion for the tribes? They want no white faith."

"All people deserve God's grace," Silas said. "Especially the uninitiated. My brethren have ministered among the Iroquois for many years."

Quayland sneezed again and resettled his askew hat. "Then why do none in this valley know your church?"

"We seek no notice," said Silas. "To instill a love of God is enough."

"Which side do you take in the rebellion?" Dowd's narrowed eyes warded another spasm.

Silas waited. "Neither. People must follow their own conscience. The Brethren recognize whatever lawful government rules."

Dowd snorted. "A banal answer. You evade the choice. Coward."

Shoulders stiffened, temper flared the Moravian's eyes. "No. We are not violent but not unwise. Some carry weapons to protect their families."

Quayland looked up. "And you?"

"I am not unwise." Silas resumed his food.

"I see no weapon," Dowd said. "And hear no spine."

"Because you choose not to see or hear," said Silas. "Your pique will not allow it. But do not doubt my will or my aim."

"You sound and look capable," the surveyor said. "How does a fit man of mature age like you avoid the war?"

"We are forbidden by church rule to serve in militia or as regulars."

"So cowards indeed," said Dowd. "Only armed revolt will purchase our freedom from British tyranny. Participate, sir. Do not watch others work the task for you."

He tapped his stiff leg with the walking stick. "I captained militia for the Crown against the French in the last war. A musket ball and rheumatism were my reward but I obtained some acres for my commission and put them to use. Land. Land is always key."

◑

Gert returned around the table. The lambs seemed an unhealthy group, wild plants ill-suited or unwilling to yield well among each other. Whether delivered by chance or

purpose she could not tell but the peculiar surveyor presented odd, his gullible manner untold by careful, quick eyes.
He glistened early fever and raw fingertips spoke hid sores.

"My husband served the same war and lost an arm."
Gert said. "The Colonials promised a small homestead for
his seven years but he passed this life broken, without payment and left me naught but his burdens."

Quayland turned toward her. "My regrets."

"Of those I'll have none." She wiped dribble from the
tureen with her apron.

"You concern me, madam," said Dowd. "I thought this
a patriot house."

"Think what you will," Gert said. "My loyalty is my
own."

Jacks entered from the front hall, filled his trencher
with bread and cheese and emptied the tureen on top. He
exchanged gauging, unspoken appraisals with the other
men and turned toward the small servant table along an
outside wall.

"There is ample room on the bench," said Silas.

The driver shrugged. "Aye, a common enough table.
But I'm a hired man, every bit, and my place is not among
you. The others will want their space. Why disturb the
peace?"

"Largess has limits," Dowd said. "You do not pay your
own board."

Jacks sat and ate, mouth open. "Could if I wanted.
Always have."

Gert approached the driver with cider and pumpkin.
"You bring strongish airs from the driver's bench."

Jacks shrugged. "A little sauce for taste. Sizes the room
but keeps the rules."

"Grumble your way," she said. "Are the man and woman
not to eat?"

The driver nodded toward the main entrance hall. "The birds linger on the stair."

Gert moved to the open entranceway. Near the top of the staircase Cotswold gripped tight Sybil's arm.

"These displays grow tiresome," he said.

Sybil twisted but did not free herself. "I want more than your indifference."

"Be careful what you wish for, my dear."

Cotswold noticed Gert, released Sybil and retrieved the heavy satchel beside his shoes.

"Forgive us. We are tardy to the bell."

"There's still meat," Gert said.

Sybil descended the stairs but looked away when she passed. Cotswold's curt half nod answered Gert's stare.

He escorted Sybil to the table beside Silas. The Moravian stood and nodded.

Quayland rose awkwardly, wiped dribbled cider from his chin and adjusted the fringes of his kerchiefs and hat. "My apologies. I did not see the lady arrive earlier."

Dowd grumbled and caned briefly up on his stiff leg.

Sybil sat on the bench and pushed stray blond hair across her forehead. "Pardon our worn appearance. A long day and an impolite road."

Cotswold placed the satchel on the floor between his feet and sat beside her.

"You have a city look, sir," said Dowd. "A proper man."

Gold-ringed fingers quickly guarded Cotswold's mouth. Head tilted dubious, he minced. "I sense no compliment."

He turned to Gert. "Madam, perhaps a brandy of taste. If not, a well agitated madeira. For the others as well, of course."

Gert liked not the gentleman and guessed his rings hid poor teeth. She pushed the bread platter toward the woman. "This be a country inn. We pour no brandy. Madeira is more durable."

Quayland smiled at Sybil. "What good deed brings you to the valley ahead of the storm?"

"My family—"

Cotswold interrupted. "Our business is our own. Trade and industry continue despite the war, as do matters of family."

Sybil's looked away, looked back. "An incomplete journey."

Cotswold ladled stew for Sybil and himself and glanced at the surveyor's hat. "A curious appendage. Did you pay for it?"

"I feel I am about to," said Quayland.

Dowd rotated the head of his walking stick in tight circles with his palm. "Pride and the bitter whim of an incautious hatter. A man should think more highly of himself."

"Indeed," Cotswold said. "We all suffer."

Silas looked at Gert. "Blunt talk. Is your table always so active?"

She carried the cider kettle and stew tureen toward the kitchen. "Is early yet. Likely the wine will decide it."

On his stool at the kitchen hearth Dayne ate from a small bowl. Face moody in fire glow, Lauch fingered chicken pieces from the simmering stew pot.

Gert handed Lauch the tureen and filled the kettle from a pail beside the fireplace. "More stew for the table room. Then bring madeira up from the cellar."

Lauch continued to eat.

"You heard me." She swiveled the pot away from him and moved past.

"I'm hungry. I want to eat." Lauch tongued dribble at the corner of his mouth.

Gert looked back. "You smell of ale. Wash first. Now, quick, before the Keeper comes."

Lauch stared hard at the fire. "Why? I'm not dirty."

Gert tore bread and cheese at the table. "You know that answer."

Lauch brooded but wet both arms and rinsed his mouth over the water barrel.

"More," Gert said.

He meagerly splashed his face. Water slow dripped from his chin.

She frowned impatient. "Why such sulk?"

"You treat me as a fetch dog. You and the Keeper both."

Gert extended a small bowl of cider. "Swallow some apple and your woe. And spill it on your coat. Will hide the smell."

Bake oven uncovered from wood coals, she finger poked for doneness a rim crusted pie. Thick smells of apples and molasses wafted.

Lauch moved close and inhaled. "What if I want pie instead?"

"You'll have what's left," said Gert.

Shoulders slumped but jaw jutted, he shook his head. His voice leaked quiet. "There won't be any for me. I want this one."

"Is not yours. Maybe tomorrow. A different pie, if made. Do the table and wine as I ask."

Lauch reached for the pie but Gert snapped his hand with an apron rag.

"To the cellar," she said. "Finish the bowl and cover your smell. Hear my words."

Face clouded by anger, Lauch set aside the cider bowl and left the kitchen.

Gert sliced the pie and placed a sliver on the table for Dayne. "Be not like your brother. Shape some candles for the meal table. Use both the three stick holders."

Dayne eagerly chewed the pie. Gert pinched his filled cheek, smiled and returned to the fire. He moved along-side and blunted the bottoms of tallow candles against the corner stone of the hearth.

CHAPTER SIX

Triple candlesticks unsteady in each hand, Dayne slowly entered the common room and stood close to the wall. Often nervous and timid around strangers, he sifted the grown-ups' faces and gestures at the crowded table for silent expectations. Tension and disagreement pricked his ears.

A man in black at the bench corner motioned him forward but he looked away and shook his head, a prisoner stiff and expressionless behind wobbly flame tips.

"I seldom discuss politics," said the coach gentleman. "No side convinces the other so what is the point? However, your rude preach begs me reconsider."

The large man with flabby cheeks busily pivoted the point of his walking stick on the floor. "Evade the issue how you will, sir. But corruption and outrageous taxes undermined the Crown and its legitimacy. To surcharge stamps, tea, newspapers and other daily activities without proper consent is heinous greed."

The gentleman's puzzled look flattened, an annoyed crease. "No consent was needed. You are subject to the King and protected by His Majesty. The British Army, not the colonial militia, defeated the French and saved the colonies. At considerable cost."

The cane walker waved an uncaring hand. "Most lives lost belonged to people born here, not Britons. We purchased our freedom with our own blood."

"Regardless," said the gentleman. "Government cannot survive without taxes and the levies were seldom paid. You but gloss disloyalty with a righteous lie."

Fingers pinched between his eyes the cane walker puffed angry. "Not words I take from any man, sir. Certainly not you."

The man in black smiled at Dayne and again gestured him forward. Tired of smoke and burnt tallow smell in his face, Dayne placed one candlestick on the floor and slowly approached with the other. Shaved too slender, several of the candles fell over and rolled on the table. Dayne went rigid, afraid of a scold.

The cane walker glared. "You are a clumsy, ungainly boy."

"No need for anger," said the man in black. "A simple accident. Easy to remedy."

Fallen candles calmly gathered, the man dripped melted wax from the basin of the table lamp into the fixture's cups and reset the candles. He smiled again and offered a snuffed candle for Dayne to re-light.

Dayne lit the wick, re-set the candle and shyly retreated behind the other fixture at the wall.

The man pushed the candles to the table center. "Now we have ample light."

The cane walker sniffed disagreeably and sat back from the candles' drift. "Tallow wicks are a smoky bother. Why thrust them so close?"

"The better for us each to see the other," said the man in black. "As God intended."

A man in an oversized red hat itched under his neck kerchiefs. "Illumination, even by the Almighty, is not always wise. What do Moravians pray for besides the land?"

"Our settlements center on the industry of hands and minds. We understand thrift but also the common good. Prosperity and safety uplift all."

"You touch the core of it," said the hat man. "Common good for common people. Rule by a foreign king across a distant ocean is contrary to basic notions of society."

The coach gentleman removed and wiped his eyeglasses. "You forget your heritage. The King is not foreign and all men are not equal, it is hash to say otherwise. There will always be an aristocracy, whether based on money or title, and the common man will always be common. English law, English custom and English tradition must rule. Not the tyranny of the mob."

"Mob or not, we have broken free of the royal yoke," said the hat man. "The only way now is for our own councils to govern."

The gentleman squinted, bemused. "Yoke? You but ruin a successful system. All have prospered these hundred fifty years of Crown rule and yet you want revolt? The masses cannot govern themselves. Rebellion only promotes anarchy."

Chin raised, the cane walker clenched and unclenched hands around the head of his stick.

"You are a bold Tory, sir."

"Of the deepest dye. Although that term is so vulgar, so Irish. I prefer Loyalist." The gentleman resumed his stew.

The hat man sipped cider. "Loyal to what?"

"A steadfast King and country. The structure, laws and ways of life carefully passed down for centuries. What has lasted so long is best left unaltered."

"The past is not the future," said the hat man. "It can never be. Current public will must rule."

Stew ended, the gentleman kept a hand at his mouth. "The mob knows not what it wants. Street views shift easy with each breeze and cannot long sustain any rational society."

The bursts of disagreement and unfamiliar words confused Dayne. Unsure what else to do, he carried the second candleholder to the opposite end of the table between the woman and the hat man. Wax dripped from the basin of the lamp onto the corner, he re-set each of the candles. The man in black nodded encouragement.

In shadows by the window the dark driver gnawed a chicken bone and hissed until Dayne turned. "Bring me a flame stick so I can see what I nibble."

Still uneasy at the driver's manner in the barn, Dayne stared.

The driver grinned and waggled the bone. "You're a skittish knob. And odd, too. I'll get a squeal yet."

Gert entered from the kitchen and collected trenchers. The man in black spooned crumbs, a final relish and offered up his wood satisfied.

"The apple pie spoke well," he said. "Crisp and heavy with molasses. A wayfarer's true delight on a cold eve."

"You fawn unneeded," said the cane walker. "The porridge will still come hasty, lumped and bland in the morn."

"Like some at this table," said Gert.

The woman softly cleared her throat. "No one asks my opinion on the matters at issue."

Puzzled, the cane walker turned. "Political discussion in a public house is not fit for a proper woman."

"Then I plead improper," the woman said. "How can I be otherwise with my avid uncle, you already see that. Women in fact hold strong social views men seldom hear because men seldom listen."

The gentleman's hand grasped her wrist. "My dear—"

"Let the lady join," said the man in black. "Our ears could benefit, surely."

Clutch withdrawn, the gentleman's annoyed frown continued. The woman dabbed and set aside her napkin, almost peeked at him and nodded at the man in black.

"This war comes from fracture," she said. "Distrust, disillusion and selfishness on both sides. The Crown is arrogant and corrupt, true. However, the patriot rabble who riot the streets flout the very liberties they espouse. How else do you heartily steal others' lawful property in the name of justice and equality? If they are the common men to rule us then we have no common future. Soon we will all speak Spanish or French."

Silence buzzed. Dayne shifted unsure, eyes alert. The woman seemed an unlikely talker.

Gert scraped the pie board with her knife. "A woman with notions. The roosters go quiet and scatter."

The gentleman cleared his throat. "Like many of her sex my niece often expresses her mind keen and at will, whether or not well mannered."

"Needed truth," said the man in black. "Many are the hands eager to revolt and take the mantle of freedom, few to do the hard work of crafting what follows."

The hat man ended a cough spasm with a gulp of cider. "Well said. To replace one form of corrupt government with another serves no purpose. Change is required but the people will decide what is best. We must trust ourselves and each other."

"Only a fool does so," the cane walker said. "But you are on the right side of it."

The gentleman turned to Gert. "Is there no wine, madam?"

She came around the table beside Dayne. "Go and find your brother."

Dayne went into the main entrance. Startled, Lauch wiped his mouth near the door to the tavern steps. His wet fingers and eyes pleaded for Dayne not to react.

Lauch bit into an apple from his pocket and carried a leather bladder past toward the common room.

Distress and disturbance groaned Dayne's spine. Lauch's words in the kitchen and unsure step brewed trouble. Afraid, he wanted to grab his brother's arm and tell him not to enter the room but did neither. He followed reluctant, disappointed.

At the table the gentleman's ringed finger tapped the table beside his tankard. "You may serve."

Lauch started forward, wavered and continued. Concerned, Gert moved to help too late.

He mishandled the bladder and spilled wine.

Dark madeira dripped the gentleman's sleeve and hand to the table and floor. "I am stained."

Lauch blinked. Dismay clamped his face.

The gentleman's curt flick failed to remove the spill. His annoyed squint seized Lauch. "How much drink did you steal in the cellar?"

Gert wiped the table spill and tankard with her apron and handed the gentleman a cloth.

"I regret the pour. No doubt you've suffered worse."

She took Lauch's arm. "Tumble it right. Or let me."

The gentleman's voice seethed. "Make him do it."

The mishap and harsh dislike in the room spooked Dayne. Arms clasped tight across his chest he swayed slight, eager to avoid more pain but unsure how to help his brother. In his mind he stepped forward to help but his body did not move.

Lauch's hands quivered. He slowly poured the wine and stepped back, relieved.

The gentleman dried his sleeve and hand with the cloth. "Come, who will join me?"

"I drink with no Tory." The cane walker covered his tankard.

The gentleman turned to the man in black. "And you?"

"Spirits are not a vice I may embrace."

"I'll share the man's wine if not his politics," said the hat man.

The cane walker huffed. "You have not the courage of your convictions, sir. Hardly a surprise."

Lauch moved around the table, Gert close at his side.

The hat man slid his tankard to a corner. "Tonight we are all but strangers, not foes."

The gentleman lifted his wine. "It appears only the adroit and clever get the wine. To the King's majesty."

"Rather to mischief and mayhem, wit and anarchy." The hat man drank.

The cane walker burped cider and shifted uncomfortable on the bench. "The Keeper's son reeks of pig and drink but what says the local boy of the war? Tyranny or revolution?"

Lauch set the bladder unevenly on the table edge. Wet fingers smeared his breeches and he glanced uneasy past Dayne toward the entrance hall.

"Or are you spineless like your father?" The cane walker pivoted his stick between broad knees.

"I have neighbors and friends on both sides," said Lauch. "The war brings fear, hatred and violence. I would stop them all."

The driver approached the table and took leftover bread and cheese. "I doubt it. The boy wields a weak bladder. Blunt talk addles him."

Lauch pulled his arm from Gert's grasp and turned to confront the others. "No. Indians wear paint and cross close upon our land. Some raid and pillage the valley. The worst is a half breed called the Beast. Skins people alive and boils them to the bone."

"Nonsense," said the cane walker.

"Truth," Lauch said. "He's burned farms, butchered families and even murdered an old widow who knelt in prayer. His tomahawk cleaved her skull down to the jaw."

Dayne winced, stiffened. He recalled such talk from the jail wagon visit.

The woman blanched and covered her mouth. "Dear God. How grotesque."

"A faithful but unfortunate end, if so," said the man in black.

The cane walker's finger chided the man. "And yet you minister such savages."

"People are savage only when provoked."

"Many rumors spread about this Beast," the hat man said. "Some claim he is a white hostage raised by the tribes but Christian educated, others hold he cannot possibly be. None doubt he is a murderer. Once he tied a dozen captured river boatmen in a line, worked himself into a frenzied dance and smashed their skulls with a war club. He leaves behind a red hand print to instill hatred and fright. A wild animal's mark, for such he is."

The gentleman finished his wine. "Atrocities occur with both sides. Part of war."

"This Beast is a myth," the cane walker said. "A ghost. The fright of ignorance and fear."

The hat man scratched under his kerchief. "No, the Beast is real enough. A rightful scourge and threat to this valley."

"Rumor is—" Lauch licked his lips and gathered his voice. "Rumor is he comes back to raid and pillage. Soon, already. Any who aid him will hang. Each here should know that."

"A bold statement," said the hat man.

The cane walker snorted. "Gossip overheard. And of what do you warn? Do you inform or do you accuse?"

The stern voice of Dayne's father came unexpected from the entrance hall. "Forgive my son's display. Sometimes he acts and speaks out of place."

Dayne turned. His father strode past into the room footsteps hard with purpose, always a sound of trouble.

Lauch pivoted abrupt and his hand knocked the bladder off the table. The loose stopper leaked madeira into a puddle on the floor near the driver.

"Your son is a clumsy alarmist, Keeper," said the cane walker. "Perhaps if he drank less of what he pours."

"An accident," the man in black said. "The lad meant no harm."

Dayne's father moved beside Lauch at the table and took the bladder. "Clean the mess and leave. Enough is done."

"I only—" Lauch began.

His father loomed closer. "Clean the mess and leave."

Gert handed Lauch an apron cloth. He knelt to wipe the floor but the driver did not move his boot. Lauch finished with the cloth and rose to speak.

"No words," said his father.

Eyes lowered but face red and angry, Lauch went into the kitchen.

"You blister your son for cheap tongue," said the cane walker. "At least he took a stand on the war. You still do not."

Dayne's father tightened the bladder cork. "This is my inn. I pulled every stone and cut every board. No one else. I owe no congress and no king for the right. Nor any of you."

"Loner's pride," the cane walker said. "Conceit. You sound a man afraid. Is it the choice or the consequence?"

"I do as I wish and as I need," said Dayne's father. "Has always been so. I regret my son's distraction."

He turned toward the kitchen with the wine bladder. Dayne quickly followed, protective of his brother and alarmed by his father's hard eyes.

Gert shut the kitchen door behind them. Dayne kept close along the wall, body low and hunched, small and away. Disturbed emotions in the room burst and rippled.

Lauch waited back turned at the water barrel. "Where is my pie?"

"None was left," said Gert.

Voice flat and lifeless, Lauch did not turn. "I knew it. So did you."

His father approached behind Lauch, angry and resolute. "When did you become such a drunken rumor monger?"

"I've a right to my own mind."

"What you need mind is me, your father."

He jerked Lauch's wine-soaked sleeve to his son's face. "Smell it. Smell the shame. Have I not told you—"

Lauch pulled away. "What if you have? Do you not always tell me what to do, what to feel, what to think? Am I a man myself or only your son?"

"Neither," said his father. "I claim no bottle sucker. Off. Off to the barn and muck where you belong."

Gert stepped forward. "Stop it, both of you! This be my kitchen and I will not have it embarrassed by the likes of this. Keeper, this be not the time or place. And you, Lauch, mind your way. This is your father you speak to."

Dayne's father leaned close to Lauch, voice cold. "To the barn. Take your stench from this house."

His brother turned. "Why? Because I am like you?"

His father raised an open palm but Gert moved in between. "It ends now, you hear me," she said. "Lauch, go on."

Stubborn fear struggled Lauch's eyes. He angled past his father and left the kitchen.

Gert glared. "You are a fool, Keeper. A fool. These boys are all you have. Your own, the last of you. You'll lose them both this way."

She glanced toward Dayne.

He turned close against the corner, eyes wide but lost, quivered by disorder and discord. Strained breaths created a faint whistle.

Gert gently touched his shoulder. "Is over now, son. To your room. Come back when I say."

Dayne edged toward the door but looked back. Rimmed by fire his father roughly stoked the grate and brooded into the sparks and flames.

Gert stomped flared embers on the floor and brushed another off his father's shoulder. "You'll burn us all yet."

◖

Empty quiet.

Dayne stood at the entrance of the main hall into the common room. The rankled words and crowd of unhappy people from the night's supper left no marks behind. Dwindled lamps puddled dim light on the ends of the meal table and the triple candlesticks once so proud and bright in his hands sat unlit, abandoned.

The hard anger between his father and Lauch in the kitchen lingered different. Their crackled noise and pained bursts of color still squeezed, disturbed. At times Dayne wished for life alone, without family, yet the notion scared him. He needed connection, roots and the lifeblood of being.

Dayne wondered where the past went, where it stayed. Memories held part but not all. Images and sounds he did not remember often nudged and confused his mind with questions, hints of events not his. Perhaps the past came back. Never ended.

He crossed to the kitchen doorway and peeked inside. Gert mumbled, hunched busy over plants and cuttings on her window work table. Dayne entered and sat a stool by the hearth. The kitten curled asleep by his feet, plump belly exposed toward the fire warmth. Smells of stew and molasses drifted and he escaped into the soft hiss and flickering trance of the fire.

Gert passed and dried trenchers from a wash tub across the hearth. Pale eyes hard and coarse like her gray hair, she always seemed worried if protective. Her infrequent inner light, rich and many colored, blended affection but also shadow. He did not see it this night.

For most of his life Dayne thought Gert his mother. She tended his needs and called him son but he was not of her, not her blood. The day he turned eight she gave him a cameo of his mother's faded image and said she died at his birth. He sensed more, a secret hidden in regret and pain. The untold mystery kept him incomplete.

Once he showed Lauch the image but his brother avoided further talk and said their father would not like it. Dayne already knew. When he proudly displayed the cameo on a leather neck strap he made for it his father turned away upset.

Yet he longed for the simple memory of birth, his beginning and purpose, confused such basic need went unheeded. Only the cameo spoke, a stranger's profile he often looked to in vain for some hint of recognition and blood bond. Its absence festered deep within him, the unhealed wound which upheaved his soul and shaped his numb silence.

"You can do the kettle now," said Gert.

Against the edge of an oven peel Dayne shucked kernels from corn cobs into a kettle set in ash piled at the corner of the hearth.

The hat man entered the doorway and scratched his long neck. "Pardon, but the upstairs rooms grow cold early. Might—"

Gert placed hearth coals inside a long-handled bed warmer. "I can work a poultice to salve that neck itch."

The man removed his hand. "No need. An interesting table tonight, ardent and brisk. The cripple was righteous rude, as was the Tory."

Gert handed him the warmer. "Both hold high airs for not much. Return the pan when done. Others will want it."

"Yes, the niece," the man said. "Of course."

He left. The kettle clattered and Dayne pried the lid to look inside.

"Not too eager," Gert said. "Peek close and you'll lose an eye."

Several kernels of popped corn jumped out to the hearth. Dayne closed the lid and ate the pieces.

Gert retrieved a small skillet at the fire and moved beside him. "A special treat tonight. Not cream but butter, the way you like."

Dayne emptied the corn into a bowl and she poured the melted butter. He chewed mouth open, slow at first but more interested as rich flavors ripened his mouth.

Gert lightly touched his hair. "I know you worry about Lauch. I will tend him later myself, once the house quiets. Eat full. Morning waits long."

Dayne finished the corn and savored its warm plenty in his stomach.

"Is time. Bring the cat." Gert handed him a lit candle nub.

Yawning kitten cradled in one arm and candle in his other hand, Dayne followed her in a small drifting pool of light through the common room and along the shadowed main hall to his room door.

"Heed the bed first," said Gert. "If too cold then the hearth. I will fetch another blanket."

She went into her room opposite. Dayne turned into his sparse room and set the kitten to the floor. Thick chill and gloom seeped the walls and he placed the wavering candle nub on the window sill.

Atop the bed quilt Dayne cupped hands around the cameo of his mother on its leather neck strap. The harsh unsmiling likeness often haunted his thoughts and dreams. He wanted to know what she looked like as a child his age and when she gave birth to him and if now she would look old and gnarled like Gert. His thumb rubbed the cover glass, a yearning for physical connection always beyond his touch.

Gert's voice came from the hall. "You do not often take your rifle to the post. What do you hunt so late?"

His father answered. "A gypsy was about this morning. Best to walk and see. The snow deepens. Will come a foot thick by morning."

"Take this to Dayne. The night turns bitter."

Hesitation marked his father's voice. "Is your blanket. Your notion."

"Take it to him. He saw and heard you with Lauch. Make amends."

His father opened the door slow, unsure and entered the room. Head and coat salted with snow, he set his long rifle and the yard light against the wall and turned.

"You forgot the lantern—" He saw the cameo and stopped.

Dayne searched his father's face, a voiceless question.

"I brought a blanket. For the cold." His father shifted awkward back and forth and extended the blanket.

Dayne stared past, empty and unwilling.

His father waited. "This morning with the hogs I meant only to teach and show what you need learn. Tonight with Lauch was the same. Your brother oft stumbles and needs reminding."

Aware he pained his father but unyielding and un-moved, Dayne blocked the words and looked only at the cameo.

"Your mother and I had differences," said his father. "Does not mean I did not care. Let no one tell you other. Talk to me, son."

Dayne shook his head once, stiff refusal. He returned the cameo under his shirt, lifted the sleeping kitten and readied his quilt and pillow.

His father blinked, hindered and confused. He set the blanket across a stool, clawed hard at his beard and re-treated from the room.

Resentment, remorse and resolve struggled inside Dayne. Such stubborn failures with his father angered, unhealed festers which gripped and guiled him even as pain and dismay flooded his heart.

He put on a scarf and woolen head cover and crawled under the quilt. Shadows shrouded the room and his brother's empty bed stirred vague misgiving. Kitten pulled snug at his chest, the rapid pulse of its unspoiled heart eased his mood.

Dayne reached back and set the wood root given by Lauch beside the nub. He thought to pinch the flame but wanted its comfort and rolled away.

Distorted grotesquely, the Peddler's face filled the window. His narrow eyes searched within. One eye widened.

CHAPTER SEVEN

COTSWOLD'S HEAVY SATCHEL and neatly folded great coat centered the bed. Two padlocked floor trunks crowded the floor.

Shirt sleeves rolled back tight despite the cold he carefully aligned the gold signet ring on his small finger. No one ever questioned the false family crest. Perception mattered, gullibility followed. Weakness he thrived on with crust and insolence, a bullied boy grown up gentleman impostor. The irony of his revenge always sustained and no longer surprised.

Cotswold turned a small shaving mirror face down.

Imperfection ruled him. Fingers traced pocked cheeks and he tongued misshapen teeth, results of childhood frailties and poor family traits. The cruel daily reminders girded his sarcasm and engulfed the deep inward place where he festered, hid. No child deserved such ridicules. So early on he refused the forward curse of unsightly, unjust fatherhood. His one good deed, the favor of his vanity.

Wistful for the indulgent manicures, hot shaves and reckless gossips of his city barber, Cotswold opened his razor and bent to the onslaught of cold basin water, a small flinch his only concession. The meticulous scour of his unlathered neck filled the room's brooded stillness, brief normalcy and routine after the frayed uncertainty of wilderness flight.

A quiet knock interrupted and Cotswold partially opened the door. His perturbed squint barred Sybil's entry and he peered into the hallway behind her. "Did anyone see you?"

"Who do you think we mislead?"

"Answer."

"No. Only one is yet upstairs."

Cotswold stepped back, widened the door and resumed his shave.

Sybil entered, shut the door and waited uneasy. Shawl pulled close, one hand strayed to her abdomen. "Why shave on such a bitter night?"

"A cold blade brings challenge, a test of proper form and resolve."

Razor cleaned on a cloth, Cotswold pressed his cheek flat and continued its scrape. "You meddled during dinner. Ever the proud peacock."

"Men and their politics. You were also bold. Rare to see you so adamant, especially with strangers."

"Self-righteous radicals, fools in fever at rebellion. A needed foil, an easy entertainment. You clutch again."

Sybil waited to remove her hand. "We need talk."

"Your timing, as ever, is errant."

"I am here to be with you. Yet you ignore me. We are both refugees and should not abandon the other. Have I not earned my place?"

Cotswold scraped precise around his creased mouth. "You were not so—burdened—before."

Sybil blinked. "Is that what you call it?"

"And you do not hide it well, either by dress or mannerism. I think you proud of the issue."

"Would you prefer shame?"

"I prefer—I prefer nothing."

Cotswold cleaned the razor a final time, tied his hair back and adjusted his cravat. "It will not aid. You know that."

"Should I have denied you?"

Wry petulance curled the corners of his mouth. "Then you would not be here. Save your pride, my dear."

Sybil stepped forward. "You promised—"

Cotswold turned slightly and she stopped.

"I provided a chance, only that," he said. "An escape from dreariness and your mother's washboard. You knew the price. I thought you smarter."

Pained confusion colored her face. "Why so angry?"

He bared poor teeth. "I want no spawn. I need no spawn."

"Spawn? Am I but a she dog gone to spoil? What if I expose you?" Anger and doubt wavered Sybil's voice.

Cotswold put on his gentleman's coat, brushed its sleeves and pulled his cuffs. "These people are rank provincials and hold no sway. No, you will not mire me. Besides, where would that leave you? Stranded here in the wilderness? With Jacks? Or is that what you two plot?"

"Only you would think that."

"I know his kind."

Sybil's hand came back to her abdomen but she forced it away. "Do not ignore me nor your child."

"Your mistakes are not mine."

She nodded, resigned. "I see that now."

Hefted from the bed, the satchel sagged Cotswold's shoulder. "Need you speak further?"

"You clutch that bag too dear. It bends your soul."

He stepped past, opened the door and glanced along the hall. "You are the one afflicted by a bastard, not I. Let no one see you leave."

Hesitant in the doorway she looked back. "Two bastards."

Sybil shut the door and turned.

Face set hard, at the hall landing Gert held a tavern lamp and the bed warmer. "I thought you might want this."

She set the long-handled pan against the wall. "Some things it will warm. Others it is best not to try."

Sybil started to speak but stopped, embarrassed. Gert descended the stairs.

◐

Dim lamp raised against the dark, Gert carried an empty basket down the tavern steps. She paused at the bottom, troubled by reddish hearth hue spread across the stone floor. The light shifted more alive, hungry than usual. An unwelcome omen.

She crossed to the cellar. The outside tavern door opened behind her and she quickly shielded the lamp and peeked around the cellar entrance. A cloaked figure stomped snow from his legs, approached the steps upstairs and climbed with measured footfall. Silas, his pack saddle and mule girth entered the faint light from the open hall door above.

Gert turned into the root cellar. Crooked shadows enlivened by the lamp shifted along narrow passages and recesses, shelves and barrels. Insistent gurgle of an unseen spring and rich earthen smells of the farm's ground harvest, its lifeblood, comforted her heart. Eyes closed, she inhaled deep and slow.

Parsnips, beans, cabbage, carrots, potatoes and beets collected for the next day's stew, Gert pulled her shawl tight against unexpected drafts of cold air. Curious, she crossed the main cellar to a partially ajar rear door. Snow danced past the lamp flicker and recent footprints trailed toward the barn.

She closed the door and placed two inner cross braces. "Lauch, this best be you."

A muffled sound in a recess drew the light. Fallen and wedged against a corner shelf, breaths ragged in the cold air, Lauch lay among dropped shoulders of meat. Ale dripped from a cask beside an empty bottle, dark wine stained his chin and throat and urine wet the soil between his legs.

Gert knelt and touched his shoulder. "Oh, child. The drink ruins you."

Lauch blinked and recoiled until recognition slowly dawned. He mumbled, meek and slurred. "He's 'ere."

"What?"

"Bar—"

"Barn? Who is in the barn?"

"Mus' 'top."

Gert set the lamp on the ground, pushed away the wine bottle and felt his head for injury.

Lauch pawed her arm. "Mus' 'top. Knots. I saw."

"You speak gibberish."

The sound of footsteps and movement filtered through the tavern door.

"Stay quiet," whispered Gert. "The Keeper cannot see this. I'll come back when he settles for the night."

She touched his cheek and rose. Lauch reached but his hand fell empty. He sobbed and weakly tilted to the side.

Gert retrieved the basket and lamp and crossed toward the tavern entrance. The Innkeeper and his rifle loomed from darkness and filled the shadowed doorway.

"You startle," she said.

"Where is Lauch?"

"Not here. Perhaps the barn."

Gert edged forward to pass but the Innkeeper did not move.

"The rum cabinets are locked," he said. "Let the tavern fire wane. Neglect may keep the lambs upstairs. Less work."

"An unwelcome brood. None like the other."

"I am not sure which yields worse. The war or politics."

"They are the same. What of Dayne?"

"He wanted no blanket. The boy quiets me for purpose."

"Too often strangers, both of you. He will learn. You will learn."

Movement rustled among shelves behind Gert. She shifted and scraped the basket against a shelf.

"Lauch's drunken talk stirred unneeded fires," said the Innkeeper. "He knows not to gossip in this house. Yet did I bark too loud?"

"He is young despite his age and wants to show his feathers. Will not be the last such. Leave him for the night. You both went bruised."

The Innkeeper set the rifle inside the doorway, hand pensive at his beard.

"I am strange tired of late," he said. "Thoughts and distractions burden, dark unease. Coldness comes and not the storm. I know not what or why, only that it waits, grows."

Gert nodded. "I feel it also. Scares me."

The Innkeeper started forward. "I told Lauch to bring meat to the spring from the smoke house. Likely he ignored my words."

A louder sound of spilled nuts or grain came from the cellar darkness.

Gert blocked the Innkeeper's path. "Let it be."

His puzzled glance dissolved into assumption and erupted into anger. "What do you hide? Lauch?"

He grabbed the lamp from Gert, pushed past and searched empty passages and recesses.

"Lauch! Lauch! Do not make me find you."

The spill sound continued. Gert groaned inward, aware what would follow.

The Innkeeper pivoted, strode and thrust the lamp at his son's drunken, beleaguered face. "Look at you."

Trapped in the corner, Lauch struggled to his knees and spilled more acorns from a shelf sack. Scared eyes pleaded. "'Tis 'im. 'im. The Beas—"

"Stop!" said the Innkeeper. "You act but a fool."

Lauch gestured helplessly at Gert. "Will no one see? I 'ound—I 'ound—"

The Innkeeper held the lamp beside the dripping cask and along the wine and urine stains across his son's front. "You found only the bottle. Did I not say the next time I would beat its stench from you?"

Open hand raised the Innkeeper moved closer and Lauch backed unsteadily against the wall. Gert tried to intercede but the Innkeeper blocked her.

"Stand back!" he said. "He gets but his due."

"The table wine was an accident," said Gert. "Lauch's talk changed nothing."

The Innkeeper whirled. "You both join against me. Why lie for him?"

He raged over Lauch. "Do not cower. Act a man."

Clumsy arm lifted to counter the expected blow, Lauch tottered sideways and dislodged the shelf. He collapsed on the ground in a spill of nuts, berries and roots.

The Innkeeper kicked at the debris and reached for Lauch but Gert shielded him with her body, back-turned fury and defiance.

"Keeper!" she said. "In the name of God I'll not let you do this."

The Innkeeper shifted but Gert angled, Lauch's head cradled to her chest. "Keeper! "Keeper!"

Rapid blinks and twitches drained the Innkeeper's face. His hand quivered and slowly lowered. "Would you have this weakling ridicule us all?"

"You cannot do this," Gert said. "Lauch is yet your son."

"Agh, then I claim him not." The Innkeeper spit at his son's feet.

Lauch flinched as if struck and began to sob.

The Innkeeper held forth the wine bottle. "Here is your beast. Its dung swallows your soul."

Gert glared and rocked Lauch back and forth. "Leave. Just leave."

The Innkeeper tossed the bottle to the ground and turned from the passage.

Lauch continued to sob, eyes barely open, voice a faint slur. "Pow'er."

"More gibberish," said Gert. "Cease."

Lauch shook his head and an insistent hand clutched her sleeve. "Pow'er. I saw."

Gert's cradle slowed. "Powder? Gun powder?"

"Bar—"

"In the barn?"

Lauch nodded and closed his eyes. "Beas—"

Gert quieted him against her chest and resumed. "I know."

◑

Soft rhythmic thuds.

The Innkeeper drummed his forehead against the wall inside his dim shadowed room, eyes wide. Roiled by the confrontations with Lauch and Dayne, failure, anguish and rage swirled, pilfered his sense of control. Reasons and excuses drifted past clouded and confused, hope and good intent ruined by temper and mistake.

On a table the dirty yellow flame of a half melted candle set in drips of wax trembled stubborn and defiant, vulnerable and exposed. Hog tallow tainted the cold air.

The Innkeeper sat restive on the bed. Above his protective mask of thick beard, fingers stiff and calloused traced deep skin creases, insidious reminders and scars of fitful life. Spiritual but not religious, he no longer doubted the nature of things ran longer than a man's years and grievous sins followed their owner to the grave and beyond. Bitter fullness tightened his throat.

Angered his right hand quivered against his will, the Innkeeper forced a determined fist. He chided himself about strength, resolve and refusal to abide his sons' weaknesses or his own.

The candle sputtered. Surrounding blackness crept closer.

Crisp tastes of rum and ale haunted his throat, ripples and blossoms of temptation which consumed his thoughts.

Lauch gulped that nectar too early and reveled lazy in its surrender while Dayne hid safe within obstinate silence away from the demands of others. The Innkeeper deeply resented his sons' freedoms and escapes.

Fury rose, turned inward. Clutched and afflicted, flawed, he but repeated his father's drunken abuses, petty spites and violent threats. Patterns of rage and regret the Innkeeper swore never to imitate yet continued on Lauch and Dayne.

Desperate for the redemption of resolve he glanced around the room. Chill void, absence. No warmth, no hiding place. His life passed not as he planned or hoped. Twenty years of hard fought survival in wilderness granted no peace or decent birthright, only diminishment, disquiet and the final rueful ebb of mortality.

Steadfast yet embittered, he stared at the dwindled candle flame.

Later in endless night, unable to sleep and trapped in troubled purgatory between rank exhaustion and an un-quelled mind, he relented and opened his blanket chest. The familiar bottle feel of the flask soothed his hand and sharp rum smell taunted and provoked, savage elixir he detested but could not elude. His dark family addiction passed square to him and from him.

He swallowed the rum, flung the empty flask on his bed and felt behind the corner ceiling beam until he found another.

Ensnared, he threw back his head and drank hard.

◗

Cold and dark choked Dayne's room.

Icy flakes hissed the window and only a faint wisp of burned wick remained of the candle. Eyes open and the kitten's exposed head ticklish at his cheek, he laid stiff and tried to ignore pockets of raw chill between quilts.

The dim shape of his brother's unused bed loomed across the room. He listened eager for Lauch's safe return but only his father's closing door and unsettled footsteps in the hall earlier bothered night's burdened silence.

Dayne climbed from bed, pulled the quilt tight against the wave of cold and felt Lauch's empty space. Door opened, he peeked into the hall and left the room. The sleepy kitten squeaked displeasure and followed beside his feet. The candle at the end of the hall burned low, lonely.

Dread pricked his senses. Among the shadows an unknown tear in the inner fabric of the inn rustled fresh, alive with disturbance and pain. Concern about Lauch and the tavern steps pulled Dayne's hand toward the knob of the closed downstairs door. Unwilling to confront his unease, he moved past.

In the kitchen he dropped wood on the fire and pushed his stool close. Lauch's wood root clutched in his lap, he faced the hearth like an animal hopeful for dawn's sacred promise of warmth and renewal from darkness.

He wanted to sleep but fear of consuming blackness jarred him awake when he drifted to the edge of escape. Ill dreams lurked. Night haunts, deep sharp feelings and random frights of a different unfamiliar world. At times similar visions intruded days he wandered fields and forests near the farm, odd goads and signs he did not want or understand, images of ancient past and indistinct future, life paths taken and not yet filled.

Often unseen presence followed or pursued Dayne on his forest walks. At times bright and protective and at others vengeful and dark, its unspoken voice murmured his mind with strange words and feelings, dim unrecalled memories.

Discomforted and cold, Dayne moved the stool closer to the fire and tugged the quilt tight around his shoulders. Exhausted, fitful sleep gradually closed his eyes.

The dream came early.

Black arrowhead on his open palm, Dayne stood entranced by the shifting veils of the waterfall above, sheltered safe within the roar of dropping water. Shrouds of fog and mist partly obscured the Indian's giant rock face but he knew it watched, waited.

Dayne rose weightless in the air. Cold spray from swollen stream rush watered his sight and he struggled not to move, afraid the dream would end and he would fall into the bouldered pool far below. A giant red spruce towered overhead, gnarled and ravaged by years yet rooted deep in the ground, a keeper of the earth.

He hovered above the fall, eyes captured by views never beheld before. Endless winter wilderness stretched along rugged mountainsides ahead and behind the distant bend of the broad river seemed a thread against deep forests, Indian lands girded by fear and mystery. Beneath him the inn, barn and fields in the narrow valley which so dominated his life sat small, unimportant.

Without effort Dayne surged forward along the stream and drifted up and down with the wind unaware of time, distance or cold. Mind empty bliss, he joyed in free movement and life unbound, the world of a bird, and wondered how far he might go, what he might see. Triumphant voice sounded deep within his being.

Escape did not last. Clouds heavy with weather gathered past the mountains and change crept the air. Unwilling to cease, Dayne pretended it away but dark brood and burden always returned.

Above empty woods Dayne stalled, unable to rise. Scared deer ran past below and chill wind hunted his face. An unseen dog barked anxious and the raw lurk of a prey beast wisped the air.

Breeze pushed him toward a small clearing and cabin. Children in hide coats played ring toss in the yard and their father raked straw into the crop shed. Dayne floated past unseen and settled to ground near a hard flowing creek inside barren woods. Angry limbs angled too close over-head, threat and omen, but thick solitude and water sound soothed his unease.

Dayne peeked around a tree at a young farm boy squat at the water's edge. With a stick the familiar stranger from other dreams pried loose stones and Dayne stepped forward eager for companionship.

The boy stood and turned. Large shy eyes framed a face pained by plea and need. He extended a smooth black stone on his open palm.

An old trick used before yet Dayne wanted to believe. He knew such loneliness, doubt, confusion. His hand reached to accept.

The boy shifted the stone back and forth between closed fists. Face distorted by spite and cruel laughter, he leered quick changing masks of Dayne and Lauch, Dayne's father and mother and himself. Each twisted into the next, bursts of different pains and emotions.

Dayne flinched. Hot scratches of rivalry and temper soured his throat. The timeless game resumed unwanted. Angry at his weakness, he turned back into the woods.

Sounds drifted past, vague and unclear. The crackle of shouts and gunshots followed. The boy hurried to the edge of the tree line and Dayne ran behind to warn and stop him. Too late.

In the clearing the small cabin burned with savage fury and its family died stricken in the yard, taken without reason or mercy. Life removed sudden. Sight of the fierce painted Mohawk chieftain and his war club over the dog's body overwhelmed Dayne.

Ancient hatred, blood lust. The horror of his enemy clear, unwavering. Fear squeezed Dayne's heart, buckled his knees. The warrior shrieked and charged forward.

Dayne fled. He wanted to fly again but his legs dragged heavy and would not lift. Arms flailed against pokes and scratches of branches and briars. He begged inward for rescue, escape but heard only the thrash and thuds of his pursuer.

Across the creek Dayne glanced back and saw the frightened, exhausted boy stalled in the dark water. He pulled the boy forward, pushed him up the rocky bank and together they lunged among desolate trees. Splashes and enraged grunts closed behind.

A second shriek, immediate and curdling, drove the boy to his knees. Dayne stopped and reached back but could not grasp the boy's arms. He stumbled down in dead leaves as the deadly war club surged just past his head.

Sound of the fatal skull crack rippled Dayne's bones. Beside his face the boy's large eyes dwindled, ceased and the smooth black stone dropped from his dying hand. A shrill cry of brute conquest etched Dayne's ears. His eyes trembled shut.

On the kitchen stool Dayne shuddered awake. Clutched tight, the chiseled edges of the black arrowhead sliced his palm.

He blinked confused, unsure if he was dead. Sharp pain creased the back of his head yet the hearth fire still burned and kitchen shadows remained as before. Afraid, he did not move.

The fire waned and cold crept, surrounded. Dayne pretended to be warm and drifted in and out of empty awareness until exhaustion closed his eyes and time passed unknown.

Loud noise winced him awake.

The driver stared close from the hearth. Kindling snapped under his heel, he flipped wood into the flames.

"Not just your prize this night," said the driver. "A cookery always warms better than a musty tavern floor."

Blankets unrolled, he stretched oversized boots rude near Dayne and the sleeping kitten.

Dayne scraped his stool farther away and slid the kitten toward him. The driver sneered, belched and rolled toward the flames.

Sleep did not return. Fire glow tinged the hearth the same awful color as the bloodied boil of the hog cauldron and Dayne forced away images of the slaughter but could not escape images of the farm boy's unseeing face, so close. Shame and regret blackened his heart. Once more he failed to speak, to save.

The horrors of the Indian warrior pounded. Painful truth sat hard, unrelenting.

The Beast was real, within and without, and came for him.

Dayne grasped the neck cameo, an embrace and plea for comfort. His mother's cruel cackle echoed across time.

CHAPTER EIGHT

THREE EMPTY FLASKS.

The Innkeeper's empty stare escaped none. In faint morning light along his bedside floor each overturned goad spoke separate unremembered surrenders. More failure, more guilt.

Sprawled chest down across unused quilts, he wanted no memory. Yet shards of night images and ill dreams notched his mind, confused outbursts of fury and torment, lost moments from the cellar and tavern framed only by the caw of certain regret.

The Innkeeper looked away and absently thumbed the hardened wax outline of a missing nub on the bedside table.

Brittle cold burdened the room. He struggled stiffly upright, pulled loose his great coat and strained to urinate in a bucket chamber pot. His piss reeked of rum.

Hurried footsteps in the hall preceded an urgent knock. The Innkeeper edged the door open and squinted at Gert.

She sniffed. Her eyes flashed suspicion, disappointment. "Is Lauch. Downstairs. Quick."

He followed into the hall but paused, reluctant to approach the door to the tavern steps but unsure why. Gert glanced back, motioned him forward and went downstairs. A shadowed veil settled, surrounded as he filled the doorway.

Gert knelt at the bottom step next to Lauch's crumpled upside down body. "Neck is broke. Dayne found him going to the barn."

The Innkeeper descended and stood grim, ungiving over his son's body.

Face down on the stone floor, Lauch's head bent hard to one side and his legs splayed behind over the steps. Frightened, surprised eyes stared above his bruised contorted mouth. Taut grasping fingers reached out desperate, unfulfilled.

Inward wince peeled the Innkeeper's spine. One fist clenched, unclenched and clawed his beard in silent cry of bitter shame and dismay. He slowly hardened, blinked and a single massive pulse pounded shut his mind.

"A lazy child, weak at heart," he said. "Stained by the bottle."

Gert touched Lauch's mottled cheek beside a trickle of blood. "Lauch was pushed, bottle or not. That I feel. He saw or heard something last night what scared him. That I know. The fear in his eyes was not but of you."

"His fear of me was just."

"Aye, and it kept him from you. Why would you not listen to his words?"

"He spoke the fool, filled with notions by Thaler and the others. You saw him. Was the drink, nothing more."

"Yet you forced him to it, not away. Was always his weakness and your own. See now the result." Gert stroked Lauch's face.

The Innkeeper retrieved a cold candle nub from the step beside Lauch's foot and slipped it into his coat pocket unnoticed.

"This is not of me," he said.

Gert rose, face blunt. "Will you not admit your part?"

She glanced past him and the Innkeeper turned. Jacks watched above from the hall door but retreated from sight.

"You have but one son now, Keeper. See you don't forget him." Gert moved beside Dayne at the hearth.

He trembled, eyes and head averted, empty milk pail clutched tight in both hands. The Innkeeper approached and lifted his son's chin toward Lauch's body. Dayne flinched.

"You have seen death on this farm before," said the Innkeeper. "Hear my words. The drink did this, took your brother. Look hard and learn. Lauch's end was ill-favored and need be remembered."

He stepped in front of Dayne to block the view and tapped the pail. "Now, finish your chores. Gert and I will see to this."

Single tear on his cheek, Dayne's eyes strayed to his brother's body before he carried the pail toward the cellar.

Gert turned to the Innkeeper. "Take Lauch up to the parlor."

Solemn and stiff, he hefted his son's body over one shoulder and trudged up to the main floor. Gert followed to the front entrance opposite the common room, unlocked the parlor door with a key from her apron and cleared a table inside. The Innkeeper passed close with the body.

"Wash your taint," she said.

"Is Lauch you sniff."

"Soon, before Dayne smells it. You were cruel with him downstairs. Ignored his hurt."

"He need be stronger than his brother."

The Innkeeper stepped back from the corpse. His son's lifeless eyes pursued, final anger and agony, an eternal grip of accusation. The Innkeeper blinked and turned away.

Gert gently touched the bruised corner of Lauch's mouth. "He looks not at peace. The fall marks him."

Her fingers closed his eyes and draped a lace cloth over his face. "I will wash and dress him later. Lauch was wrongly seen. Harmed no one and sought only the same for himself."

"Say naught to the others," said the Innkeeper. "Is not their concern. I will bury Lauch when the storm clears. But no ceremony. Nothing to recall this shame."

"Keeper—"

"Nothing. The wake tonight will be his end. Then the ground."

Gert stared hard, face flushed by anger and doubt, an unspoken question he would not answer. "Why peer at me so, woman?"

The Innkeeper fled to the door but looked back. Mouth opened to speak, explain he stayed silent and left the room.

Gert turned to the body, adjusted the face cloth and smoothed hair at Lauch's forehead. Her hand lingered, fear and doubt unresolved.

"Forgive us, child. Winter is a harsh time."

She locked the parlor, returned to the tavern with a rag and bucket and on bent knees scoured death's taint, real and imagined, from the bottom step.

Matted with snow, Dayne entered and waited beside the filled milk pail near the steps until Gert finished.

"He is in the parlor room," she said.

Dayne hefted the pail with both hands, lurched over the dark wet stain on the first step and climbed toward the hallway. Gert followed and unlocked the parlor door. Dayne searched her eyes.

"Not forbidden," she said. "Not today."

Gert took the pail from his hands, set it on the floor and knelt before him. "Remember your brother as he was. Not as he is."

Dayne entered alone and stopped. Unsettled past emotions and festered secrets rankled the crowded forsaken room. Vague shapes, noises without color.

A harpsichord and spinning wheel beneath the shuttered front window and forgotten child toys and games waited, stuck in time. Moth ravaged old clothes, dresses and faded needlepoints reeked musty decay. Gert once told him some of the unfamiliar items belonged to his mother but she and his father rarely spoke of the room and always kept it locked, a mystery not his.

Gert moved alongside and touched his shoulder. "This is where Lauch was born. Also you."

Taps and heavy footsteps descended the second floor stairs and approached along the entrance. Pinched and winded, the cane walker peered from the door.

Gert quickly shut the door and returned beside Dayne. "I cannot explain this death and have no answers. Not yet. For now it just is. Like it will be for all of us."

Her eyes searched, questioned.

Unwilling to reveal his pain or emotion Dayne stared empty, numb at the floor. He knew not how or what proper way to say goodbye.

"I worry for your heart," Gert said. "Is no shame to be upset or cry."

She tugged his ear, stood and left him alone.

Dayne slowly approached the body. Memories and feelings flooded yet blurred and yielded no comfort. Life without his brother seemed lonely, wrong, unkind punishment.

Stymied by the face cloth, he heaved and snorted pained, strangled sounds. Denial of a final chance to remember and touch Lauch's face, unexpected, seared and confused his heart.

Dayne needed to see his brother's eyes. He hoped their last images remained etched inside, the final pieces of Lauch's path and the truth of what happened in the night.

◑

Fire glow stained Gert's coarse hands red as she stirred porridge at the kitchen hearth. Brow clenched, she worried the cause of Lauch's death. The smell of drink on the Keeper and clouds of doubt and guilt in his eyes lingered rude reminders, unwanted truths she pushed away.

Cloth pulled from her apron, Gert lifted the pot from its trammel and entered the common room. She set the porridge on the meal table beside stacked trenchers, bowls and platters of bread and cheese. Dowd and Quayland sat ends of one bench, Silas cornered opposite.

Dowd sniffed the pot and huffed. "Madam, you serve bare gruel once again."

"New bread," said Gert. "Make do. Is not a morning for cookery."

He reluctantly spooned porridge to his trencher. "A miserably cold night. Fitful bedding and loose ropes. The morning goes not much better."

Silas filled and cupped hands around a new-filled bowl. "I rested well if not warm. Anything hot is welcome."

"You sided with the Tory last night," said Dowd. "Why?"

"The Brethren have no preference, nor do I," said the Moravian. "Our mission and faith are all that matter."

Unhappy at the porridge, Dowd took up the bread and cheese but did not pass the platter. Silas waited, reached and exposed reddened areas on knuckles of his right hand.

"Your hand goes bruised," said Gert.

Silas nodded. "A bent saddle nail and wayward hammer."

"So you say." Concerned, Gert filled noggins from a cider kettle.

Dowd drank. "Your cider holds too much grit."

She turned. "And you too much air."

Oversized hat tilted uneven, Quayland coughed into his handkerchief. "A restless table already. Cold's pall stirs early."

Cotswold entered and settled across from the surveyor, satchel close beside his leg. Jacks followed behind, heavy boots willful loud on the floor, and sat the servant table.

Quayland rose in anticipation of Sybil. "Is your niece not to join?"

"She inhabits her room and blankets, indisposed by the cold," Cotswold said.

"A loss we all share." The surveyor resumed his bench.

"She can sit a chair by the kitchen hearth," said Gert. "I'll find use for her hands."

Cotswold's smirked, bemused. "I am afraid she does not cook. At least not willingly or well. And not here certainly."

"I am surprised you would ask, madam," said Dowd.

Gert wiped hands on her apron. "Why? Likely she knows how to work a needle or cut roots by the fire, airs or not. How better to spend a chill morning?"

She started toward the kitchen door but stopped. Resentments spilled sudden, an urge to speak of Lauch to the unquiet takers who disturbed her house. Also need, to remind his killer her wrath was sure.

Gert returned beside the table. "The Keeper's older son is dead. Found twisted, fallen on the tavern steps at first light."

Quayland glanced from his bowl, concern masked by mannered condolence. "Sympathies to this house. He was but a youth."

Filled spoon in his wounded hand, Silas paused but did not look up. "An accident, surely."

The driver chewed cheese mouth open but did not look up. "It happens. To drunks."

Cotswold squinted doubtful at the porridge bowl. "You make it ominous. What says the Keeper?"

"He has his own mind, as do I." Gert liked none of them.

Dowd shifted slightly toward her. "Whom do you accuse, madam, and of what?"

"I accuse none yet," she said. "Still each of you brings something dark, ill or untrue to this inn. Little happens beneath its roof by chance."

Gert's glance lingered on the missionary's bruised hand. "The truth remains hid for now but I will find it. All here should know."

◑

The truth scolded and mocked.

Dim candle held aloft, the Innkeeper could not tell which truth.

The narrow cellar alcove where he found Lauch the prior night showed fury and violence. Toppled shelves, overturned baskets and scattered nuts littered wet ground beside an empty wine bottle and abandoned meat. Drips from a cracked rum cask and stale urine thickened dank air. Stray chickens from the smoke house clucked and pecked beside his boots.

All seemed familiar, yet apart, unremembered. Cruel, nameless insinuations he could not deny or admit. Blind doubt, bitter resentment and woeful resignation soured the Innkeeper's throat, the unyielding harness of fearful guilt.

Aching hands trembled despite his will. Unwilling to touch the wine bottle he toed it to a corner crease behind the shelf. Debris sorted, his heel scoured fresh dirt over the stained ground in vain pretense of normalcy.

"Dying is easy, son. Takes no strength. You leave me and with much to do. Just like your mother."

Gert carried a basket into the cellar from the tavern. Unable to hide, the Innkeeper simply stared.

Gert gathered vegetables from larder holes in the earthen wall but did not look back. Lauch was killed, pushed for purpose. You know that."

"Why ponder it? Serves no good." The Innkeeper covered his hands and retreated away from the alcove.

"I told the lambs," said Gert. "Regret and apology. But none were true surprised."

She cut rotten gourds and potatoes into the slop bucket. "The driver looked down on Lauch from the hall without reaction. And last night the missionary came late from the barn. Saw him pass in the tavern. At table this morning fresh scrapes and bruises marked his hand."

"You try too hard." The Innkeeper picked up a broken chair back from the ground.

"And you not enough. I will have my answer."

Gert finished with the basket and bucket and turned "The slop is ready for the hogs."

"Is Lauch's for doing."

"No longer."

"Then for Dayne."

Concerned, Gert looked past him toward the alcove. "Not this day. He remains to himself, as he should be. His brother he was close to. The wake tonight will fall hard on him."

"Double work now. He need earn his keep."

"Dayne is yet a boy. See you leave him that."

The Innkeeper turned abrupt, voice low. "I cannot tend this farm alone. Nor with only an eleven-year-old's hands."

Gert waited. "What choice?"

She opened a large pottery jar and stirred pickled pole beans inside. "The land will survive. But Dayne's silence will worsen. You are his father. Talk and end the quiet."

"He spurns me and offers little chance."

Jar drained, she placed the beans in her basket. "Dayne's mother and now his brother are gone. He knows not why, only that much abandons him. He angers."

"His eyes speak harsh to me every day, woman. Think me blind?"

The Innkeeper set aside the chair back and kept his eyes apart. "His moods are surly like hers. And he favors her to look at."

"Is that what draws your ire? You will lose him, and soon, if you do not act."

The Innkeeper grumbled. "Have him set wood for the hearth. See he does it. The lambs will come down for the tavern fire."

"They already bleat. None like the cold." Gert extended the slop bucket.

"Let them shiver. I am to the barn."

He took the bucket, with his boot scattered chickens at the rear entrance and emerged into the cold. Storm had gathered in the night. Wind-driven white veils blurred past and thick snow shrouded the barn yard and fences. Icy flakes needled his uncovered head and hands and salted his beard.

At the slaughter pen hogs huddled in a corner near the mounded mass of a frozen victim. The Innkeeper emptied the bucket alongside, grim at the lost meat. Winter always tolled the farm.

Defiant, he confronted the harsh swirl and taunting wind. "Go on and blow, hard if you want. I'll not bend."

Dayne's earlier tracks led to the barn. Large door pulled ajar against a drift, he slid inside and breathed deep of familiar laden smells. The farm provided sustenance and the inn hard currency but the barn bridged and enabled both. Its simple, repetitive chores always provided purpose, renewal for his troubled mind.

The heavy freight tandems and empty coach filled the corridor, stark briars in morning gloom. The Innkeeper's hand ran along the shattered wheel lashed on back of the coach and shut an open passenger door. He distrusted the gentleman and his driver. Few fled to the wilderness in winter unless forced.

Horses led from stalls and tethered beside a hay sled, the Innkeeper removed soiled straw and placed fresh bedding. The Moravian's wary mule refused a bit or lead.

The Innkeeper waited, bridle and rope loose between his hands. "You're proud like your master. But you will take my lead."

He stepped forward. Jerusalem raised his neck, moved sideways and blocked the stall door. Approached again, the unsettled mule snorted and refused. The Innkeeper thought better, forked hay over the gate and returned the horses to their stalls.

At Dowd's tandems he stepped onto the axle hub of the rear wagon. Tight stretched canvas, nailed crossed leather straps and thick doubled ropes beckoned his touch. Heavy freight was not uncommon along the wilderness road but he doubted Dowd's story why the drivers abruptly abandoned the trip. The wagons' lurking presence and hidden cargo edged uneasy. He wanted no complications.

A loose knot and ripped corner caught his hand. "Agh, Lauch. Son, are you a thief as well as a drunk?"

Urge to pry further fluttered and tempted the Innkeeper's fingers. Yet the cargo was not his to know and the cripple paid with clean silver coin, the absolution of commerce. He pulled the cover taut and stepped down from the axle.

Across the corridor the bell of his Welsh Red cow clattered soft but persistent. At her stall he broke ice in a water bucket with the pitchfork, snapped dried cornstalks and rubbed her long neck. Grateful for the warm touch, forehead against her broad brow he fed two halved apples brought from the cellar as treats.

"After me who will take such care?"

The cow shifted, ears cupped and large liquid eyes alert. Wisps of movement in the barn disturbed the air. The cow grunted, shuffled and the Innkeeper stepped back into the corridor. Small birds fluttered anxious, unseen in shadowed rafters beyond the loft line overhead.

His eyes roamed the barn and taut ears listened. No other disquiet followed and he pulled the sled down the corridor to the rear entrance. The braced door remained intact and the ground nearby unmarked yet the subtle gnaw of intrusion grew, an unwelcome taint of trespass.

The Innkeeper glanced back along the barn, unhappy he left his long rifle in the cellar. A careless error he would not repeat. His grip tightened on the pitchfork.

Around the corner he threw hay for goats and sheep kept in rear stalls and returned with the sled past the door into the main corridor.

Snow crusted blanket wrapped over his great coat, Jacks stood on the rear axle of the freight tandem and with a knife pried a rope knot from the canvas cover.

The Innkeeper stopped. The blatant affront inside his barn welled slow fury. "Leave the freight be."

The driver did not look up. "You come quiet, unexpected."

"Go no further."

Jacks lifted a small rum keg from the wagon. "The cripple will not miss my little taste. Knew it was here. Spiced my dreams all the night, it did. A thirsty man and his drink need not wait."

The Innkeeper dropped the sled rope. "The man's property is his own."

Jacks did not stop. "And fine sturdy wagons too. Deep, full sowbellies for serious cargo. But what's inside? No simple freight, that be sure of. Else why such ropes, why such straps?"

"I shelter no thieves."

"Knot was already loose, I'm not the first. But who do I follow? Your son, the weakling drunk? The surveyor? He has nosy, untrue eyes. The preacher? He likes the barn late when no one watches."

Pitchfork poised, the Innkeeper stepped forward. "Go no further."

The driver grinned and trailed his knife along the corner rope. "C'mon, Keeper. What lies hid? A rich one's spoils or a smuggler's contraband? A wee peek is all. Don't tell me you've not thought it."

"No thieves."

"Why pass the chance? I'll knot the cover back after the look."

The Innkeeper leveled the pitchfork at Jacks. "No thieves."

Grin gone and knife in hand, the driver stepped down from the wheel. Blanket shrugged from his shoulders, his hard black eyes gauged.

"Or is it you, Keeper? You yourself, out here all lonesome with no one to see. Is that the truth of it? Maybe you're the secret meddler."

The Innkeeper angled dirty tines close in front of the driver's face, voice final. "Enough."

Jacks considered, sheathed the short blade and spread his hands. "That fork makes you. Will not always be so easy."

He retrieved his blanket from the ground, glanced back sullen and left the barn.

Pitchfork set aside, the Innkeeper stepped up on the axle. Strong rum scent pricked his nose and lured stiff hands. Hesitant, he returned the keg to the wagon but traced ripped canvas and outlines of hidden freight until he forced his touch away.

The wagons would prove a bane. He knew it but re-tied the knot and dropped down.

Birds fluttered again overhead and the Innkeeper quickly climbed the loft ladder with the fork. Overhead the ceiling rope and pulley drifted, creaked and small dark finches chirped and hopped nervously in rafters.

He moved slow among piled hay and stalks. Shadows darkened corners and disturbance wisped the air. At a muffle behind he wheeled, pitchfork thrust. Scared field mice skittered and hid along the wall.

"Who is here? Show yourself."

Uneven stillness. He descended the ladder and looked along the corridor. The mule and horses watched, heads outside stalls and ears cupped, silent witnesses. Pitchfork readied, the Innkeeper approached the coach and opened its door. Empty.

He glanced at the loft line again and turned to the cow's stall. The Welsh Red chewed stalks unconcerned.

Wind gusts moaned and whispered, frank jeers and chides. Annoyed and confused, the Innkeeper retreated into the corridor.

"This be my barn," he called. "Mine alone."

His words faded with his breaths in the cold. Above, a brief flurry of wings bothered the quiet.

CHAPTER NINE

Along the upstairs hallway Gert carried a large pitcher, wash basin and cloths on a tray. She knocked on the door at the far end and entered the room.

Open trunks and valises spread across the floor and bed. Eyes burdened and remote, Sybil wistfully smoothed a bright green satin dress against her front and quickly dabbed a stray tear from her cheek.

"You fret," said Gert. "Do I intrude?"

"No, please. You are the only other woman in this house. I welcome such company."

Gert filled a bedside wash basin with water from the pitcher. "Fresh water and cloths. The cold hampers this morning. The hot will not last but a start."

"Thank you. I need to get clean."

Sybil clung to the dress. "All my life I wanted a green satin dress. Real satin, smooth and soft to touch. To wear at a ball and every eye on me as I dance."

"And now?"

"Now I have it."

"For how long?"

Sybil's expression sagged with the dress. "A while yet. Perhaps."

She forced a smile and displayed a tasseled dress shoe. "Paper soles. Quite comfortable, stylish."

Gert took the shoe, bemused by the bottom and dropped it aside. Rough fingers roamed the dress unimpressed. "Not durable. Little use on a farm."

She stepped back, an overt appraisal. Frayed by hard worried travel, Sybil sat well-scrubbed if not well bred.

Worn large brown eyes arched a pleasing face beset with the first declines of age. Strong shoulders and coarse hands belied her pedigreed air.

"You study me harsh," Sybil said.

"You were pretty once."

Sybil smiled faint, wistful. "More interestingly plain, or so I was told. But who knows what men really see. Kind of you to say, though."

"Your past knows work."

"Is my stain that obvious?" Sybil's face faded to sadness.

"Only to me. The marks never leave, child. Your eyes and hands tell it."

Dress set aside, Sybil flexed blemished hands. "I am embarrassed by what you heard and saw this morning. He is not my uncle, I think you knew that. An easy pretense he believes effective."

"His use of you will work ill in the end."

Sybil nodded. "My mind wrestles that though it should not. Lately I see him more for what he is, what he has become. Yet part of me wants to believe his heart is not as cruel and cold as his manner."

"False hope pains more than no hope. Your words to him were plain, true. Let no man make you a fool."

Gert crushed dried flowers into the water. "Some scent to help the water."

Sybil rose to the basin, filled her hands and absorbed the warm rinse and scent. "Such a simple gesture. So often needed, so often forgotten."

She lingered eyes closed, excess water a quiet drip. "I am sorry for the Innkeeper's son. He seemed unclear of himself and lost to his father but a kind child. Cruel, the accident."

"If such it was."

Sybil dried with a cloth. "You cannot think it intentional."

"That riddle remains."

"I hope not. The angers of this war destroy much already."

Gert emptied the tray and turned at the door. "Your man means to leave you. Soon, sure. Why stay?"

"A maidservant's daughter has few opportunities."

Sybil's fingers briefly strayed back to the satin dress. "He was an escape from drudgery, the means to somewhere, something else."

"And the driver?"

"A ruffian. There is dislike between the two. But he may have use."

"He tracks you hard. Be careful what you start or finish."

"I have few options. You do not know what I risk in this."

"No, I see your things, the fancy dresses and heavy trunks. Full but empty. More I see unhappy, doubtful eyes. Scared eyes."

Sybil looked away. The edge of the dress sagged to the quilt. "I am scared. I could not stay behind without him but now feel the price. My belly sickens each day and each night and this rude travel makes it worse. Rutted, miserable roads and constant jolting, shaking. Then this cold and storm."

Her hand opened and closed across her abdomen. "It stirs often this morning."

"Choice or consequence? Your belly?"

Sybil angled slightly away. "I want no child. Nor does he. I blame myself but pretend this is a gift from God. Life can be no other. Yet I do not know God. A horrid admission, I realize."

She turned, eyes stricken with guilt and question. "You are frank, wise. Tell me what you would do."

Gert stepped close, blunt. "Do not punish an innocent for sins of the parent. That burden stays where it belongs."

"Bleak future for a single mistake."

"Regrets always run free. Only the final end matters. Your course already yields sour. Do not make it worse. Survive. Survive until the choice, the outcome are yours."

Sybil turned. "How? I refuse to be old, another's maid and have nothing."

Anger sharpened Gert's voice. "Like me? Kettles and rags seldom tell all the tale. I know your ambitions, your wants. How else have I stayed here these long years, apart and alone, willing myself to go on? For what, strangers on a road? No, child. For me. For what my hands and mine alone yield. Always one day for me."

"I am sorry. I thought you more receptive."

"I know what you do and why. Men often underestimate a woman's guile. Use that. I do and to my aid."

Hand paused on the door knob, Gert did not look back. "Where does your man run?"

"He will not tell. I think it Canada."

"What carries he in the heavy satchel?"

"His soul."

Gert opened the door. "A kitchen hearth warms best. Finish here and come down when ready. Extra hands at the fire always find work."

◗

The sharp edged quill scratched across the paper. Neat, precise letters and numbers by a practiced, steady hand. All unseen.

Quayland valued exactitude. So did his masters.

Perched on the bed in his room, survey journal open across his knees, he imagined the invisible writing as it would appear when later revealed between inked lines of routine chart entries.

Juice of lemon, a simple trick centuries old yet still effective, the perfect concealment. No incriminating codes or ciphers to prompt a hangman's noose, just direct heat from fire or candle to darken and expose hidden words.

Rind gnawed, he rolled the quill in juice spit onto his palm and finished the marks. Notes on Loyalist, Patriot and

Indian sentiments, troop and militia movements, valley landmarks and condition of local forts and strong houses all detailed by a surveyor's keen, experienced eye. Worthy treachery.

His cough spasm dissolved into a faint fevered smile. So far no one knew his secret.

Or him. His awkward manner and oversized hat, facile habits and clever affectations others ridiculed often shielded scrutiny. Few considered him a threat. The genius of self-derision.

Neck sores busied Quayland's fingers. The illness crept steady, bubbled his skin and he feared it worsened, an unwanted delay and setback. Providence and purpose, he reminded. Always providence and purpose.

So he welcomed the early winter storm, crowded inn and mystery of Dowd's stranded freight as unexpected puzzles to solve. Fresh work, a role to play and new secrets to write.

Quill set aside, Quayland rose to muddied field stones and pebbles collected on the small bedside table. Earth seeds, oddities and conversation pieces, easy enablers of polite indifference by others. Yet to the trained eye behind the similar surfaces lurked different colored natures and cores, like people. A lesson proved time and again in both his lives. He returned the rocks to the table.

Coiled measuring chains and bundled marking posts piled neat the corner floor. Son of a royal surveyor, as a boy Quayland learned to measure and plot in the family garden to the bother of his mother and siblings. Later he travelled with his father and absorbed teachings about rivers, lands and forests. The learned, practical skills instilled stature, accomplishment and experience with all manner of people, the perfect foundation to one day wander back woods devious and ask detailed questions of strangers. Quayland hoped his father, a man of simple wisdoms and clean spirit, would understand his use of the gift. All was God's unerring, unseen hand.

He unkinked a length of chain and lifted his father's glass-topped compass box. Edges smoothed by years and countless touches, the box held the assurance of truth and constancy, guidance for his steps and his soul. But unclear fate clouded his recent sense of direction and purpose. Unwanted finality drew too near too soon.

His hands glided over the old wood anxious for warmth, stability. Chill premonition and void replied. The loss of an inner, true compass pierced deep. Scratched by doubt and worry, he set the box aside.

Yet his journey north proved uneventful. Despite strong tensions and open unrest the valley escaped actual scourges of war. That would likely change in spring when the armies increased their reach and the Iroquois took the war path, matters his work would help shape.

Rebellion was not his nature although he understood the value of land. Rapid colonial expansion west into Can-tuc-ee and the Ohio Territory yielded fertile soil, unending forests teeming with game and navigable waters full of fish. Further settlement promised trade and dominion, the evil lures of vast wealth and false gleam of new empire.

The future always collided with the past. He preferred the certainty of the latter and the known cradle of tradition. Change stirred disorder, heresies and weaknesses of human nature. The loud arguments for revolt guised politics, class and greed as democracy, natural law and commerce. Such principled arrogance hid the vain glory of a grand unneeded social experiment for which thousands would die needless.

Quayland frowned. Continued social order required his rigid duplicity. He held no other explanation, only conviction his righteous God would not permit wander astray were it not so. In the end he was but a steadfast link in a divine chain. His duty was not to question, only adhere.

Or so he prayed.

Religion came early in his life. Fundamental, unwavering faith joined to the veracity of numbers and logic of nature. He saw no inconsistency, only compelling, complicit antagonists. Order and truth derived from chaos and uncertainty. Plan, purpose over chance, randomness. Fate over choice. God's will always. Ambiguity be damned.

Nausea notched Quayland's stomach and quibbled his loins, a grim precursor. Countless struggles against rugged terrain, cold weather and brackish water often exposed him to sickness yet he sensed troubling difference in his current ailment. Deeper and more attached within, the fevers, chills and weakness intensified.

He rose, adjusted his neck kerchiefs and glanced back. The open journal's neat ink entries and invisible words in between briefly renewed his vigor. Penmanship's reward. He thanked his early schoolmaster and picked up the chamber bucket.

To further his designs Quayland often used a local ally or pawn, witting or not. Indirect influence worked best to provide distance and prevent suspicion. The varied people at the inn presented a difficult group to assess but his growing illness made his plan clear.

Gert.

◗

Amulet grasped at her neck, Gert murmured an incantation over Lauch's body in the parlor. She cleansed his ashen face and hands with a cloth dipped in scented water.

"Sweet basil. Will soothe your passage to what comes after."

Her touch lingered over his bruised mouth. The sign of violence angered, unsettled. She folded Lauch's arms across his chest and placed a garland of dried yellow fennel in his fingers.

"To keep evil away."

She hesitated, a last look. "You do favor your mother. Just not so much as Dayne."

Eyes closed, Gert etched Lauch into memory. Turned. She drifted among the parlor's once favored clothes, furniture and objects. Snippets of words and faded blooms of lost emotions emerged, fleeting images and distant remembrance. Lies, tattles, jealousies and ridicules blurred with laughter, games and innocent young girl dreams in a former life tapestry, separate and remote, hers yet not.

Along the front wall she paused over the harpsichord, a source of frequent emotional tugs of war with her younger sister.

"Your favorite. English made, brought all the way from London. You insisted father buy it yet would not teach me to play."

Gert smiled, primitive and triumphant. "But I did anyway, without you, despite you. Poor jaundiced sisters we were, both of us. But now tis mine. Just mine."

Fingers playful above the keys, she mouthed a silent melody. Outside the front wall notes sounded in time with her hands. Puzzled, she stopped and glanced at the shuttered window. The notes continued, clear and meant for her.

She left the parlor and opened the inn's front door. Top hat and frock coat matted by snow and face mottled by cold, the Peddler played a mouth harp in rag-covered hands.

Gert clutched the neck amulet. "Vengeance!"

The Peddler finished the melody and lowered the harp. "A melancholy song. Full of pain, regret and much guilt."

"You come on me too quick."

"Ask me inside, make me yours. I prey no other way."

Hesitant, Gert stepped back from the door.

The Peddler entered with his pack and jagged birch branch. Protruded, lizard-like eyes widened, narrowed and his exposed tongue sifted the air.

"Spirits of life," he said. "Also fear, anger, disarray and death."

The Peddler stepped into the parlor. "A once busy room, musty and no longer used yet surged with secrets. Yours."

"Yes."

"Lonely paths."

He fingered fringe on a once colored hat ribbon. "The past never fades. The present never changes. The future watches, unforgiving and spiteful."

Gert kept her hand on the amulet. "I do not deny my choices. Or what follows."

"Will not be enough." The Peddler's exhale whistled cold.

Stood beside Lauch's body he rocked slightly back and forth, eyes closed. His hand curled and uncurled slow just above the face cloth.

"The dead son," he said. "Troubled no more."

"He was never happy here."

Eyes flashed open, he snatched the garland and turned on her. "The neck charm will not help. Or the dwindled yellow flowers."

The Peddler returned to the hallway and Gert locked the parlor door behind. Trinkets and shells jangled from the pack, he followed her through the common room.

Inside the kitchen the Peddler brushed cuttings and sprigs hung from ceiling beams and sniffed potted plants on the work table at the window.

"You reek deep," he said. "Careful, clever baits open for all to see. Do the others know?"

"None bother."

He removed his top hat. A burden strap of corded moose hair and tree bark held the pack to his scaly, blemished head. Odd swirls and shapes marked skin on one side of his face. He knelt at the fire and slowly unwound frozen rags from discolored, frostbitten hands.

"You smell hard of the earth," said Gert. "I thought you different."

"Why? I am for you."

Gert glanced anxious toward the empty doorway, worried the Innkeeper would come too soon.

The Peddler did not look up. "What will you tell him?"

"Does it matter?"

"No."

Footfalls approached across the common room. The Innkeeper appeared in the door, saw the Peddler and strode angrily forward. Gert blocked his path but he pushed past.

"Gypsy!"

"He has no coin and barters for the floor," said Gert. "I said we would grant a bowl and blanket."

The Innkeeper turned on her. "With death already in this house you invite more?"

"He is but a tinker," she said.

"Aye, and what else brings he? Yesterday I ran him off and now he strange appears and with Lauch dead. The barn went pilfered last night. Let him deny his part."

The Peddler folded his hand rag. "I lay content with small birds and the red striped cow. Others brought the thieving."

The Innkeeper grabbed the poker beside the hearth and thrust its tip to the Peddler's forehead. "You lie."

The tinker did not flinch. "Am I alone?"

Gert moved alongside the Innkeeper. "You see his froze hands, his hard skin. We cannot cast him back to the storm."

"He is a wild animal and deserves no favor."

"Perhaps," said Gert. "Yet he may have use. No harm will come to see inside his pack."

"That choice is mine."

The Peddler rose with open hands. "A bitter night and cold. I am fortunate to feel the warmth of your fire."

The Innkeeper kept the poker close on the tinker's head. "You stink of filth and rot."

"I am older than you."

"And have no place here."

The Peddler bobbed his forehead firm against the poker tip. "What is it you fear?"

"I fear no man, gypsy."

The Peddler continued to press his head. "Perhaps then a boy?"

Ire stiffened the Innkeeper's face. "Leave my sons be. They are not for you."

Sudden grin warped the tinker's face. Long-nailed thumb and forefinger scratched corners of his mouth and wide unforgiving eyes, one brown and the other green, goaded and imposed.

"Like me not, strike me not," he said. "The snow still flies and the Beast still comes. Be bold, Keeper. Choose well."

Gert stepped to intervene but stopped. The battle of wills was a test for each man and not hers to decide.

Doubt clouded the Innkeeper's expression. Surprised, he blinked and lowered the poker. "He stays but the night, weather or no. And he works for any meal."

Poker dropped loud on the hearth, the Innkeeper glared harsh. "You best be a tinker and only that. Or I will skin you like the vermin you are."

The Peddler showed no triumph. "I look forward to it."

The Innkeeper pulled a tomahawk and scalping knife from the tinker's rope belt. "No Indian tricks."

"Do not think this makes me toothless."

The Innkeeper gestured at the birch branch angled against the hearth. "You had no such wood before."

"Is soft and takes my cut. You will see its use."

The Innkeeper glanced at Gert, dark accusation, and left the kitchen.

She ladled stew over torn bread and extended the trencher to the Peddler. Misgiving rawed her throat, edged her voice. "I hope I make not a mistake to bring you here."

He greedily fingered and tongued the food. "Late lament. Serves no purpose."

Gert turned away but looked back. "The song. How did you know it?"

"A special gift."

CHAPTER TEN

Dayne mourned.

Knees drawn close and collar upturned, beside the small spring pool in the rear of the cellar he skewed uneven back and forth, mind stained by images of Lauch's body on the drink room steps and parlor table.

Unforgiving grief, anger and emptiness both suffocated and heaved difficult breaths. Once more separated by death from his family, Dayne knew not where his brother went or why. He wanted to follow so Lauch would not be lonely and scared like him.

The spring's insistent gurgle gradually eased his heart. Lauch's ancient tree root clutched close, he blew wispy breaths in offer of warmth and self and wished his brother to reappear. Unplayed games remained, walks among fields and jokes by the fire. Another season, another harvest at least, not such abrupt and final end. The coarse wood refused his pleas and Dayne set it aside dismayed.

By his shoes the kitten squeaked displeasure at lack of attention. He flicked water to quell the nag and the cat moved away.

Dayne brooded within water sound and dense earth smells. Carved into hillside against bedrock beneath the inn, the spring and earthen rear cellar provided storage for the farm's food and secret haven for him. Narrow passages and nooks created places to hide and barriers against others, an escape where brittle stillness mirrored his silence and accepted his quiet wallows.

Tubs of cheese, butter, milk, eggs and lard crowded the dark pool. Lauch said its water came from a pond high beyond the farm's rear orchard through secret caves. His father called it an Indian crawl, a place to conceal and shelter if marauders attacked the inn.

Dayne rose and wandered the passage between the spring and drink room door amid lifeblood scents of old river loam and root vegetables stored in dirt wall grottoes.

Door pushed slightly ajar, Dayne listened before he entered. The empty room whispered quiet distress, the faint rustle of unclear disturbance.

Gert carried a pail and sack down the steps from the main floor. A stranger with long stringed hair and odd tall hat followed behind and eased his laden pack and a birch staff to the floor. Dayne ducked behind the bar counter and peeked around its edge.

Gert set the sack and pail on a table. "The lambs come down soon. Core these apples and stay hushed, apart. I want no fuss. Give the Keeper not a reason to change his mind."

The stranger lingered over the step where Lauch died. "You scrubbed hard but the taint remains. All here are guilty."

"They will bleat other but lie the truth."

"Not just them."

Gert started up the steps, looked back and continued. Hat, staff and pack propped in the corner, the stranger moved to the hearth and pulled ice fragments from sparse hair. Head tilted side to side in rhythm with the tick of a mantel clock, his finger stilled the pendulum.

Dayne angled to see the man's face but could not. The stranger peered at mail and public notices on a board by the outside door and rummaged a coin from the postage tin beneath.

The kitten pawed Dayne's breeches and he bent to push it away. When he looked up the stranger sat cross legged on the corner floor beside his pack, thumbed apart an apple and tongued the seeds.

The click and thump of the cane walker and his stick groaned the steps. Bundled in great coat and scarf, he warmed his backside at the fire and loudly farted. Relieved, he rubbed snuff from a small box into his gums and drifted to a window beside the outside door. His finger searched the empty postage cup.

"Your secret cupboard is bare," said the stranger. "Others proved faster, more agile."

Startled, the cane walker turned to reply but stopped. "An unmannered beggar. How did you sneak in?"

"I followed your smell."

"A rude, unlikely tale."

"Why? Your shite draws many flies to the barn." The stranger cored another apple.

The cane walker thumped along the hearth and peered at the stranger but kept disdainful distance. "You look both culprit and tattle. I like not that you roamed the barn unattended and rummaged my freight."

"Other things I do you will like even less."

"Curious cheek for someone face marked like a slime toad."

"Nature makes slime." The stranger tongued his lips and glanced toward the bar."

Dayne retreated behind the cellar door, stopped and peeked again through a knothole in the bar.

Stick pointed at the stranger's pack, the cane walker smacked his jowls and stood stiff. "Yet you are the one who carries a meager estate. Is it lack of ambition or indolence which finds you so?"

"I am a wanderer and seek only shelter and fire for the night, a full belly and dark idles to tell. What follows after is fate."

"Yours or the fool who lets you overnight?"

"The end is the same."

The cane walker angled to the steps. "Thieving bread

and buttermilk is hardly worthy aspiration for any man. Even a filthy beggar liar like you."

The stranger bit an apple core and spit seeds on the floor near the man's boots. "I like buttermilk. And I am a liar. How else is truth revealed?"

"You do not amuse, sir. Our conversation ends." The cane walker lumbered up the steps.

The stranger tapped his hat. "Then scurry. But was your burp what shamed the air."

The kitten patted past the bar corner and across the tavern floor. Dayne grabbed too late, nudged the door and winced at its creak.

He quickly retreated into the cellar and hurried along the passage to the spring. His leg tipped the tree root into the pool but he dared not reach back and hid in a small crease behind sacks and barrels in the corner.

Fractured silence rumbled Dayne's ears. Huddled and anxious, he waited several minutes before he crept out and listened at the passage corner. Odd presence drifted yet no sound or threat. At the pool edge he searched dark water for the lost root, puzzled why it did not float on the surface.

Dayne turned and froze, eyes burst wide. Indian moccasins and leggings loomed inches from his hand.

The stranger's leathered, marked face looked down above. He dangled the annoyed kitten by the top of its neck. "I know you do not speak."

Rigid and surged by fear Dayne struggled, caught like a field mouse between urge to flee and inability to move.

The stranger's nose and tongue sifted the air. His unhurried, shameless hunt beast stare settled on Dayne.

"The silent dreamer," he said. "You are young."

Dropped on its feet, the kitten hissed and sought safety behind Dayne's leg. Dayne slowly withdrew his arm from the spring and edged backward on his shins.

The stranger pursued. "A fine spot for your sadness. Quiet, safe within the earth."

He reached close past Dayne's face, opened the lid on a pail in the spring and licked fresh cream. His body reeked of decay and deep unstirred woods.

"Harsh, what happened to your brother," said the stranger. "Its pain burdens your eyes, your heart."

Dayne looked away, unwilling to be studied, unsure how the stranger knew. He continued to retreat.

The stranger stepped closer, finished the cream from his fingers and returned the lid to the pail. He knelt and his rag-covered hand lightly circled the surface of the spring.

"Not all of life is seen at first. You must core the apple for much lies hid beneath the surface. Secrets old and dark, like in your pool."

Hand slowed, he snatched below the water and lifted up the root. "Ancient pine. Dense. Strong. It sinks deep unlike most wood. Yours to shape once more."

Offered the root, Dayne waited wary. The wanderer's blunt eyes, one green and one brown, squeezed and swallowed him. He reached unsure but the stranger held firm and drifted a long fingernail across Dayne's wrist.

Intense cold and searing heat both trembled Dayne's forearm and cleaved his chest. Fright tightened his throat.

"Fear is wise," said the stranger. "All creatures hunt, both light and dark. Most are false, clever, deceitful. Some have interest in you."

He clicked several times, an agitated bird sound, and released the root. "Your heart beats strong. The time for your voice will come. Remember to use it."

Dayne quickly lunged away with the wood. Buckets, barrels and crates blocked his path along the other side of the spring and he turned, desperate and trapped.

The stranger was gone. Dayne peered at the empty corner of the passage, uncertain and uneasy. Ears taut, he waited and slowly returned beside the spring.

A black and gray object lay on the ground where the stranger stood.

An owl feather.

◑

Dayne sat at the drink room hearth, chin rested on arms folded over drawn up knees. He fingered the feather in his pocket, unsure what the gift meant.

He hated owls. The unnatural turn of their heads, large unflinching eyes and eager sharp claws scared. Often chased among farm fields like a prey mouse, at times he heard their harsh screeches close by his room late at night. He knew they watched, waited.

Dayne glanced to and from the stranger shrouded by dim shadows on the floor beside the steps. He seemed both light and dark, truth and trickery. Busied with sinews and trinkets on his pack, the stranger paid no heed but Dayne sensed the wanderer also watched, waited and brought dark purpose, upheaval.

Rough cuts of a saw and pound of a hammer on nails drifted through the closed door to the cellar. Lonely, hurt sounds yet also stubborn. His father.

Dayne dropped fresh wood on the fire. The blackened logs underneath collapsed and smoke escaped the fireplace. He stepped back disappointed. Lauch stoked the hearth better.

The cane walker pinched Dayne's shoulder and peered down knotted and stern. Waggled fingers demanded the poker and he jabbed and prodded the fire into shape.

"You would do better with a proper stack," said the heavy man. "Wood burns more ably when spaced."

Across the hearth the driver mouthed pipe smoke and his dark eyes followed Dayne. "A laggard chore boy. Lazy."

Uneasy between them, Dayne retreated to the large wood pile along the outside wall. He gathered pine cones and small kindling to a bucket and avoided the driver's following eyes.

The gentleman rose at his table opposite the hearth, moved to the fire near the cane walker and cleaned his spectacles with a cloth. He minced, annoyed when the large hat man joined from his chair near the outer door.

All seemed reluctant, carefully apart. At different times they shifted front and back to the fire, too warm on one side and too cold on the other.

The cane walker flapped his great coat and leaned heavily on his walking stick. "Taking the correct measure of a new fire is a doubtful endeavor. The bane of winter."

"Indeed, tedious," said the gentleman. "More so in a crowd."

"On the contrary," said the hat man. "I find a good hearth always brings people together."

The kind man in black entered from outside and shook snow from his hat and coat. "The storm is bitter. Angry cold."

The hat man angled to open space at the hearth. The others grudgingly edged further away on the corners.

"You are to the barn again," said the cane walker.

The kind man eagerly warmed his hands. "Yes. I tend Jerusalem regardless the weather."

The cane walker shifted his backside to the fire. "He is a mule."

"Also a companion."

"Yet an odd foray on such a morn." The red hat man scratched his long neck.

An apple cored with his thumbs, the stranger cackled but did not look up. "Dinner fowl. Trundled on spits, twisting this way and that for the best flavor."

The cane walker pivoted, stick pointed. "You have been warned prior, sir, about your incautious tongue."

The stranger spit apple seeds. "Truth comes rude."

The driver shifted on his stool and blew dense, riled smoke. "Why does the Keeper let a half breed red bastard among us? He's a stench even from here."

"Strange folk oft wander country roads," said the kind man. "He is but another. No need for hasty contorts."

"He is no tinker despite the pack," said the cane walker. "More a criminal with clumsy ruse and brazen provocation."

The gentleman left the fire and resumed spectacles, book and foot warmer at his table. "The hat and frock bespeak a wilderness fool or wayward piper. The Innkeeper rubs his coins hard, if indeed the vagrant pays."

At the wood pile Dayne tried not to move, confused by the angry voices.

"Are not all entitled to shelter in a storm?" The kind man unwound his frozen scarf and walked past toward the stranger.

"Like you I am new here," he said. "You do not appear an Iroquois. Perhaps a Lenape from the south? Or a Susquehannock?"

The stranger cored another apple. "One, sometimes both. Or all. Perhaps none."

"You speak without native cadence or idiom," the kind man said. "Were you educated by whites or Christian missionaries?"

"I know their lies," the stranger said. "False nature. But I learned to bend the bow and found the true way."

The red hat man turned. "Were you a captive?"

"Often. Beware. My pretty speech is but a ploy and sap for the unwary."

"Tell us why Indians take scalps," said the cane walker. "A hideous, heinous custom. Is it the bounty paid by the British or just innate brutality?"

With his small knife the stranger slow peeled an apple in a single long piece. "The head tops the soul. Scalping is a warrior's final triumph, his enemy's final indignity. Both redcoats and blue pay well for the deed. Both want fear in the other."

He flicked blond fringe on his leggings. "Women scalps are much sought. Longer hair makes the best trim."

The gentleman glanced up from his book. "Such foul pride does not impress."

"He admits bold to white murders," said the cane walker. "A savage, unashamed and untamed."

"Yes," the stranger said.

"Violence against whites comes no different than ours against natives," the kind man said. "Why despise them for what we ourselves do?"

The driver pointed his pipe stem. "Twill feel otherwise tonight, missionary, when he lays his blade against your scalp while you sleep."

Dayne placed the bucket of sprigs and chips on the hearth. Each man's words carried brood, trouble and he wanted no more. Shoulders slumped and hands deep in coat pockets, he circled among rear tables to avoid the others and moved toward the steps.

The red hat man stilled a rasped cough. "Trinkets and trifles have use on a farm but tinkers here are rare. Tell us how you survive the wild."

"I steal, I snare, I kill. Then I eat, like you. A beast." The stranger deep bit and chewed an apple.

"There is an Iroquois renegade by that name," the hat man said. "A marauder, murderer. What do you know of him?"

The stranger glanced at Dayne among the tables. "A harsh truth of the forest. An evil twin. Kills for bloodlust, spite. Dominion."

"Rumor says the Beast comes back to this valley to war for the Crown," said the hat man. "On which side are you?"

Coy, the wanderer blinked once. "I crave neither noose. As the season demands, such a creature am I."

He lifted a portion of the hide shirt beneath his top coat. "Once the Beast tried to burn me dead but a sudden fierce rain came. True grace it was. Confusion, escape. He still hunts me. I still hunt him."

"So you know this Beast," said the kind man. "The stories are real."

Distracted by angry bubbled skin on the stranger's side, Dayne caught his foot and a chair leg scraped the floor. He winced expectant but the unwanted noise faded without rebuke. Dayne breathed again and looked up but recoiled, ears covered.

The stranger screeched sudden, severe. "The owl is out. Wise men flee."

Above the steps the door opened. Gert descended with a filled tray and Sybil carried a kettle behind. Frightened, Dayne hurried past both to the main floor.

Gert turned. "Why such haste?"

"The Keeper's vulgar new guest regales us rude," said Dowd. "The boy took not to it."

Cotswold glanced from his book. "Unneeded displays. It finally ends, I think."

Startled by the Peddler's unexpected presence and appearance, Sybil moved quickly from the steps. "Dear God. A leper!"

"But a wandering tinker," said Gert. "Brought by the storm."

Sybil kept her distance. "If true then I am at fault, sir. My pardon."

The Peddler slowly chewed a bit of apple and sliced another. His finger flicked the front of his throat. "Pardon is not my nature."

Jacks removed his pipe and sat upright. "Watch your manner, filth. The lady made nice."

Gert placed honey and water pots, sacks, small bowls and mortar and pestle from the tray on the table in front of the fire. She glanced unhappy, regretful toward the Peddler and the lambs.

Sybil set the kettle on a trammel at the hearth, joined Gert at the table and adjusted her shawl. Jacks' covetous eyes followed and Cotswold squinted at the driver.

"A public tavern is no place for decent women," said Dowd. "Do you both intend to remain?"

"I scrub this floor more than any man drinks upon it," said Gert. "And is years since anyone thought me a decent woman. You cannot deprive the only common hearth."

"Decorum matters even in the wilderness," Dowd replied. "The spectacle at dinner last night was quite enough. This is unexpected."

Gert turned. "Only by you."

"Let them stay," said Quayland. "We can discuss issues besides the rebellion, surely."

"All spoke their minds last night," Silas said. "A free exchange. No harm was done."

Sybil nodded at the two men. "Tolerant gentlemen who remain so. Thank you. The woman of the house and I renew our affront to society yet bring a small bribe."

Cotswold's mouth creased. "My niece continues her poor choices and misplaced humor. They will cost her again."

Hesitation lowered Sybil's eyes but she turned to the bowls, resolute. "I asked for melted chocolate against the cold and instead was offered what sounds like coffee."

"A shrewd hostess," said Quayland. "Coffee is the new tea, a common drink for common people. Decidedly un-English and so quite popular."

"An eager way to deprive the Crown and its merchants of revenues," Cotswold said. "Trade always trumps war."

The surveyor shifted. "You sound a man of tariffs. A bureaucrat."

Cotswold's hand rose to shield his crooked mouth. "Basic commerce."

Gert moved beside the hearth, paused for Jacks to retract his leg and pushed the kettle closer to the fire.

Dowd caned away, flipped the sides of his great coat and stiffly lowered to his chair. "Coffee is a bitter sauce best found in less reputable drink houses."

"The less reputable the better," Quayland said. "Bold havens where all men may discuss public affairs without offense."

"Simple democracy," said Silas. "A community of voices. The artisan and the aristocrat together. Let it be so here."

Jacks belched smoke. "Pipe rubbish."

"Even so, you are free to speak and join," Silas said. "Let no fear of reprisal prevent it."

"I fear none in this group," said the driver.

Cotswold's finger but not his eyes sought the Moravian. "False liberties and excess are best not encouraged. You see what besets me."

"The true gist," Jacks said. "Common stays common and not good enough."

Cotswold smirked. "Common is common."

"You speak apt for a Tory, sir," Dowd said. "Peeved by class. But you are true correct. Artisans and aristocrats are different breeds, not the same. Disloyalty, murmur and sedition do not make them so. To hold otherwise posits but rank comedy."

Quayland adjusted his neck kerchiefs. "You've not been to the same drink houses in Philadelphia as I."

Dowd turned on the surveyor. "No doubt venal abodes of drunkenness and stupor. Open sores upon the city."

Sybil smiled innocent, defiant. "You argue spirited once more. Yet again what of the women? Have we no voice?"

Cotswold minced. "No, my dear. You do not, regardless how much that pains you."

Spasms puckered Dowd's face and annoyed fingers flexed across the head of his walking stick. "Indeed. Scripture recites women are the weaker vessel. The man leads the family as God intended. Was Eve who was seduced by the serpent."

Gert emptied green and red beans from the sacks. "Aye, but little goes done on a farm without a woman's touch or use. The plants and animals know it, enough for me. Men see not past their own wants or the serpent in their pants."

The tip of Dowd's stick loudly struck the floor. "Proper tongue, madam. Even from you."

Renewed sounds of the saw and hammer intruded from the cellar.

"The Keeper evades his duties yet again," Dowd said.

Gert turned. "No. He tends his oldest son alone as he should."

"A grim task," Silas said. "No parent should live to bury a child."

Quayland wobbled to his feet and approached Gert at the table. "Lighten the air for all. Tell us of your coffee."

She crushed red and green coffee in the bowls with a pestle. "Such seeds are unknown to this valley and travelled upriver with an Albany boatman. Before that a sea captain's wife brought them from afar."

"Beans," said Dowd. "They are called beans."

Gert stared curt. "Seeds."

"A warm delight and indulgence of home, gentlemen, regardless," Sybil said.

Honey and hot water added to the mix, Gert handed bowls to Quayland and Silas.

The surveyor sniffed the paste, baffled. "My regrets."

Silas nibbled paste from his finger. "It carries a harsh grit. Perhaps later."

Cotswold refused his bowl and resumed his book. "I think not."

"No, and I'm a drinking man." Jacks guzzled his tankard of cider instead.

Dowd sniffed and turned aside. "Your irksome trick goes astray, madam. What you foist is not coffee."

Gert stiffened. "It is in this house."

Sybil tugged Gert's sleeve. "Forgive me but I thought—"

The Peddler rose. "I will eat it."

Open-mouthed, he crunched the mash and crudely licked the bowl.

Dowd clucked. "You exceed your manners, savage. Your bowels shall exact bitter recompense."

The Peddler tapped his hat and bared rotten teeth. "Go, throat at me. But I grin at you."

◑

Hardened by anger, Gert roughly scraped the last coffee paste into the flames of the kitchen fire.

"Burn. All of you."

She cared not for the bitter seeds, one reason she offered them to the lambs. Yet the hint of ignorance and poor choice stirred embarrassed regret.

Silas' voice came from behind at the edge of the doorway. "I apologize for myself and the others."

Gert did not turn and thrust the bowl into a wash tub. "My skin runs thick enough."

"Regardless, a rude display."

Silas stepped closer. "You were right to remark earlier at morning meal about the Keeper's son. He was young but open and spoke against those who would come to this valley to do harm."

Hot water poured into the wash tub, Gert lathered a rag with dark lye soap. "And you?"

"I hold no ill will for any just man."

She glanced at his hand scrapes. "Which side is just?"

Silas showed his knuckles. "This morning your look did not believe me. Was a stubborn nail, only that."

"So you say."

Gert scoured trenchers and bowls with the rag. "You carry a humble mask but it does not hide all. You are a used man. A man with secrets."

"More regrets."

"All have those. Your face tells different than your words. You walked into this valley for purpose. Why here? Why now?"

"To do good, not mischief," said Silas. "If war dawns in full the Iroquois will decide your fate and that of most in this valley. Better if they embrace a common faith or bond."

Gert continued with the rag, eyes away from his. "You bring more than religion."

"Life is more than religion."

"The nature of the tribes is violent. War suits them."

"All the more reason for my journey."

"Others will fight you. Know that."

"They already do."

Gert stopped. Water dripped from the rag. "Who?"

"You are not blind."

She turned slightly, insistent. "Who?"

"All have reason."

"Agh, no answer."

Finished with the tub, Gert dried hands on her apron and turned toward him. "You come odd and with a peculiar faith. What says it to a guilty soul?"

Silas fidgeted the round brim of his held hat, reluctant. "You live harsh, you and the Keeper. Such is plain. Your troubles I will not guess and do not judge. All guilt can be cleansed. None are beyond grace or final redemption."

"Some deserve it not."

"God's choice, not ours."

"His choice oft runs hot, bitter, cruel," she said. "And what of fate? Are the guilty not forever bound to their sins?"

"We each make our own sojourn with God," said Silas. "Faithful and joyous or difficult and dreary. We choose."

Gert opened a side oven in the hearth and used a long handled peel to rearrange loaves of bread baking on large cabbage leaves. "What changed you? I do not think you always so pious."

"My brethren have a saying, 'Be still and know I am the Lord'. Quiet your mind and your soul will follow. One day I understood. My past faded. My future beckoned."

Gert shook her head. "Is the past what weighs. You still carry old burdens. And are not so quiet within."

Silas smiled. "Sometimes I lapse."

He nodded and turned toward the doorway but looked back. "Frank talk is part of faith, the sharing of good will and truth. So I will warn. Trust none here. On pain of this inn, on pain of your life, trust none here."

◐

The Innkeeper brooded beside a small cellar window. Sawdust drifted past in pale light, his life's unsettled dross. Outside the glass raging storm shrouded his farm and kept it from him. Inside the glass doubt and shame tormented his heart, kept it asunder.

He wanted no part of the others in the tavern. No new troubles, no new burdens. Yet beyond the closed door treachery, vengeance and war gathered resolute, certain. Their taints riled his house, bitter smoke. Devil's fire would follow.

He confronted its proof. Cobbled from warped boards and rusted nails pried from stray planks and a broken shelf, the unfinished coffin angled upright against a bench. Its open dark maw, unyielding and forever, mocked. The bane of the living and blunt, utter answer to faith.

Years earlier his father placed a polished cherry wood coffin in the family parlor, proud of the frequent conversation piece. As a child the Innkeeper ignored death's daily reminder and with siblings used the box as a centerpiece for games and make believe. Once older he no longer saw its innocence and wondered at his father's morbid, distorted obsession.

Rough lengths measured with his boot, he hewed the wood in fits and starts over a table. The short saw often bound and his swollen hands struggled. Despite use of a drawknife to shape the lid, the uneven boards vexed his will and taunted his eyes.

"Poor wood and joiners but will have to do."

The Innkeeper shifted uneasy, frayed breaths brief bursts in the cold. Clouded images of the prior night, vague swirls of question and blame, twisted and punished. He recalled only part of his cellar confrontation with Lauch. Jumbled emotions and words from an angry second scold with his son on the tavern steps only confounded, agitated.

"Who did this, son? Who put you in this box? Say it was not me."

Lid placed on the coffin the Innkeeper traced its rough corners, splintered a finger and trailed blood along the wood. From his coat pocket he retrieved the melted candle nub found on the tavern step above Lauch's body and set it on the bench.

His marred finger tapped the hard tallow. A silent witness to what happened, the stubborn goad ignored his desperate pleas for answer or truth.

His oldest son died. He did not know how or why.

Loss bottomed the Innkeeper's gut like dropped entrails of the hogs he slaughtered. Mouth twitched by recrimination and hurt he faded, emptied.

Resentment and denial gradually seeped his mind until they roiled his veins and choked his throat. Sleeves ripped back, he found no scars or outward brand of guilt. Enraged by the absence, his eyes narrowed on the offending candle nub.

Savage hammer blows shattered the wax. Strength spent, the Innkeeper heaved for air and release.

Bent nails clutched tight in his fist, he lurched toward the tavern door.

◗

Soft, warm, protected.

Fur on the kitten's tender belly and under its chin soothed Dayne's jealous fingers. The upside down cat yawned, stretched and rolled off his lap to the bed quilt.

Dayne's room creaked with cold. Icy flakes hissed and gathered against the window over his bed and outside wind drafted the late afternoon grayness. Scarf pulled close at his neck, he pretended the bony chill did not reach within.

After the noise of the drink room Dayne hungered for quiet apart from others. Troubled and confused, he did not know what Lauch's wake would be or mean. He wanted to see and remember his brother's face again yet feared the finality and loneliness of what might follow. The void of Lauch's unused bed already saddened his thoughts and eyes. Dayne needed no reminder of his loss.

The door opened and Gert entered.

"You stayed hid this day," she said. "Finish it now and start over. The inn and farm will next be yours. You will be the new keeper."

Dayne slowly shook his head.

"I know, child," Gert said. "Your spirit runs different. Yet we all suffer what burdens come. You will grow to it."

She lightly touched his hair. "Come and say goodbye to your brother. Bring the young cat if need."

Dayne retrieved the kitten and reluctantly followed Gert into the hall. At the corner into the main entrance he slowed and stopped. The parlor door loomed blunt and dark. Violence lurked behind, secrets and torments and memories not his yet which he somehow shared. His brother's body waited inside, prey of the same unwanted past.

Dread and anger struggled deep within Dayne's chest. His face emptied, hardened.

Gert knelt before him and took his chin but he looked past her. "You will get through this. Your will is strong, I feel it."

She rose. "Be kind to your father. Is his sorrow, too. All ours."

The key from Gert's apron did not fit into the door lock. She probed and squinted at the key hole as his father stepped into the hall from the meal room.

"Bent nails," said Gert. "You seized the door."

His father stiffened and scratched his beard. "No wake."

"You cannot—"

"No wake. None."

Mouth open to reply, Gert stopped and blinked twice. Stunned anger corded her neck and hard shells of betrayal and disbelief creased her face.

She spoke low and measured. "The drink ruins you, Keeper. As it did your father and as it did Lauch."

Dayne retreated. Intense colors of long held fury and resentment between Gert and his father burst his sight. Unable to shutter he angled away, back tensed but shoulders and arms crumpled, and shrank upon himself.

Gert's stare rose toward his father. "What is it you fear now? What secret do you hide this time?"

Chin jutted, his father glared defiant and unflinching. "Do not speak to me of secrets."

With the heel of her hand Gert thrust sudden and violent against his father's chest, stepped closer and thrust again.

Pain and abandonment exploded Dayne's heart. Confused muted cries strangled his throat and inward he wildly waved his arms to shield further harm. Outward he moved not at all. The scared kitten wiggled free of his hand and fled down the hall.

"You show your cruelty," Gert said.

"Is the best way."

For who? You deprive your sons of each other and you deprive me. This is my room, was always mine. You know that."

"Was also hers. I never gave it over."

Gert's voice quivered cold and accusing. "Nor did you ever look to see what was wrought within. You but left that burden to me."

She pivoted to Dayne. "Look hard at your father. Look hard and remember this shame. Remember last night and what befell your brother."

Gert started past into the meal room but turned. "What you do here is a sin, Keeper. A horrid, horrid sin."

His father refused to look at her. "Bucket your puritan words, woman. Both of us already earn our place in hell."

CHAPTER ELEVEN

BUNDLES TIED NEAT.

Lesson primers, alphabet woodcuts and books necessary for a proper schoolmaster lined the floor of Silas' room alongside his pack saddle, mule girth and bedroll.

So far the ruse worked.

His fingers roamed a paddle-shaped board retrieved from a stack, its cattle horn cover worn smooth by countless eager young hands. The frayed carry rope, once attached to a pupil's belts and breeches, stirred strong memories of his board years earlier.

Double-sided, the hornbook listed vowels and consonants with simple illustrations and verse. His eyes quickly found the desired dictum: 'Many are the afflictions of the righteous'. The core irony of religion. Oft recited as a child, Silas learned the words' truth only as an adult.

His finger traced the red Christ Cross painted in the book's upper corner. The symbol evoked a faith and way of life he once forgot, rediscovered and now misused. Sanctity turned artifice. Belief turned manipulation. His unique gift, his damning sin.

The board proved it. Moravians stressed education as a clearer path to understanding and serving God. Despite many cold mornings on hard benches, mirthless instructors with quick switches and frequent punishments for bad behavior, Silas embraced learning and persuasion early. Each served him well.

The brim of Silas' round hat drew his hands. More irony. The plain fashion of his religion made him stand out and earned trust he did not deserve. Others thought him different, including the Innkeeper's young son. The boy's eyes spoke hurt, anger and fear much as his did at a similar age. He wished the child a different, truer outcome.

His older brother also died sudden, young and without explanation or goodbye. Maybe fever, maybe his lungs. No one knew and only guesses, questions remained. Anger and a deep crisis of faith followed and Silas abandoned his religion and rural life for easy city allures. At first a saddle maker's apprentice, he chafed at the tedium of sewed leather and cobbled boots and found his true home on rough streets where cleverness, self-reliance and moral agility provided excitement and instant reward.

Years of crime, gangs and civil disobedience held sway. Often arrested, he played all sides against the others as an informant to avoid jail. Betrayed by a friend, he eluded the final wrath of authorities and adversaries through escape into the anonymity of the wilderness. Retreat and rescue from himself.

Silas returned the hornbook to its place and opened his childhood devotional text of verse beside him on the quilt. The familiar scriptures and watchwords with quilled margin notes by his father reassured and oriented, his earliest roots and reminders of an honest faith he never quite conceded to. He wanted to believe the promises of redemption, salvation. Life and doubt always intruded.

The devotional and chance encounter with visiting Moravian clergy changed his course. Emotionally adrift after his flight from the city, return to the basic rectitude of his childhood faith granted refuge and renewal. He talked his way into a schoolmaster post and wandered deep into the countryside to heal. Yet his clandestine nature never fully dimmed and when local military officers lamented lack of insight on Indian loyalties in the coming conflict, he offered himself as a missionary educator and spy for hire.

Treachery masqueraded as salvation. The perfect disguise. His fraud granted seldom questioned travel across Continental and British lines, stature among strangers and offers of meals and lodging along the road. No epiphany or moral crusade, simply the shrewd blend of distinct talent and background with opportunity.

Silas shifted on his bed. Its old ropes sagged and husk-filled mattress sacks bit rough and uneven, bare improvements from the hard ground he too often knew. Jaded weariness toiled his thoughts, vague alarm he could not resolve, an odd vulnerability.

He unrolled his bedroll on top of the mattress, the comfort of habit. An ivory handled hunting knife loosed from a sheath on his calf, he wristed the blade back and forth, mood restored by its steel glint and cruel shape. His hallmark and often savior, he gave and expected no quarter, no forgiveness, no second chance.

Yet he never eluded the dilemma of conscience.

Silas pretended he spied reluctant. Instead he preached reluctant, uncomfortable declaring for others what he denied himself. During the prior year he converted a band of Lenape Indians to Christianity, an awkward process he felt unworthy to lead as a lapsed believer. Banished by tribal elders for renouncing their native faith, the converts did not survive the passage west to the Ohio Territory. As the hornbook dictum foretold, a righteous affliction Silas would forever carry.

Still he prospered. When war arrived he counseled peace and neutrality as a missionary and most Lenape refused a fight not theirs and continued cautious relations with the British and Continentals. For Silas a job well done, a role well played and coin well earned.

Now he sought the Iroquois.

Their decision to fight or abstain determined the fates of the valley, its vital trade routes and possibly most western settlements in several colonies. Crafted influence and accurate, timely information promised its owner decided strategic advantage and Silas handsome reward.

He thumbed recent stitches on the mule's girth, an unlikely concealment for the detailed maps and letters of safe passage carried from both sides in the war. Two masters, two fees, four choices. Straightforward duplicity.

Until the freight wagons in the barn interfered. A dangerous unknown Silas' employers would want addressed, he suspected the cargo contained war contraband for the Nations. Others pried the canvas covers before him, possibly the Keeper's dead son or more likely the surveyor or crude tinker. He was not the only curious carrion.

His prior effort to uncover the hidden truth of the wagons ended unfinished when the Innkeeper returned to the barn unexpected. So his answer would come with the dawn while the others slept. If found he could claim he but tended his mule again.

Yet the plan sat wrong in his mind. A nagging pall of unwelcome finality obscured his sense of future and leaked doubt, misgiving. He chided the lack of nerve and resolved not to yield. Later he would seek the margin notes in the devotional, the last vestige he owned of his father, and center himself.

Silas sheathed the knife, left the room and listened in the shadowed hall. The quiet rooms of the others beckoned, an unplanned opportunity. He approached the surveyor's room at the far end, careful not to creak the floor, and reached for the knob but stopped.

Instinct warned. Too much risk, poor timing. He quietly retreated and turned the corner at the stairs. Quayland ascended from the main floor.

Silas brimmed his hat as they passed.

◑

Wicked proof. The telltale of his guilt.

Breaths loud and hurried, the Innkeeper bent close over his bedside table and the dried tallow mark of the prior night's candle nub. Crooked nail in hand he gouged the wood clean, blew aside the residue and stopped.

Dayne's door opened and shut across the hallway. Soft steps faded toward the main entrance.

Mind roiled and etched by his son's distraught face earlier outside the parlor, the Innkeeper grimaced anguish, remorse. His effect on Dayne seldom mirrored his purpose yet he often stymied, betrayed and incapable of any other result.

Anger followed, selfish and strong, an instinctive shield. He filtered away regret, sought no pardon. The wake promised only deep hurt and unspoken recriminations.

He wanted neither and knew the price of his choice. Gert stomped and flouted her ire but would mend when needed. Dayne would brood longer, more quiet and stubborn. Reason and revenge now girded their resentments. It mattered not.

Unable to quell the tremble in his hands, the Innkeeper confronted his cold and sparse room. The clothes chest and ceiling corners beckoned, bottle places where pernicious temptation and habit lurked. The ghost taste and smell of hidden rum, an insistent itch and scar, crawled his throat and nose. The Innkeeper yearned for refuge, slowly yielded, rose and almost surrendered. Only a final twist of will turned his fists away.

On the bed quilt the Peddler's scalping knife and tomahawk waited, goads of a different dilemma. Painted carved symbols marked the knife's bone handle and tomahawk's long shaft. Simple and efficient weapons of annihilation honed to brutal art, the nightmare fears of every white settler. Odd foreboding tightened the Innkeeper's gut. Uncertain fear.

He placed the weapons inside his belt, ornery defiance borne of disquiet and dread, the illusion of control. His hand reached for the more familiar feel and reassurance of his rifle and he left the room.

Door to the tavern steps pushed closed, he continued through the common room to the kitchen doorway. Hunched in blood red glow of the hearth Gert mumbled, set the heavy stew pot on the trammel and stretched her stiff back.

The Innkeeper seldom recalled her young. Always gnarled and edged, she lingered her life unaltered as he did his. Progeny of the earth, progeny of the farm. Neither escaped.

She turned. The Innkeeper started to speak but her angry, unforgiving expression stopped any words. He receded into shadows.

◑

Dayne gathered ash into a bucket on the drink room hearth. The fire burned close but not warm and he swept weakly at the stone. The ignored kitten pawed pieces of pine cone at his feet.

Confused and agitated by the disturbance between his father and Gert over Lauch outside the parlor, he festered. The unfair refusal of a last chance to see and say goodbye to his brother ripped Dayne's sense of self and family. Bitter new cold squeezed dark his heart.

He glanced toward the stranger on the floor near the steps. Unaware and indifferent, the wanderer worked an apple press to drain juice into a pail. Dayne turned disappointed.

On his stool across the hearth the driver prodded the fire with a poker. "Ain't much of a redskin is he, boy? Ugly crude skin and fool of a hat. Why look at him? Look at me."

Dayne shrank and refused eyes but the driver waggled the poker near his feet.

"Said look at me. I'm the one talkin'."

Dayne stared at the floor. His cheek twitched anxious.

"Speak up," said the driver. "Or you'll feel the back of my hand."

At his table in front of the hearth the gentleman shifted annoyed on his foot warmer. "The boy is mute. Leave it."

The driver shook his head. "Naw. He's a gamer, this one."

Dayne edged away, resumed his sweep at the hearth and waited before he looked up.

The man in black pegged and trimmed new heels and soles on a pair of Gert's worn shoes at a nearby table, a mended harness curled under his chair. He smiled, eyes kind.

Neck kerchiefs adjusted, the red hat man rose to the hearth from a chair and opened his coat to the fire.

"Your skilled hands surprise," he said to the kind man. "You've sewn leather and cobbled before."

"Industry serves society and so also God. The Brethren teach a durable faith. In the wild a man's hands are oft his purse."

The kind man rubbed charred wood against the new shoe leathers. "Parson's polish. Conceals many missteps."

Throat cleared, the cane walker rearranged his girth on his chair. "Soot for shoes. You show a shabby cleverness, sir. Needed for a man who walks his life in front of a mule. Bravo."

"Better than behind the mule." The hat man loudly blew his nose and dug a nostril.

The man in black smoothed the last heel peg. "I am fortunate to call Jerusalem a friend."

The driver dropped fir springs as lure and the kitten pounced. "The youngling cat has a good frisk. Is partial to me."

He tried to grab the kitten but it hissed and fled to the harness beneath the kind man's chair.

Dayne slid forward but stopped, unsure what next to do. The kind man's eyes spoke trust and calm yet odd sadness. Specks of pale yellow light wavered around him.

Offered the charred wood, Dayne waited shy and the man dabbed soot on his nose and on Dayne's, A simple gesture, a pleasant itch. Dayne smeared the grit with his hand and gathered the kitten.

The kind man extended a folded scrap of paper removed from an inner pocket. "I copied this rhyme as a boy about your age. It eases the mind with truth. Perhaps it may help you."

The man opened the scrap but did not read. "If buttercups buzzed the bee and if boats were on land and churches at sea. If ponies rode men, if grass ate cows and if cats were chased into holes by the mouse. If precious life could be bought for half a crown then all the world would be upside down."

He playfully cupped Dayne's ear. "One day your voice will come. Unhindered and loud. Your own."

Dayne's finger followed the scrap's creased lines and scrawled marks. He knew some of the letters but no words. The soft flow of the words lingered.

The driver barked rude behind. "Enough play. More wood."

"Why pester the child?" The kind man glanced past Dayne.

"He's the Keeper's whelp. Is his work, not mine."

The gentleman glanced impatient from his book. "You continue, an unnecessary bother."

Dayne tensed again, unsettled by the quick hardness in the lambs' voices.

The kind man rose, collected wood from the wall pile and stacked the grate. Dayne returned to the hearth edge away from the driver.

The cane walker struggled up and limped on his stick between the outside door and window. "Cold and dark already rule. The chill aids me not. Would that winter be over."

"Full war comes with spring," said the red hat man. "Why hurry it?"

"Liberty and triumph should not wait."

"War solves little," said the kind man.

"What does a Quaker know of fighting?" The cane walker pinched between his eyes.

"Man's vanity. Not God's glory."

The cane walker waggled the head of his stick. "The vanity is yours, sir. War is a noble tool, the means to a proper end. Conquest builds nations, empires, prosperity."

The driver smacked his pipe empty against the hearth stone. "War is all working man's blood. Spilled so the spoils go to the landed and lorded, the officers and the gentlemen. I'll wager none here could long suffer the heel of a sergeant major's boot."

"Have you served?" The red hat man gnawed his peel.

"Did my time. Didn't like it much."

The door above the steps opened. Gert carried a tripod cider kettle down and set it over fresh ash she spread near the fire. "More hot apple. Will ease the night's chill."

"We return to further test your sensibilities." The sad woman followed with tankards, glanced at the gentleman and sat at a table beside his.

"I know this displeases you," she said. "But there is little else here for me to enjoy." Candles lit at the fire, Gert filled lanterns on tables. She noticed the soot on Dayne's nose and dropped an apron cloth across his arm but he wanted to keep the mark and did not wipe.

"We discuss the war once more," said the hat man. "What says the woman of the house?"

The cane walker grumbled and stomped back toward the window. "By all means ask the cook."

"War here is personal," said Gert. "Grudge and slight, blood feud against old wrongs. No noble flags. Brings a keen, harsh edge to it."

On his blanket the stranger worked a sinew strip between ragged fingers. "The tomahawk cleaves close for purpose. None like its wrath."

The driver turned toward him. "Says the butcher and brute."

"Peace and kindred spirit should overcome the arrogance of arms," said the kind man.

Coat pulled tighter against the cold draft, the cane walker returned annoyed toward the hearth. "Weakling words, sir. Your black dress and timid air show lack of spine."

Concerned, Dayne looked up. Quiet anger filled the kind man's face.

"I am a man of faith and so will ignore your barbs," the man said. "Plain dress and plain speech promote equality and harmony, a way to better one's worldly body for God. Neither occurs without deep pride or spirit."

The cane walker dropped the metallic tip of his stick against the floor. "The Pharisees in Solomon's temple held such notions of ritual and dress yet murdered our Christ."

"All sin," said the red hat man. "Even men of God. None are blame free."

Dayne's chin slumped against an upraised knee. His eyes drifted with the voices but he tried to close his ears and retreat within. Too often grownup words brewed confusion, dislike, disturbance. He preferred his quiet.

Gert scraped a chafing dish at the hearth. "You scab each other hard."

"Yet they complain incessant about female claws," said the woman.

"Tiresome. Tedious," said the gentleman.

The kind man handed Gert her shoes.

"A useful guest," the sad woman said. "How does your church regard women? Most do not."

"Must we?" The gentleman winced.

"The Brethren teach the joy of kinship and congregation," said the kind man. "Many of our women read and write and so enjoy God's word direct in their lives. They share music, craft, literature and embroidery."

"Only the sewing matters," said Gert. "A woman's life yields best from daily torments and constant work. That and a good house garden."

The stranger rose. "Deceivers, betrayers, liars," the stranger said. "And you, plant witch, join."

He dangled a noose shaped sinew. "The religion you speak is false, a shameless reed. Hollow."

"Not so," the kind man said. "Christian faith provides truth, salvation and eternal joy."

Twisted, the noose unwound slow in the stranger's hand. "Only nature holds truth. You pray with your lips."

The hat man removed his peel. "Do natives not believe in God's final judgment? In the glory of grace and the pain of damnation? How do you seek heaven and avoid hell?"

"What whites call heaven is but the double of this world, done better," said the stranger.

The hat man coughed into his kerchief. "Yet we flourish and your people wither."

"The fat and lazy always sing happy. Until rotten seed brings no harvest."

The cane walker flicked the stranger's top coat with the point of his stick. "And what of your fruit? You come paltry, meager, a crooked life toted in a decrepit pack."

"The shell of the Great Turtle is old. Older than the world. Older than you will ever be." The stranger twisted the noose again.

"Now you delude. There is no great turtle, only a righteous God." The cane walker turned and fanned his great coat to warm his backside at the fire.

"Yet none here are righteous. None." The stranger dropped the sinew and a toad skin on the table in front of the kind man.

The man in black rose. "You make harsh without cause. I asked no trouble."

"Bothers oft come undeserved," the stranger said.

The cane walker snorted. "The Quaker, guiled by the savage."

Sinew and skin thrown into the fire, the kind man rose to confront the stranger. "Why mark me so?"

The stranger's frog eyes blinked slow. "You fool no one, missionary. Every twelfth man is a Judas."

Dayne did not know the word yet the edged silence of the others quivered his ears. The burdened room waited.

The gentleman looked up over his spectacles. "A curious assertion. To what and against whom?"

The cane walker peered hard at the kind man. "He brands you a traitor. Is it true?"

"No man is pure. I am only Silas." He sat.

The cane walker's jowls smacked doubtful. "An honest man would defend himself more ably."

The red hat man removed his mouth peel and stepped forward. "We mire needless. A dismal, sorry group. Dour, short tempered."

The sad woman turned in her chair. "Pray let us change that. Surely it will benefit all."

"Indeed," said the hat man. "Let us play like children at heart, joyful to be warm, fed and sheltered from the tempest."

He produced a wooden fife from the pocket of his great coat. "Music is the cure."

The cane walker pivoted on his stick. "You overstep decency and betray the common fire. I object. Where is the Keeper?"

The hat man approached the man in black. "You look a player."

"I have wailed trombones from rooftops, yes. The Brethren like their music spirited, loud."

He puffed cheeks and mimicked the horn sound for Dayne. "I also know spoons."

The hat man turned to the gentleman. "And you, sir. Will you join our happy interlude?"

"I have no skill nor ear for music. A childhood illness. My regret."

The driver blew a cloud of pipe smoke. "Fire up your whistle and maybe I'll show my boots. But likely the ladies will not want the jolly songs I know."

The hat man looked at the woman. "And how do you regard music?"

"I am ardent, if unschooled," she said. "Boisterous song and praise in church are fond memories."

The gentleman rumbled his throat. "My dear—"

The woman pulled her shawl tighter. "I will add where I can."

"Then we but require the consent of the woman of the house." The red hat man turned to Gert.

She wiped hands on her apron. "Has been long since I enjoyed song. Of dance I am not so prone. I'll wait to jump."

At the corner blanket the stranger's hand revealed a mouth harp. "Play hard. Play full. Out do me."

"Ah, an ancient lyre," said the hat man. "Then tis settled."

He blew a string of sounds on his fife, coughed fitful and chanted loud but wavered. "Lift up your hearts my heroes and swear with proud disdain. The wretch that would ensnare you shall spread his net in vain. If Britain empties all her force we'll meet them in array and shout huzza, huzza, huzza for brave Americay."

Dayne stared at the fife, unsure how it worked, curious at its bright sounds.

"You but bastardize the march song of the British Grenadiers," the gentleman said. "And humble proud tradition."

The hat man bowed slight. "Indeed and on purpose. What better way to show freedom from royal tyranny."

"A pointless pursuit. Not a surprise." The cane walker returned to his seat.

Dayne's father came down the steps, rifle in hand. An imposing shadow at the edge of firelight, he stayed separate and wary. "Why such noise?"

"You hide again," said the cane walker. "A poor host."

The red hat man cleared another cough. "You arrive timely. We are about to spread our wings."

He played a quick melody on the fife and danced a jig, gangly ankles and knees high, shoes erratic thumps on the floor. Kerchiefs trailed from one hand and the other held his hat in place. Several times he lost balance and almost stumbled.

Trencher spoons gathered from a table, the kind man played against his palm and thigh. The woman slapped hands and the stranger flicked his mouth harp. At the hearth the driver banged soup ladles against kettles, smoky pipe clenched in his mouth. Gert swayed slight, almost willing.

Dayne grinned, pleased by the strange bursts of noise and unexpected movements. The red hat man whirled and posed and shadows stretched happy across the floor. Welcome change.

The hat man extended his hand to the woman. After a glance toward the gentleman and Gert she accepted.

Hands raised toward each other but untouched, the hat man and woman stepped back and forth and in circles.

"An unholy mix and bald affront," said the cane walker.

The gentleman's mouth creased hard, grim. "She is already demeaned."

The hat man separated from the woman, again played the fife and lunged a final jig. Exhausted, he leaned breathless against his chair.

"A poor flourish but all I can muster," he said. "I am spent."

Kettle and ladles set aside, the driver approached the woman and slapped stray ash from his foldover boots. "I'll finish the job. But mind, dance like you mean it."

The stranger's crooked grin widened beneath mischiefed eyes. "A fine, bold rooster at last. Cockle-doodle-doo!"

The woman hesitated. Gert stepped forward but Dayne's father moved in front.

"Enough," he said. "It ends now. Go no further."

◑

With his rifle barrel the Innkeeper's prodded the Peddler, his pack and pine knot flame from the tavern through the cellar door. Thick shadows and cold gloom weighted close.

"You give in to others," the tinker said.

"None will rest easy with you free."

Pack set beside a ceiling post, the Peddler squatted on the ground. "I saw no frolic in you for our dance. A missed chance for song. Yet a brief smile on the face of the boy."

"Do not meddle where you are not wanted, gypsy."

The Peddler extended his hands to be tied. "My tomahawk and knife gleam and glow on your belt. Both happy at your touch."

Finished with the rope, the Innkeeper retrieved the pine knot.

"Let the light remain," said the Peddler. "I have use."

"Set any fire and you'll burn hard in it." The Innkeeper set the knot flame out of reach on a shelf and turned toward the tavern door.

"You carry the long gun anxious," said the Peddler. "Be aware. Pain and surprise follow the dawn."

"Speak clear."

"Your eyes will tell the tale. But you may not see."

"Gibberish."

The Innkeeper closed the door, leveraged a doubled length of rope around its handle and tied the ends to a post on the bar counter. Across the room he tested braces on the outside tavern door and window and turned, rifle crooked in an arm.

No remnant of the music and floor shuffles echoed yet the driver's unneeded dalliance with the woman brewed trouble. Smoke and cider smell tainted air rife with unease.

The others slept near the hearth bundled in great coats and blankets, differences and station suspended until dawn for basic comforts of warmth and light.

Dowd huffed loud, stiff leg outstretched from his too small seat. The surveyor mumbled and twitched across four chairs, vain hat held in place by his kerchiefed hand. The missionary reposed upright, quiet but unsettled on his chair.

Cotswold sat apart at his table, mouth creased and squint intact. A chair leg anchored his satchel handle to the floor. The driver lay against the hearth corner rolled in blankets.

Unhappy mounds. Unwelcome intruders. Tolerated for their coin yet despised for their presence. Bleating lambs.

The Innkeeper returned behind the rear counter and once more tugged the ropes on the cellar latch. He fingered spigots on ale and rum casks for dryness or drips and padlocked the drink shelves.

Dim yellow light filtered from a small cellar wall hole and he bent to look. Lauch's open coffin loomed upright against a bench, placed for him to see in the pine knot's flicker. Lonely, insistent notes from the mouth harp bruised the silence.

Fury swelled the Innkeeper's neck. Hidden guilt revealed, his fists clenched and unclenched and he reached for the latch but turned away, unwilling to cede any reaction. Hole covered with a bar rag, the Innkeeper retreated to a table at the edge of firelight and looked back uneasy.

The bitter goad remained even if he could not see it. The Peddler knew of the candle nub.

Around him wind and snow hissed the outside walls and brooding new blackness stirred. His inn moaned and trembled an animate warning. Upheaval came with the dawn. The Innkeeper sat heavy, inhaled the pervasive cold and placed the tomahawk and scalping knife ready on the table beside his rifle.

The tavern steps gradually pulled his eyes. Pierced and fragmented by Lauch's death, his day ended as it began. No clarity, no insight, only sadness and regret, rage and resentment. He choked off further feeling.

Exhausted and alone he awaited the long bleak hours of deep night, teased by hope of rest and sleep he knew would not come.

◑

Dayne shivered on his corner stool at the kitchen hearth, face bundled between scarf and wool cap, the sleeping kitten's head close against his neck. He did not want night to rule but cold dark swirled without heed.

Logs on the grate glistened, white hot bones behind pale flame. Smoke, kettle food, dried plants and fresh dough for morning bread weighted dense air.

Cocooned in quilts and shawl the sad woman slept on her chair, face slumped toward one shoulder, fingers raised as if warding a blow. Across the hearth Gert's uncovered head defied the cold, her open eyes narrowed but asleep above her blankets.

End of day images and emotions drifted Dayne's thoughts. The drink room surprise of music and happy movements, so loud and sharp, already faded as did the words of the kind man's paper gift. He touched the end of his nose, sad little of the black soot remained.

Darker broods soon intruded. Lauch's ruined body on the steps, the stranger's unsettling presence, the coach driver's cruelness and Gert's and his father's hard faces at each other. He did not understand the reasons, only the pain and confusion.

Dayne needed the blood root of family. Yet no grief or shared dismay colored his father outside the parlor, just anger and shame. Disappointment and resentment brewed bitter defiance, wrath and Dayne pondered how to force open the locked parlor door and free his brother's spirit. Afraid new visions and visitors lurked the night, he wrestled against sleep until weariness gradually closed his eyes. Restive, fitful dormancy followed.

The dream came late.

Dayne sat on a large flat stone beside a bend in an unknown river. Wooded mountains framed the valley beyond and storm clouds gathered the sky above. No sounds but brisk wind and the push of water. The current moved swift, a passing mystery and he wondered how fish breathed and saw in the dark world of the river.

Powerful wings pounded close overhead. Dayne ducked and a large owl screeched past wings spread and claws extended. It perched the lone limb on a tree sheared dead by lightning and stared back, head rotated, wide eyes frank, ruthless. One claw expectantly tapped the wood.

Bitter fear and panic burned Dayne's throat. Owls often hunted him, he knew not why. Stalled and shrunk inward, angry defiance and survival rose and he hurled handfuls of rocks at his enemy until he spent himself and all the stones.

Dayne closed his eyes. He floated effortless, free in utter blackness. Warm, content, quiet. He did not know who or what shape he made, only that he was.

Distant rhythmic thumps, double drumbeats, surrounded. A giant turtle swam past, majestic and supreme, intense shimmers of lights and colors. Dayne touched a corner of its shell.

Smaller specks gathered. Slow blossoms of feeling and thought, reawakened fragments of distant memory, passed into and through him.

Another presence drew near, a ghost shape of scattered veins of light and dark. Kindred spirit grew into familiar reflection, a face or faces. Dayne realized too late its cold menace.

Changed sudden into the awful bloodied snout of a frenzied feeding wolf, the reflection's cruel amber eyes sneered hate, death, and pulled Dayne forward. He screamed.

Gert's image, younger and blurred by maternal white shrouds, welcomed him even as she peeled away a separate hidden part of his soul. His lost self raged loud and harsh, bitter words and violent emotions which pierced Dayne's core. Gert took it away hid in a blanket.

Silence.

CHAPTER TWELVE

The Innkeeper struggled awake in early morning grayness.

Head slumped on an outstretched arm he blinked at the tomahawk and scalping knife close at his face. His clawed hands ached stiff. Groggy yet taut in rife cold, he sat up and glanced toward the cellar door. The guard rope remained intact. So did the bar rag.

At the hearth Dowd dropped fresh wood on the dwindled fire, flipped his great coat up to warm his front and rumbled his throat clear.

Huddled beneath layered blankets, Quayland moved alongside. He coughed and extended hands greedy for warmth. "I wrestled the night. A poor slumber."

Dowd moved further away. "You worsen, sir. And now ooze damp with fever despite the cold. Do not lean so close."

He stalked on his stick toward the Innkeeper's table. "Where hides the Quaker? He was absent and the outer door unbraced when I awoke."

The Innkeeper turned. Against the wall the door brace lay upright and rumpled blankets topped the missionary's empty chair.

"He goes constant to the barn alone." Dowd said. "For what purpose?"

Alarm and unwanted complication sprouted raw in the Innkeeper's throat. "You meddle."

"And you ignore. Prudence dictates caution."

Dowd moved but stopped. "Where is the morning pot?"

"Upstairs."

"You demand I climb two flights of stairs to empty myself?"

"Is your lily what's full."

"This is a tavern. You remain maddeningly inhospitable." Dowd returned to the fire but kept pointed distance from the surveyor.

Jacks unbuttoned his breeches over an empty ash bucket at the hearth corner. "I'll christen a pot for you."

"You are indecent, sir," Dowd said.

Jacks angled sideways, a pretense of modesty, and urinated.

"A reassuring, healthy morning sound," said Quayland. "Truly the most ardent of spirits."

Dowd turned away. "I am at a loss."

"A fine righteous pint of piss. Will take a strong man to match it." Jacks re-buttoned and toed the bucket forward.

Cotswold minced and squinted without his spectacles. "Entertain us no further. Stoke the warmer for upstairs and rid us of your company."

He lifted his feet. Jacks frowned, irked and defiant.

"Do it," said Cotswold.

Impatient with the petty confrontations, the Innkeeper hefted his rifle and approached the bar counter. He stared at the rag stuffed in the hole. Harmless and innocent in pale morning light, its memory yet swirled. He undid the rope from the counter, lifted the latch and with his rifle barrel edged open the cellar door.

The coffin leaned upright against the bench beside a burned down candle nub. Lid askew, the box beckoned the Innkeeper forward to look within. He glanced away, glanced back and succumbed. A crude corn cob figure with straw limbs and mud beard leered next to a toppled rum bottle and dark stain.

The Innkeeper shattered the bottle with the rifle butt and mangled the figure with his fist. He wheeled, gun raised, and confronted crowded, watchful shelves. No Peddler, only an empty blanket on the ground.

"Show yourself."

"I have no taste for hard drink," said the Peddler from behind. "Your snare is gone, taken. A gesture of aid and goodwill."

The Innkeeper pivoted. "Why this taunt?"

"A reminder and lesson." Frayed rope dangled from the Peddler's uplifted wrists.

With his rifle barrel the Innkeeper waggled the shreds. "And this gypsy trick?"

"Quiet tenacity of the beaver. A worthy skill." The Peddler clicked his teeth.

The Innkeeper stepped back irate yet confused, wary. "What broken mischief brought you here?"

"Fireflies."

"In winter?"

"Midsummer's eve. A warm night full of spirits, good and bad, an awakening. Fireflies danced the darkness and showed my path here."

"More gibberish."

"I watched you and the boy several times. You saw me high up on the ridge. I wanted you to know, to brood."

"I summoned no conjurer."

"Matters not. Some commotions quiver deep in the forest."

The Innkeeper kept the rifle aimed. His stiff hands ached and the barrel drifted more than he wanted. "You know I will not yield."

"No. Is not your nature."

The Peddler slid fingers along the coffin edge. "A sound, sturdy box. Yet cold already hardens the ground and you will not bury its secret until spring. Can your guilt hide that long?"

"Do not speak of Lauch. You knew him not." The Innkeeper closed the coffin lid and dragged the box into a narrow alcove between shelves.

The Peddler wagged the cob figure's bent straw arm. "Reckoning creeps close, Keeper. Your burdens show. The woman and the boy, they see. The stubborn tree cracks and crumbles."

The Innkeeper knocked the taunt to the ground and stomped it. "A poor likeness. You will need more goads than a straw man."

"I have others."

Bewildered anger and humiliation seared the Innkeeper's throat. Dark torments pounded his chest. He did not understand the need.

His rifle rose to the Peddler's face. "You paint a second mark beneath your eye."

"Blood root. A new tear. For the next departed."

◑

Key poised, Sybil's hand trembled. Fear of discovery. Wavering resolve.

Confronted by a locked dome trunk on Cotswold's bed, she weighed boldness against need. His growing indifference and sarcasms stirred open divide between them and she sought some portion of his hidden truth, either reason to stay or reason to flee.

She undid the lock.

The room door opened. She turned, startled and without excuse. Jacks filled the doorway.

"You move bold at last," he said. "How did you take the lock?"

"The trunk was once mine and I have a second key. He is unaware."

"You are serious then and mean to leave?"

"How else could I be here? His recent looks chill my heart. What you did last night did not help."

Jacks set the foot warmer aside. "I liked the look on his face. Surprised and fussed his pride, needed work. He comes here soon. Best hurry."

Sybil opened the lid. Shipping ledgers, manifests and customs records with official seals and ribbons stuffed the trunk.

She stopped. "I expected more. Different. Something."

Jacks moved close alongside, crude smile lopsided. Thick smells of ash, spilled cider and stale pipe breath oozed from him. "You give too easy."

Shawl pulled tighter, Sybil shifted away.

The driver lifted the shipping records to the bed. "These trunks frogged my mind from the start. No more."

"Careful," she said. "He will know the arrangement."

Jacks tapped the inner trunk bottom and pried loose an edge. "Knew it. A cheap hoarder, like the weasel he is."

Crisp red and black New York, Pennsylvania and Continental currency notes and English pound and shilling bills stuffed sacks beneath folded newspaper.

"A leprechaun's pot, only paper not gold." Jacks fingered the brightly inked bills and inhaled the distinctive richness of new paper money.

Hesitant, Sybil opened a sack but stopped. "I did not think it true."

"Why? He swindled both sides, clear. Did you not know?"

"I oft wondered but dared not ask."

She reopened the sack and lightly touched the notes. "Such money cannot be real."

"Real enough. No wonder the thief runs hard. A hanger's noose'll stretch his neck if caught."

"I grow nervous. Put it back." Sybil returned the money to the trunk.

"Back?"

"Is tainted."

"With greased luck. Use it or stand a fool."

Jacks pocketed a handful of bills from the bottoms of two sacks. "For services."

"We have no time," said Sybil.

A slow footfall approached up the stairs and paused in the hall. Jacks grabbed the warmer and readied to block the door but the steps continued past. He returned the sacks and records to the trunk and re-clasped the lock.

His blunt look held her. "I know your secret and his. We come partners now, you and I. Say it."

He leaned close, low voice insistent, coarse fingers on hers. "Say it."

Uneasy, Sybil looked away but waited to break the touch. "A difficult choice. Allow me time to make it well."

"Finish this, what you start. Or I will."

◐

Clusters of squat smoky candles. The illusion of warmth.

Just beyond the candlelight shadows lurked corners and floors in Gert's cold, colorless room. Watchful, waiting, patient.

Eyes slit, her head drifted side to side over a smoldering bowl of juniper sprigs. "Deceive the deceivers. Protect me as I sleep. Especially now."

With a sewing needle she deepened interwoven spirit lines etched into her headboard. Other carved lines framed the window and talismans of bone, shell and hide adorned walls.

Brittle wreaths of dried vines and flowers, old garden bonnets circled by tattered ribbons and a faded torn wedding apron draped wall pegs, dusty memories and keepsakes.

Gert opened the rough-hewn floor chest. Coarse bony hands, always scarred and never young, hovered over a favorite secret. She no longer looked in mirrors, no longer doubted or anguished the harsh unfairness of her appearance or guilt of her years. Her vain younger sister, the Keeper's wife, took others' eyes and always teased Gert's rough reflection. So Gert kept their mother's hand mirror, often fought and wrangled over, carefully wrapped in Dayne's bloodied birth rags as triumph and reminder. Prettier did not always win.

Rag and mirror set aside, her fingers roamed Dayne's infant clothes. Flat wooden buttons special made for him, not the usual ties or knots, shirt with bone body splints he hated, pudding cap torn by toddler chew marks and his first woolen breeches she made when he turned six.

Her child. One she always wanted, never had and took. That Dayne would not speak was unkind if just payment for her act. His quiet struggles bothered him dear and at times his eyes accused, questioned. She wondered what he remembered, what he knew, and hoped it was not the truth.

Her child. Gert wanted to keep Dayne young and innocent, aware it could not be. Already he changed, marked and stained by the farm and his father. She eased what she could and he watched and listened, aware beyond his years, his way misunderstood by others. No different than her.

She closed the lid and left her room for the kitchen. At the hearth she placed a steeping kettle and bowl on a tray, carried it into the hall entrance and climbed the second floor stairs.

The driver rounded the corner and descended past without gesture, face unbalanced by dark grin. He troubled the woman and his lack of surprise at Lauch's body on the tavern steps lingered ill.

Gert's footsteps slowed and quieted along the hall. The surveyor's partly open door at the end seemed a careless invitation. She peeked around its edge.

Bundled in blankets on the bed he chewed lemon rind and wrote in a journal open on his knees. Gert knocked and pushed the door.

The surveyor coughed, wiped his palm across his breeches and closed the journal. "An unexpected visitor."

His splotched, fevered face and neck concerned her. "Your skin burns hard."

"My throat has the pip and I grow dizzy, weak. No fire warms me and I quiver yet my sweats and rashes are torments."

Gert set the tray on a table beside small tarred field rocks. "This brew will unbind your throat and lessen the chills."

The surveyor lifted the kettle lid. "A daisy tonic? I am not dead. Not yet."

She filled the bowl from the kettle. "Pale chills need heat to balance the body's humor. Feverfew will warm your blood. A half portion first, only that."

He cradled and sniffed the offering. "You are a kind woman to treat me so. Or are you the plant witch the gypsy called?"

"He is a tinker."

"More hides there, I think."

The surveyor drank. "Is strong, bitter. Again."

"Drink too full and there will be other pains."

"Again."

Gert refilled the bowl.

"The tinker said the Moravian is a Judas," the surveyor said. "Did you believe him?"

"The gypsy needles all with his stings."

"But what is goad and what guile?"

The surveyor gulped the brew, returned the bowl and scratched pale red scabs at his neck. "I shiver still. This house yields no warmth. Even my ink nearly froze last night."

"Fire here never seems to keep," said Gert. "Although once the house nearly burned."

She soaked a cloth. "Wet your skin. Will aid the rash."

Kerchief loosened, the surveyor wiped his neck and forehead.

"You move odd handed," said Gert.

"Left handed, yes. A mishap of nature. The Latin for it is 'sinister'. Now you know all my secrets."

"Latin?"

Quayland nodded. "Does it disturb you?"

Gert shrugged and turned to the tray. "Use both my hands. Always have."

The surveyor returned the rag and set the journal and quill inside a saddle bag draped over a chair back.

"You are an interesting woman and see more than you say," he said. "Your words on your husband's service and loss of land are too common. You should make inquiry."

"Women have few such choices under whichever side. Mine is only what I take."

"And this inn?"

"I run it as my own."

The surveyor's bleared eyes searched hers, an unspoken question. "The curious bruise on the Moravian's hands still bothers. Did you believe his story?"

"No. Events hold reason, purpose."

"Indeed."

He displayed his hands, a dirty kerchief in one. "I carry no such marks."

"Yet you ask many questions. Others comment on your curiosity and what it holds."

The surveyor smiled faint, forced. "I assure you I am but a simple man who means well. Only that."

Gert squeezed the rag empty. "We are all believers. What else justifies our sins?"

Cough spasm rasped his voice. "You are a faithful woman, resolute. I sense it. Very soon the war comes here in earnest and the Nations will take sides. Blood will flow. It already starts."

"You are no surveyor."

"A surveyor cannot save you or this inn."

He touched her arm, unsure but insistent. "Much depends on what I do. Will you aid me?"

Gert waited. No one, not even the Keeper, knew which side she took for war. None ever inquired.

The surveyor released his touch. "You said your loyalty was your own. Now is its time."

"Do not ask more than I am able."

◑

Shielded from view, Dayne sat chin to knees beside the kitten and an empty milk pail on the top drink room step. The house quivered and groaned, restless cold and lingered misgiving. Smoke and ash burdened stale air.

Grownup voices drifted past, short unfriendly crackles. He wondered if his voice would sound such to others. Most used his quiet as excuse to ignore. Only Lauch and Gert at times sensed his deep loneliness and despair, even if they knew not the reasons. His father did not understand. Resentments and frustrations, anger and stubbornness, too often broke their awkward, infrequent efforts to reach out.

Dayne remembered nothing of his birth and early childhood. The blind search for his root always went unanswered. Willful, pained silence and rebellion, the penance of the unclaimed, resulted. At first he thought Gert his mother and she did not pretend other yet he never sprouted, never knew his real mother's bosom. Not until he turned eight did Gert reveal the cameo and open the truth, a partial story shrouded in shame, unspoken guilt and the emptiness of death.

Often Dayne studied his mother's faded face in vain hunt for his own. He seldom saw any sign of himself in his father. They shared only dark moods and temper. Even Lauch seemed a stranger at times, a missed bond.

On the stone floor below his brother's pale light no longer lingered. Eyes closed, he held Lauch's wood root tight against his chin and hoped, believed. Only shadows of violence and hurt answered. The bitter crush and void of another death, another loss stymied his heart.

He knew not what came after life, if anything. An end without light or feeling seemed unnatural but vague notions of God stayed an uncertain mystery, religion a grownup confusion. Yet Dayne did not doubt omens, spirits or the struggles of darkness and light. His haunts came too real.

Pieces of the prior night's dream returned, mixed images and feelings. He wished to again float safe and free in the dark surround of water, sustained by its relentless drumbeat. But the owl's cruel swoop and hateful false mirror face of himself interfered.

The kitten peeked from the empty pail, jumped free and patted down the steps. Dayne took up the bucket and followed.

Fire and brood hissed the room.

At his stool beside the hearth the driver scratched beneath his great coat and idly flipped worn playing cards into a random pile on the floor.

"The morning crawls," he said. "The long chill makes it no better."

The driver glanced up and Dayne avoided among rear tables to the large wood pile along the outside wall. With a hatchet he trimmed small sprigs from logs and collected pine cones to the pail. He did not like the hard stay of the driver's eyes on him.

Kerchief at his mouth, the red hat man shivered and coughed on his chair near the fire. "I find no comfort in this fire despite the heavy burn."

The cane walker pushed aside a trencher of breakfast remnants at his table. "Thin cheese and cold porridge, Indian mush. A poor first meal hampers the day. The Keeper masquerades parsimony as thrift and shorts our board for purpose."

He overturned a game board marked by squares and lines and looked at the gentleman. "I would court you for a game of nine man. But I sit with no Tory."

The gentleman squinted up from his book, annoyed by the intrusion. "Common tavern dullness. I shall manage the insult."

Last card flipped, the driver stood and approached the board. "I'll play you square up. A full man and common enough."

"I think not."

"Said I would."

"Another time."

The driver spit stray pipe tobacco and ground it into the floor under his boot. "Afraid you'll lose to the likes of me, is it?"

"Remember your station, sir." Jowls clenched, the cane walker waved his stick as a shield.

"Gave you equal chance at the piss pot this morning," said the driver. "Too prim to take it. Now this uppish gall."

The gentleman cleared his throat. "Cease. You were warned prior."

"Aye, and what of it?" The driver turned abrupt.

"Our music filled night changed little," the red hat man said. "Another fulsome day."

Unsettled by the stiff dislike of the men for each other, Dayne edged sideways with the pail of cones and springs to the hearth. He missed the kind man in black and glanced at the man's empty chair. The dark nudge of loss, vague and uncertain.

Hopeful, he fingered his pocket for the paper scrap but instead found the owl feather and glanced toward the stranger on the floor beside the steps.

The wanderer did not look up and tied sinew strips around an end of the birch branch sliced into thin strips like a fan. With a flint he shaved bark from the wood above.

"Why do you always stare at the Indian, boy?" The driver started toward Dayne but stood over the blanket instead.

"Squaw's work," he said.

"The Giver of Life is a woman," said the stranger. "You and all who begat you exist only from her wiles."

"You're still a squaw."

The red hat man rose from his chair, coughed into his kerchief and approached the game board. "I will maintain the peace and do the honor."

"Nonsense," said the cane walker. "You but bring your fever to me."

"A single game. Besides, I am a poor player, an arse. Embarrass me. Take my money."

Hesitant, the cane walker pivoted his stick in a tight circle.

"You have no one else," the hat man said.

"Play your own coin. Winner keeps, loser laments."

"Of course."

The hat man sat at the table. "Games are a gracious hobby. A fitting repast for the keen and sporting intellect."

"Do not make me regret."

Pennies removed from under his coat lapel, the hat man set his edge of the board and picked up a halved silver coin from the other side.

"I have not seen a Dutch lion dollar in years," he said.

"A mistake, sir. Return it."

The hat man extended the dollar. Unwilling to touch hands the cane walker tapped the board instead. Dollar retrieved, he replaced it with a smaller coin.

"A pence," said the hat man. "Odd how we revolt from Britain but its currency still rules our lives. Few citizens can even count in dollars and cents."

"Indeed, a bastard system. We should have more pride and foresight."

The cane walker carefully aligned his pieces. "I contested the missionary last night. A slow, guileful player and poor finisher. I doubt you will fare better."

He moved a coin along a marked line to begin the game. "Do you find your carrot pate a disadvantage?"

The red hat man slid one of his pieces on a different line. "Should I?"

"It furthers an ungainly appearance. Why a surveyor?"

"An important, learned profession. Difficult but righteous work."

"Not learned at all. Are you honest, your measuring chains precise?"

"Yes, and well used."

"I doubt it. Surveyors are instigators, land thieves, legal liars. No better than squatters."

"You sound a man aggrieved."

"I have shot at more than a few of you, sir."

The hat man loudly blew his nose. "Another reason to continue our mutual dislike."

At the hearth Dayne mounded ash into a large tub and swept stubborn residue with a straw besom. Frustrated, he used a rag to gather streaks and clumps left behind on the stone.

The driver sat heavy on his corner stool and poked the fire. "You made lazy and let ash pile the morning."

He toed the abandoned piss bucket toward Dayne. "A special chore. Empty this."

Dayne took the bucket handle but smelled its content and stopped.

"You've spilt piss on yourself before," said the driver. "Do it again."

Dayne left the bucket and resumed the rag.

The driver's rough grin dissolved. "You're no mute. If I grabbed your neck you'd squeal loud as one of your Daddy's pigs. Tell me I'm wrong. Go on, tell me."

He goaded Dayne's shoulder with the poker.

Dayne stiffened, angry at the rude voice and touch, and fled to the steps.

The stranger tightened sinews on the birch. "The dark one cannot hurt you. He has not the power and knows the wrath of it."

He extended the branch. "An Indian broom to help your way. Scrape smooth the handle and make it yours. You have the flint already."

Dayne waited. He sensed no threat and reached.

The stranger held the broom. "The owl found you. Also the wolf. You will see them again."

Head cocked, he released the broom.

The door above the steps opened and Dayne's father descended, rifle in hand. He grabbed the broom and moved Dayne from the wanderer.

"Take nothing from his hand," he said. "He seeks your touch, your breath. Give him no power."

Dayne pulled away and stood on the far side of a table.

An angry chair scrape intruded. Across the room the cane walker struggled up on his stick at the game board. "You are a cheat, sir."

The red hat man backhanded his runny nose. "Why? Because I take your coppers?"

Jowls agitated like a furious rooster, the cane walker retrieved coins from the board. "You claimed you were a poor player."

"I lied."

"This game is over."

Broom dropped on the fire, his father continued toward the outside door. "I am to the barn. Dayne, bring the pail."

◐

Icy flakes driven by biting wind gusts stung Dayne's face and hands.

Deep snow shrouded the rear yard and he struggled against the knee high mass. Twice he fell forward with the pail and salted himself. His father gouged ahead toward the dark loom of the barn and did not wait. Behind him the cane walker lunged ungainly, one hand at his cape collar and hat and other on the useless walking stick.

Prior tracks led from the drink room into the white haze but none returned. Others from the front road crossed and mingled near the barn and his father followed one set to the pasture fence.

Unable to open the barn door against the snow, Dayne and the cane walker huddled in the wind until Dayne's father returned. He took the pail from Dayne, dug away the snow drift and creased open the door.

Dense gloom wafted inside the barn. Dayne's labored breaths trailed in brittle stillness of disturbed quiet and dank smells of dirtied straw and long stabled animals itched his nose. Open stall doors for the cow and mule stirred more misgiving about the kind man.

The cane walker wiped at snow crust on his face and cape. "I see no Quaker yet his tracks lead here. Mischief, thievery. You waited too long, Keeper."

"Be not so quick to accuse."

Dayne followed his father toward the freight wagons but both stopped sudden. Strong movement lurked shadows beyond the dim shape of the coach along the corridor. His father cocked the rifle slow, face grim.

"What? Why uneasy?" The cane walker snorted a nostril clear.

The enraged mule burst forth in a fury of raised hooves, neck thrusts and bared teeth.

Rifle knocked to the ground, Dayne's father pushed him beneath a tandem and scrambled alongside. The mule bit a wheel spoke, its teeth hard scrapes on the wood just above Dayne's head, and a hind leg kick splintered part of the wagon sideboard. Dark powder from the tandem's bottom sifted on Dayne's face.

Jerusalem circled fierce, wide-eyed and bellowed an angry, anguished shriek and haw. Agitated horses inside stalls reared and banged, cries added to the tumult.

The cane walker hid behind barrels along the opposite wall near the door. "Do something, Keeper. This be your barn."

Bursts of sharp colors and sounds crackled Dayne's mind, instinct or perhaps simple awareness, the bond of the injured. Confusion and fear surrounded Jerusalem, not open hostility.

His father's reached toward the rifle and Dayne knew he would shoot the mule. Crawled out behind the wagon, Dayne stepped over his father's outstretched arm. He edged forward, arms wide to increase his size, and slapped a hand against the pail.

The mule charged again.

Dayne's heart plunged and he winced. One knee almost buckled but he continued to slap the pail. Jerusalem's hooves gouged the ground and his massive neck and chest stopped just short. Loud snorts burst visible in the cold, inches above Dayne's face.

Pain spilled from the mule's eyes, the sharp hurt of loss Dayne knew too well.

His father scrambled to the rifle, rose and aimed in a single motion. Dayne held up a hand.

"Shoot, Keeper!" yelled the cane walker. "Shoot!"

Dayne shook his head and hoped his father understood. Finger curled around the trigger, his father hesitated.

The cane walker rose and jabbed his stick. "Shoot, damn you! Kill the wicked beast!"

Rhythmic slap of the pail resumed, Dayne advanced. Jerusalem weaved back and forth but retreated into shadows past the coach.

Dayne followed to the end of the corridor. Snow blew through the partly open rear door and tracks, human and large animal, led into the white swirl of the side pasture. Dayne pulled the door further ajar to provide the mule an escape but after a final anguished bellow Jerusalem withdrew along the rear of the barn and watched.

Dayne returned to the front and sat on the milk pail near the freight wagons. Drained and overwhelmed, he could not stop the stark quiver of his hands.

Faded white light and faint voices, wisps of Indian words he did not understand, lingered from the mule's stall. Dayne looked away. Jerusalem was not the end.

Eyes and mind squeezed shut, he pleaded inward for the fury and upheaval to end. Numb grayness came instead, emptiness relentless and unhurried. There was no escape.

Dayne approached the stall. Head down, his eyes rose slow to the round black hat upside down on straw inside. Dark drips stained the brim and dirt. Above, worn shoes proudly soot-blacked at a warm fire the prior night dangled too high off the ground, stilled forever.

The kind man hung from the ceiling beam, scalped and throat cut, mule girth tight around his neck. An open vacant eye and swollen discolored tongue distorted his unready, defiant face. Desperate fingers splayed stiff, useless. From the chest a knife handle protruded and an empty sheath wrapped one lower leg beneath his rolled up breeches leg.

Rending loss and coarse brutality welled raw Dayne's throat, forced his stare.

Pinched and narrow eyed, the cane walker stepped alongside. His hands flexed hard around the head of the walking stick.

"A sad remnant, regardless the man," said the cripple. "The savage slipped your snare, Keeper. Admit it."

Face tight with anger and disbelief, Dayne's father stood near the body. "Why say it was the gypsy?"

"Who else would kill in such a manner?"

Dayne knew the stranger brought change, disturbance. That he also brought death did not surprise. The owl feather spoke it.

His father stepped in front to block view of the body. "This be not yours to see yet you always do. A curious plague, no different than others' weakness. Quiet be your affliction."

His father moved aside and Dayne once more stared at the corpse. He needed to look and remember, needed an answer to explain the kind man's end. None revealed and he turned away to sit again on the milk pail across the corridor. His fingers scratched black grit on his neck. He wished it was soot.

Death seemed an ugly poison, an unfair separation and end. Life removed for no reason. He knew the hurt and loss of those left behind but what of the dead? He hoped they did not feel the lack of light and being.

Mind and heart filled, he decided to think and feel no more. He shrank. Withdrew within and closed his eyes.

Inside the stall the Innkeeper watched his son. His honest act fell unheeded, rebuffed by hurt and disappointment. Another wayward failure between them, another mutual resentment.

He returned to the body. Scrapes and blood splatter in the dirt showed struggle and he knelt beside square heel gouges from the missionary's shoes and mingled moccasin prints.

The cripple entered. "I cared not for the Quaker, if such he was. He wore his religion too proud. It did not save him, nor the hidden knife."

The Innkeeper looked up at the knife handle protruding from the missionary's chest. "The blade is a sign. For us."

"Yes. A prideful, devious killer."

The Innkeeper left the stall. Hesitant, he approached Dayne and squeezed his son's neck and shoulder. Dayne flinched and dipped away.

"You did well with the mule."

Untaken, the words hung between them. The Innkeeper waited but knew not what else to say and turned toward the freight wagons.

Black residue marred his hand. He sniffed and awareness crept, an unwanted itch beneath his beard. At the rear freight wagon he knelt beside a small spread of black dust on the ground by the mule damaged wheel.

Dowd stumped alongside. "A costly encounter. I will need a wheelwright unless you are capable."

The Innkeeper rose and turned on him. "You haul gun powder."

The cripple pursed, stepped back. "Yes."

"Why?"

"A trade item often in demand. Always a market."

Angry dismay squeezed the Innkeeper. The haven of his barn went awry, spoiled by the stupidity of outsiders. Jaw clenched he swayed slight, voice flat. "Why?"

With his stick Dowd scraped straw and dirt over the ground stain. "Be careful what you start."

The Innkeeper stepped on the wagon axle hub and held up the cut tarp corner. "Others already nibble your bait. What reason?"

"Which others? You trespass, Keeper."

"Why gun powder?"

"The wagons and freight belong to me." Dowd swatted his stick across the wagon corner.

The Innkeeper wrenched the cane free and pushed it hard against the cripple's chest. "But the barn is mine."

Tarp sliced with the scalping knife, the Innkeeper removed woolen blankets he threw at Dowd's feet and lifted a small damaged keg. Black powder spilled over his hand.

"Answer," he said.

"My business is my own."

With the tomahawk the Innkeeper punctured another keg. Rum dribbled down his leg and he tossed it aside. "Powder and drink. Why?"

Dowd shook his head.

The Innkeeper hefted a box, glared when Dowd reached to block him and wedged it open with the tomahawk blade. Rifle flints and balls.

"I gave no leave for such," he said.

Dowd waited. "Was not my choice to strand."

Cross straps cut and canvas wrenched open, the Innkeeper wrestled a heavy oblong crate from the bowel of the wagon. He pounded, splintered and pried its lid with the tomahawk and pulled free the grim hard shaped wood and cold steel glint of a musket.

He clenched, scalded by such an unwanted find. "The other wagon?"

"The same," said Dowd.

"How many?"

"More than a hundred."

The musket's gall sagged the Innkeeper. Despite iron will and years of careful neutrality, tumult and war at last took his inn.

He looked away, voice quiet. "Which side?"

"Does it matter?"

"It will to others."

Dowd shifted on the walking stick and pulled his cape close.

The Innkeeper set aside the musket and stepped from the axle. Dayne watched close, concerned. Both their lives upheaved yet again.

The Innkeeper gripped tight his beard, let it go.

"We carry," he said. "The freight cannot be easily defended here."

CHAPTER THIRTEEN

GERT MURMURED an incantation.

Huddled over her crowded kitchen work table she removed cover cloths from plants and lightly fingered barren stems, dried cuttings and seed pods.

"The cold chases you every year and yet your hearts endure. Behold the new born sun."

She smiled and pulled a quilt back from the lone window. Faint daylight filtered across her face and the plants.

The Peddler's voice came from behind. "You are a relic."

"Not so much as you." She turned.

Seated on Dayne's stool at the hearth, the tinker traced his long fingernail along etched lines in hearth stones above the fireplace.

"Witch marks will not aid," he said. "Here or in your room."

"The chimney is open to the night and so unguarded."

"Yet you invited me inside."

Gert centered plants in the window light. "You came unaware. And hexed me with music before I could say different."

"An easy ploy. A poor excuse."

She knelt and used a combed ladle to skim cream from shallow milk pans on the floor. "The Keeper's cow milks little in winter. Two days yield for a bit of butter."

"Yet he keeps the boy at the pail."

"As his father did him. Dayne and he are stubborn. Both share the same blood yet are separate, different in broods one from the other."

Gert set a small bowl of cream aside on the table. "The boy likes his taste."

"He is the remnant, the sole seed," said the Peddler. "All that will endure."

"Then I am content." Gert tended trenchers in the wash tub.

"And your sister?"

She paused. "Unhappy, ungodly, a living taunt. Loved naught but herself. The boy should have been mine. So I took him. She was no mother."

"And the other?"

"Dark, unhealthy. An evil root best weeded before its sprout."

"The Keeper?"

Gert resumed her scrub. "His eyes asked, not his heart. He wanted no answer. Only an end."

"What between you?"

"Maybe for a time we thought it. No longer. On that we knew better."

The Peddler flicked residue from beneath his nail and slowly scratched along the corner of his eye. "And the boy?"

"He wonders. Parts of him go missing but he was saved. For us. From her. A good deed."

"It will not save you."

Gert poured steaming water into a stick churn, drained it out a bottom plug hole into a tub and set the churn in the tub.

"A churn is always a toil," she said. "The morning cold makes it no better. Keep the shift constant or the butter will not form."

"I have moved a handle before."

"Indians do not break butter."

"I am not always an Indian."

Gert added cream through a sieve cloth over the stick hole and set chicken bones on top of the churn. "Tokens cleanse the butter. And hinder ill spirits."

The Peddler slid the stool alongside the churn, fingered the hole and licked the cream. "Not so sweet as a man's soul."

He moved the dasher up and down.

Gert cracked eggs onto a long-handled peel she placed in the hearth oven. "You summon more than expected. An uncertain surprise."

"You sought the torrent. Why question its path?"

"And if the flood runs harsh, unfair?"

"Nature unchained is cruel. Unforgiving."

Gert removed the peel. "What of choice? Fate?"

"False answers for the weak."

Matted by snow, the Innkeeper entered the doorway rifle in hand. He stopped, face grim. "Why let the gypsy upstairs?"

Gert scraped fried eggs to a trencher. "Dayne has no want or patience to sit the churn. The tinker works for his feed."

"No food," said the Innkeeper. "Only irons."

"What happens?" Gert set aside the trencher.

"The missionary hangs dead in the barn, scalped and trussed for me to find. The gypsy escaped the cellar and was in the cripple's wagons early. There are tracks."

"All beasts leave sign," said the Peddler. "Not all sign is true."

Gert turned to the tinker. "Why kill the missionary?"

The Peddler continued to churn. "And the Lord said, 'Send a man out in secret that he may see the nakedness of the land. And so the spy came to the house of a wanton and lodged there.' Listen and hear the word."

Rifle poised, the Innkeeper stepped forward. "Too much happens where you saunter, gypsy. You come a pestilence."

Eyes hard, the Peddler released the dasher and slowly spread empty hands. "Always."

The Innkeeper turned on Gert. "You wrought this turmoil. You and your unholy notions."

"Save your bellow. You know nothing of holy. Ask Lauch." She pivoted away.

The tinker snatched and swallowed an egg, resumed his tattered top hat and rose to the door. "You are bold strong this morning, Keeper. A man of purpose. But where does it lead, I wonder?"

Inside the barn the Innkeeper pulled frozen snow from his beard. Nettled by the wind, his uncovered face and hands itched false warmth.

The gypsy seemed unaffected. He sniffed deep, eyes wide then narrowed. "Fresh blood. To stoke and worry the day."

Huddled miserable on a barrel near the rear tandem, Dowd pieced together lid portions from the broken musket crate. Struggled upright, he pointed his stick toward the mule's stall.

"Your savage handiwork uncovered at last," he said.

The cow bell's soft clatter approached from shadows at the back of the barn. Dayne led the snow crusted Welsh Red forward to its stall.

The Innkeeper took the rope, touched the cow's slight neck wound and lowered his head to her broad brow. "Was she out?"

Dayne nodded.

The Innkeeper wheeled angry on the Peddler. "You were warned from the cow prior. Why ill-treat my stock?"

"Those who watch also see," the Peddler said. "A tender spot."

"There are no watchers. Only you."

"Your eyes are your own."

Cow placed in its stall, the Innkeeper returned and rifle shoved the Peddler across into the mule's stable. Dowd caned stiffly to the stall gate. Dayne turned his back, arms clenched tight, an unwilling and unable witness.

The Peddler confronted Silas' corpse without expression. "Death seldom comes pretty."

"At the churn you showed no surprise," said the Innkeeper. "And none now."

"What difference? Your heart and mind are set."

With his boot the Innkeeper toed rounded foot prints beside pooled blood on the ground. "Moccasins. You were here."

"Before or after?"

The Innkeeper stepped close, angry voice low. "Do not mock me or my barn. Take down your cross."

The Peddler overturned a feed bucket, stood on its bottom and extended a rag-covered hand toward the Innkeeper.

"Don't be a fool," said Dowd.

The Innkeeper handed over the tomahawk from his belt and stepped back, rifle poised.

Paused by familiar heft of the weapon, the tinker smiled slight and swung the blade harsh against the ceiling beam. The girth sliced and the tomahawk fell to the dirt. He caught the splay-armed body against his chest and carried it from the stall.

Dowd stepped back. "Feral brute."

The Innkeeper retrieved the tomahawk and a small colored bead beside the stall post. Bead rolled between his fingers, he dropped it and picked up the saddle and round hat.

In the corridor a loud anguished snort exploded from the shadows. Saddle and hat dropped, the Innkeeper hurriedly lifted his rifle. Jerusalem hooved the ground near the coach.

Dowd wheeled awkward. "Keeper—"

Corpse across one shoulder and face marked by dried blood, the Peddler stepped in front of the rifle barrel. "All creatures grieve. Mules are no different. Did you learn nothing from the boy?"

Anger and confusion knotted the Innkeeper's mind. Too much happened too fast and the Peddler knew too much of it.

"I should short you right now," he said.

Instead he lowered the gun. "Next comes the freight. You make this foul burden and will finish it. You alone."

He retrieved the saddle and girth and pushed the barn door ajar. Cold gusts and icy flakes swirled inside. Dowd grumbled, upturned his cape and left the barn.

"I do this for no one else, my brother." The Peddler carried the body outside.

At the door Dayne waited, the colored bead in one hand and round black hat in the other. The Innkeeper passed him and followed the tinker through the door.

The wind and snow bit fierce but the Innkeeper pushed them away stubborn, unwilling to yield. Half way across the rear yard he remembered his son and turned. Dayne stood small and alone at the barn door, a damning ghost.

The Innkeeper gestured for Dayne to approach but he did not.

Concerned the Peddler broke too far in front in the storm haze, the Innkeeper wavered. He glanced again at the barn but the door was empty.

Bitter gall took his throat. A simple mistake, a brief lapse. He meant no harm but already knew he would not be forgiven.

Head down he turned toward the inn and deeper into nature's white ire.

◑

Grief. Abandonment. Fresh hurts and loss to ponder, endure.

Rigid on a stool near the drink room hearth, Dayne eased no warmth or comfort from the fire. Deep unwavering cold moldered inside his coat and throbbed his fingers. Harsh images of the butchered body inside the mule's stall seared his mind. The round black hat in his hands yielded but brief memories of the kind man's friendly eyes and slow sturdy smile. All faded too fast.

Weary sadness weighted. Dayne received life as an unexplained daily awakening but the empty cruelty of death caused doubt, fear and failed belief.

His father's disregard at the barn door added more pain, confusion and their slender bond dwindled further. Dayne's husks of isolation and resentment thickened. Stubborn silence was his only escape.

Around him the room shuddered disturbance and violence. Stacked boxes and crates from the freight wagons filled the back wall and corner. Powder horns, buckets of flints, shiny musket balls and bullet molds covered the rear floor. Blanketed in front, the kind man's body protruded the knife handle. A horrid, spiked taunt Dayne's eyes could not avoid.

The stranger swayed over the corpse, eyes slit, uncovered head spotted by snow remnant. Dayne searched his face for answer, purpose. None came, only his father and the clink of an iron shackle from the cellar. Used on hogs, the awful chain galled. Dayne refused to watch and turned away.

The Innkeeper passed his son, clutched brief by regret, and approached the gypsy. "You pride your kill."

The Peddler spat on the floor beside the body. "He was careless and saw not. The prayer becomes prey. A useful lesson."

At the steps the Innkeeper shackled the tinker's ankle to a chain placed around the post.

"You treat me special," the Peddler said. "I shall remember it."

Gert descended from the main floor. She frowned hard, distressed at the piled weapons and covered body, and sought the Innkeeper near the bar counter. "Why this crude display?"

"The barn is unsafe, the cellar crowded," he said. "And there are pheasants to flush."

The Innkeeper gauged the others in the room. Wrapped in blankets and sodden great coat, the cripple glared pinch-eyed and florid from his chair opposite the hearth. Nearby, the surveyor gnawed his lemon peel, pallid and frail with fever, shifting gaze intent on the cargo and Dowd.

Satchel by his feet the gentleman read at his table, picked cheek pocks and looked curious at the corpse. Hands in her lap and angled away from the body, the woman glanced frequent, worried toward her man. On his stool by the hearth the driver stole sullen looks at the woman and ground ash from his pipe with a piece of bark.

"None are clean," the Innkeeper said.

The driver rose, approached the body and nudged the blanket with his boot. "Spit like a bird he is. What righteous airs got him. Only an ass rides a mule."

"I thought him polite and well-mannered," said the woman. "A modest man of God."

"Behold him now," huffed the cripple. "Modest indeed. Humbled, humiliated."

The gentleman folded his spectacles. "You proffer a dangerous house, Innkeeper. Two nights, two dead. Coincidence no longer."

"Do not ignore the human cost," Gert said. "Both the missionary and Keeper's son had names, lives. Now lost."

"Life is for the living," said the gentleman. "The dead are best removed, forgotten. Of no use."

Gert stared cold. "Aye, that be the cruelty of it. Some will forget."

The surveyor removed his mouth peel. "A harsh but needed reminder. All must seek salvation when they can for death and damnation are sure to come."

"You sound a puritan." The cripple disagreeably stretched his stiff leg.

The driver pulled the blanket to expose the body's wounds. "He looks damned for good."

"Death is rain," said the Peddler. "The path of all life. Its return, its nourishment."

The woman shifted and looked away. "I cannot imagine such an end. We saw such butchery only two days ago."

The gentleman grasped her arm. "My dear—"

She pulled free. "Up the mountain road, scant miles from here. A small cabin, the family murdered and mutilated by Indians. To see it again so close so soon is unnerving."

Annoyance creased the gentleman's mouth. "My niece exaggerates."

"She talks true," said the driver. "Stopped the coach and saw it plain. Him, too."

"That was unwise." Smirk gone, the gentleman stiffly closed his book.

The surveyor removed his peel. "You said nothing of this prior."

"No reason," said the gentleman. "Little could be done for the victims at our passing. And was best not to inflame. No doubt such slaughters occur on both sides."

"Regardless," said the surveyor. "If marauders are close then risk is at hand for all."

"The valley depends on such news," the Innkeeper said. "Lives depend on what people see or hear. Silence does no favor."

Quayland rose and bent unsteadily over the body, one hand for balance beside the knife handle in its chest and the other against his neck kerchief. He emptied wild nuts, hard candy, handwritten Bible verses and a small wooden crucifix from the Moravian's pockets.

"The poor missionary was in fact poor," he said. "He leaves behind little but curiosity."

The surveyor turned to the Innkeeper. "Have you yet searched his room? That should be done apace."

Gert touched scraped knuckles on the missionary's hand. "Even the righteous are not always true."

"He was hardly righteous." Dowd struggled to his feet. His stick lifted the blanket to reveal the empty leg sheath.

The woman glanced back, averted her eyes again. "Must you leave the knife so? And the blanket, please."

"Such violence speaks purpose," said the surveyor. "An unkind message from the killer. None here are safe."

Dowd waggled his stick toward the Peddler. "Was this savage's work. Bloodthirsty, sharp and gruesome."

Gert returned the blanket over the wounds and without expression wrenched free the knife. "I will clean the body later. All are entitled to some final dignity."

The Innkeeper displayed a musket from the splintered crate toward Dowd. "You gamble hard with my inn."

The cripple turned. "The freight is not yours to interfere. What you do is theft, sir."

"My house, my choice," the Innkeeper said. "Explain yourself."

Dowd flushed, indignant. "Duly bought and paid for. Property of the Continental Army."

"Can you prove that?" Quayland coughed into his handkerchief.

"The wagons go to Fort Stanwix across the river near the portage for Oneida Lake," said Dowd. "A new garrison rebuilds the redoubt on Wood Creek."

The surveyor patted his brow. "Why do its soldiers not aid your transport?"

Upset at the questions, Dowd waited. "The floods last week severed my path and all communication. The fort is unaware my drivers fled. The haul is unexpected, secret."

"So you have no papers," said the Innkeeper.

"Not for you."

The surveyor blew his nose. "The answer of a smuggler, gunrunner."

"I like not your tone nor your manner, sir." Dowd pursed and jutted his jaw.

Quayland stepped close to him, soiled kerchief purposed in front. "When were you last at Stanwix?"

"My business is my own."

"Hardly the assertion of an honest man who faces the noose. Who commands the new garrison at the fort?"

Dowd stepped back from the encroachment. "Mind your ill hand rag. I want not your disease."

Quayland stopped but scratched his neck. "So you fetch supplies for a post you have not visited and for a commander you do not know. We do not believe that."

"Believe or not, I care not," Dowd said. "I will still deliver my freight."

The Innkeeper trusted neither man. The musket burdened his hands, spoil of the worst kind. "Why avoid the road north of the river? It ends at Stanwix."

"That route is often beset and ambushed," said Dowd. "I moved south to negate such."

Quayland took the musket from the Innkeeper, examined the barrel and firing lock and held it toward Dowd. "An English imprint, English made. This is a Brown Bess, the standard field arm for the British Army."

"You are hardly a military man." Dowd stared.

"He is not the one under inquiry," said Cotswold.

Surrounded, Dowd weighed his response. "The guns come from dead and wounded on the battlefield, including Redcoats. A common practice. The militia and Continentals cannot afford the purchase of new weapons."

Jacks dribbled musket balls cupped in his palm back into a box on the pile. "Palaver, all of it. Too long, too easy. These muskets and shot say what he's about."

The driver tapped his pipe on a small rum cask. "Though the man has solid taste for drink."

Dowd's jowls quivered belligerent disbelief. "I did not kill the Quaker. The savage did. He accosted the man last night and made threats. Let him deny it."

"Words," said Quayland. "This powder and these weapons damn you."

"An innocent man cannot be damned," Dowd said. "But any who treat this mockery like an unholy Inquisition shall be."

He stomped toward the Peddler and jabbed the tip of his walking stick against the floor. "The missionary was scalped by this savage who sits bold among us tainted by the blood."

Cross-legged on the blanket the Peddler's eyes opened slow. "Hark! A fallen angel sings me awake."

He rose, removed his top coat and hat and slowly lifted up his hide hunting shirt. Cords of small animal bones, claws and feathers dangled beneath a purple and white shell neck gorget. Callouses, scars and strange markings marred his discolored, scaled torso.

Arms wide, he turned toward the hearth and Dayne. "You all peeked earlier. Know me now. See me true."

Dayne angled to look. Concerned, the Innkeeper quickly stepped to block his son's view.

"The beggar is a newt," said Cotswold.

The woman pivoted, repulsed. "Dear God. This is a perversion."

"An odd exhibit. Daunting, unneeded. Curious." Quayland resumed his peel.

Dowd pointed his stick. "What further proof of his deed? The brute stays a brute, a vicious animal. Bloodlust, raw and unchecked."

The Peddler's long fingernail sliced the air toward the cripple. "I am an animal. Wild, untamed, dangerous. And animals eat."

"You are sick, a heinous toad," said Dowd.

The Peddler unfurled his thick tongue. "Said the fat fly."

Dowd hissed. "You'll hang."

The Peddler grinned rotten teeth. "Toads are slippery, more clever than you."

Disgust and spittle cornered the cripple's mouth. "You'll still hang."

Gert approached the Peddler. "Why so proud? Why such stir?"

He lowered the shirt. "I do not fight fair. Is not my nature."

"Enough," said the Innkeeper. "Stay hid as you did before."

He took the musket from the surveyor. "Marauders in the valley covet this freight and will kill to get it. The inn becomes a target, as do each of us."

Quayland nodded. "Above all else these arms cannot end in the hands of the Beast."

"You flame false fear," said Dowd. "Superstition. There is no Beast."

"So you say," replied the surveyor. "None feel the same. Not now."

"Life is cheap if savage murder be ignored," Dowd said.

Jacks spit pipe juice at the fire. "Half breed Indian slime and a false gun runner. What else lurks this house?"

The Innkeeper dropped the musket to its crate and took the bloodied knife from Gert. "The missionary's death will sort itself. If not, I will summon a magistrate when the storm clears."

Gert carried a blanket from the freight pile to Dayne at the hearth and fingered snow from his hair. "I know, child. Much pain and noise. But you are strong. You will bear this, as will we all."

Knife in hand the Innkeeper moved beside her to speak to his son but paused, unsure.

Dayne's dark stare trembled, accused. He shook his head, shed the blanket and placed the simple black hat over the kind man's covered face. At the steps he hesitated, almost glanced back and climbed into shadows.

Gert turned to the Innkeeper. "He is angry, disturbed. Too much happens. Leave him be."

"He rebukes, riles without cause," the Innkeeper said. "Why detest me so?"

"He has seen you before with such a knife," said the Peddler. "He knows its work."

The Innkeeper's jaw tightened. Once more he paid a price not his.

Rifle gathered from the table, he gestured for the tinker to pick up the body. "Finish your task."

The driver taunted the gypsy. "Now you tote your own noose. It fits you, Indian."

Followed by the Innkeeper, the Peddler carried the corpse into the cellar. "You will need more crooked nails."

"No box for the stranger," said the Innkeeper. "Outside."

"Cleansing is an ancient ritual of hope, need. Why deprive him?"

"A clean shirt and shoes matter not to a corpse. The dead are dead."

"Only if the living do not remember their paths."

The Peddler propped the body at the outside door. "You know I did not kill the Judas."

"His scalp says otherwise."

"I added only the blade after. He felt none of it."

"A poor choice what draws attention."

The blanket parted and the missionary's accusing eye and swollen face confronted the Innkeeper. He blinked and glanced at Lauch's open coffin in the alcove. Pleading, unclear words rushed his mind but he did not speak. He saw no clarity, no end.

The Peddler's finger lengthened the painted tears beneath his eye. "Rue runs bitter."

"Why speak such of what you know not?"

"And the Life Spirit confounded their tongues so they might not understand one another."

"Answer clear."

"What you do not see is the answer."

"Gibberish."

"Truth."

The Innkeeper prodded the Peddler with the rifle barrel. "Not a word I take from you. Finish it."

Outside door opened, the tinker hand gouged a trough in thick snow drift along the inn wall. Icy flakes quickly crusted his shirt and head. "The storm stays hungry. You feed it anew."

"Put him deep. I want no reminders."

The Peddler placed Silas face down. The Innkeeper tossed the round black hat on top of the blanket and wiped the knife clean against the snow.

"A hunter's blade, stout and firm of purpose," said the gypsy. "Many are its trophies, its pigeons. But no avail said his God."

Corpse covered with packed snow, the Peddler stopped and with his teeth tightened unraveled hand rags. "Journey words for his spirit?"

The Innkeeper added the knife to his belt, closed and braced the door. "I knew him not."

CHAPTER FOURTEEN

The Innkeeper carried the mule's girth and pack saddle up the second floor stairs from the main entrance. Regret at the missionary's cold burial weighted his steps. Although he simply refused another unwanted corpse in his house the decision lurked uneven, a mistake.

He opened the door to the Moravian's room.

Quayland turned and quickly plumped kerchiefs to hide neck sores scratched red. An unstrapped blanket roll and two open rucksacks lay on the bed.

"You pry without leave," said the Innkeeper.

The surveyor resumed unabashed. "It must be done. The real reason for the Moravian's death stands open before us. We need but see."

The Innkeeper set the saddle and girth on the floor.

"The room is almost unused," said Quayland. "That of a man who meant to leave? Or one who never truly arrived?"

The blanket roll contained camp utensils and the rucksacks clothes, candles, toothbrush, reading glasses, ink, worn writing quills, dried berries, jerky and wrapped cheese.

"A basic kit," said the surveyor. "Little else."

The Innkeeper searched the quilt and coarse husk mattress over the rope bed. "You were hard on the cripple downstairs."

"Deservedly. You had the same mind. The missionary sat a humble ride but seemed other. A creature of the road, keen and of certain prowess. The hidden leg knife proved it."

"He worked his fare."

"You are always blunt, shrewd. Perhaps too much so."

Inside a book of verse on the table Quayland uncovered a hand drawn map of the valley with trails, landmarks and Indian villages noted. "Did he ever say what tribe he ministered?"

"No. The Oneida have suffered preachers in the past. They and the others are less war-like than the Seneca and Mohawk."

The surveyor's marred fingertips drifted slowly across the map. "Rumor holds the Oneida favor the Colonials. Perhaps a clue to the real Silas."

He extended the book and map but the Innkeeper hesitated, unwilling to touch any taint.

Quayland frowned and dropped the book on the bed. "You refuse my hand. I am not yet a leper."

"Yet."

At the wall the surveyor knelt and opened sacks beside the Moravian's work apron and tools. "Leather seemed an odd trade for a schoolmaster."

"Good shoe and harness work always finds a man a cot."

Other small tied cloths contained fruit and vegetable seeds.

"He was also a would be planter," said Quayland. "Yet another side of the man well hid."

The Innkeeper retrieved a worn hornbook from the floor and fingered the short rope loop from its handle hole. When a youth he knew neighbor children who schooled occasional with a travelling minister and used such boards. He wanted one but his father did not believe, would not allow. He set the hornbook aside.

Quayland picked it up. "Imagine the hopeful hands and unhindered minds which held this. I wore such a board on my belt for first school. You?"

"My father's homestead yielded lessons enough."

The surveyor flipped the hornbook and recited a prayer from its back, "Praise God From Whom All Blessings Flow. A simple, tidy sum of religion. But you are not a believer."

"Why ask?"

"You walk oppressed, burdened of spirit. Without the joy and certitude of faith."

"I see no joy in faith or the faithful," the Innkeeper said. "The harvest of seasons and till of land are my belief. Neither is certain but each holds survival, renewal. I ask nothing else."

Quayland blew his nose into a dirty kerchief. "No God? No heaven and hell?"

"Life and death come as a whole. The same as for animals or plants."

"So no final judgment? No grand fate?"

A leather pouch from the rucksack emptied wooden tops and clay marbles into the Innkeeper's hand. "Each day yields only nature, toil and peculiar chance."

The surveyor kept the kerchief poised. "What of choice and free will? Surely you believe in sin and salvation."

"Unsteady words. Fraught, easy anvils to break upon. Salvation is preacher talk, fear. The bait trap of the self-righteous. Only guile and guilt, wrath and retribution are real. Those I do not doubt. Whether divine or not, what does it matter?"

"Yet you yourself are tormented."

The Innkeeper set aside the pouch. He seldom talked religion with strangers, unwilling to reveal his thoughts, aware few agreed. "Each person makes their own mind, their own choice."

Quayland wobbled and balanced a hand against the wall. "Excuse my earnestness. An uncle was a lay preacher and I learned of God from the task of his voice and scold of his hand. True faith came later. I am still its herald."

The surveyor returned the lesson board to the floor pile. "Different views, different sides, neither untrue. Trials yet loom for both our ways regardless."

Quayland cleared his throat and toed the saddle and girth. "We find no answer. The final mystery of the Moravian but deepens."

"A farmer who turns all stones often rues his find."

"I am more curious than you. I do not hide it."

Spasm passed the surveyor's face and he clutched the chamber pot from beside the door, kerchief poised at his mouth. "A sudden stomach urge. Forgive me."

He left the room and footsteps hurried along the hall to the lavatory closet.

The Innkeeper stood over the Moravian's meager belongings. The man's riddle remained. Events and not questions would solve it.

Gert carried a tray and kettle to the doorway. "What find you?"

"Little."

She glanced past into the room. "Purpose is hid in both these killings, Keeper. Glean it or more will come."

The Innkeeper tapped the tray. "The surveyor's neck and gut worsen. Your plants and potions do not work."

He left the room and descended the stairs.

Gert waited as the surveyor retched in the water closet. Ill sounds brought ill waste, a chore Dayne would avoid. Her morning burden made worse.

She continued along the hall and entered his room. The open survey journal, chewed lemon rind and stained quill beckoned on the bed.

Her rapt, wistful fingers glided over precisely inked letters and symbols and edged the quill's feathers. The shapes of words and their sounds on paper always puzzled and her eyes strained for the secret words hid between the lines.

The door creaked and Gert quickly pulled her hand as from a stern paddle.

"Soon you will know all my secrets," said Quayland.

Bleary and slumped he wobbled, front breeches buttons undone and big hat askew across his head. Chamber bucket in one hand, he held the mule girth and verse book in the other.

182

"More brew," Gert said. "Will aid your fever and cough."

The surveyor pulled his breeches together, waddled into the room and set the bucket on the floor. "A rude exercise I know but I suffer at both ends. A soldier's unkind lament."

Gert filled a bowl from the kettle. "You were a soldier then?"

Confused and regretful, Quayland placed the girth and book on the bed. He turned away and buttoned his front. "No. Yes. Once. Long ago."

Neck kerchief fluffed, it dropped lower and uncovered fresh scabs. Gert stepped back concerned.

"Is not the pox, I swear," he said. "The ague. Only that.

"Your skin blossoms. The sores deepen. There are white flecks."

Kerchief widened, he reached toward the bowl but stopped. "Please. I cannot desist now. Remember your word. Do not forsake me."

She left the bowl on the table. He sat subdued on the bed, blanket pulled around his drawn shoulders, and drank.

Gert glanced at the girth. "Why the mule belt?"

"A guess. The threads on the chest pad are new. What better place for a leather worker and humble road missionary to conceal?"

Quayland removed a small knife sheath from the cuff fold of his great coat. Trembled hands struggled to cut or loosen the threads.

He smiled feebly. "My fingers are no longer nimble."

Gert waited, accepted the offered knife and pried the threads. Two wax sealed envelopes and small tightly folded sheets of symbols and numbers hid beneath the pad.

The surveyor opened the envelopes and read. "Safe passage transits from St. Leger and Dayton. The puzzle at last comes clear, I think. Behold the real Silas."

She glanced at the letters and handed each back. "What of it?"

"Our humble preacher was no simple man of God, that be sure. He served both sides, two masters. Or perhaps none."

He studied rows of random digits clumped in groups on the sheet. "A rudimentary code. But for who and for what? And what cipher?"

"You speak unfamiliar," said Gert.

"The language of betrayal. The tinker said true. A Judas lurked among us."

Gert refilled the bowl at the table. "The missionary's glance moved watchful, close. A mystery and more than he seemed. But I thought him kind."

"Perhaps. Duplicity often is."

"He had interest in you. Said you were no innocent. And to trust no one."

"Slender honesty."

Gert extended the bowl. "Drink further and wet the skin."

Quayland dabbed his neck and fingered pages of the book. "These verses likely hold the key. Words to obscure words. Faith used as deception."

He looked up. "You still peek at me askance."

"You are relieved the missionary is dead."

The surveyor continued with the book. "I relish no man's demise. But he came a threat to this valley. Also to you and this house. These finds show it."

"The Keeper's son was no threat yet also murdered."

"The lad was unlucky. In what he said and what he knew. Victim of a war he did not fight."

Quayland sipped. "Tell me you believe in fate, purpose. For what we find here, now, in this very room."

Gert shook her head. "I know only choice, chance. Is consequence what rules."

"Ah, the vice of free will. The apology of all sinners."

The surveyor looked hard, direct at her. "I say it simple.

God directs our paths, each of us. In our hands are our own fates and those of many who live near. We need only solve the puzzles of those killed. Are you still with me?"

"On that, yes."

Empty bowl placed beside his journal, he resumed study of the numbered sheet and verse book. "I will return these to the Moravian's room when done."

"Would be wise if I re-sew the threads."

"You are an able accomplice."

"And then?"

"We await God's plan."

◑

Cotswold peeked through the crease of his room door. Gert carried a tray past from the surveyor's room and turned the hall corner down the stairs. Door closed, he hefted his satchel to the bed and removed heavy cloth wrapped objects he uncovered on the quilt.

Metal printing blocks. His lifeblood. His vanity.

Counterfeit currency. The fraud and illusion of unearned wealth, status. The insidious revenge of a poor wharf worker's son and former tea pot engraver ignored by proper society.

Long nimble fingers traced the blocks' sharp etches to test, validate and restore his soul.

Such flawless calligraphy and detail rarely came to the black market and merited a rich premium he always exacted. Consistent paper thickness and grain, quality inks and an artist's natural touch separated his craft from rampant back alley forgeries. That keen businessmen did not detect the false art attested his skill.

Money's distinctive smell tickled his nose. Real or not, its rich scent always stimulated. Cotswold almost smiled.

Both the Crown and colonial governments hoarded coin and bullion. The policy devalued paper bills, increased prices and created strong demand for counterfeits. Many merchants and banks purchased false bills for use in daily commerce to save legitimate currency. Forgery became an impartial conspiracy of the street, open to all for complicity by all. His salvation.

The crime merited death and to lessen suspicion he printed small face amounts and used shovers, tradesmen who bought the paper for pennies on the dollar and easily placed the notes into circulation through countless hand to hand cash transactions. The combination of capitalism, opportunity and greed absolved all guilt.

Yet he harbored no illusions. A useful but unwelcome parasite, Sybil and others tolerated his sarcasms and cruel indifference only because of false perceptions. He pretended partnership in a shipping firm. In fact he was a clerk and knew one day the charade would end. And though he feared capture and prison he worried more over worse humiliation, a return to the grinding poverty of his youth.

Against the perfection of engraved metal his untended hands and nails irked. Fastidious in habit to overcome physical flaws, he enjoyed indulgent manicures by his barbers and vicious gossips at his gentlemen's club. Life in exile seemed improbable, a cruel unkind interruption.

Just three months prior he preened on the cusp of grand opportunity. An intermediary of the Crown inquired about engraving new plates to flood New York's teeming harbor trade in worthless notes. The British did not balk at his excessive price in gold but war intruded.

Royal troops surrounded the city and horrendous firestorms from bombardments left almost a fourth of its residents homeless. Floods of desperate civilians overwhelmed authorities and lawless gangs and squatters roamed streets at will amid the chaos. Without friends or shelter Sybil and he barely escaped the charred ruins of their lives into unfamiliar, violent countryside.

Circumstance connected him with Jacks, a joinder of necessity already regretted. He took a wilderness route north to avoid crime on main roads and began the demeaning daily exposures of an unwanted journey.

Plates carefully re-wrapped and returned to the satchel, he turned but stopped. Black threads placed on the trunk locks, indicators of disturbance and intrusion, lay on the floor. Eyes squint, he peered close and sniffed.

Frank mustiness from the driver's filthy great coat lingered separate along with a trace of Sybil's familiar body powder, a jarring joinder and simple explanation.

His key unlocked the trunks. Creased money bags, carelessly re-folded, and stronger mixed scents of Sybil and Jacks confirmed blatant violation. He expected betrayal by one or both but not together. Such base indignity and personal defilement he would not tolerate.

His fingers picked pocked cheeks. Sybil's profound absence of gratitude and judgment grated most. More possession than passion, she endured his moods in return for dresses, finery and the pretense of being an almost lady. At times he enjoyed her wit, wiles and outspokenness but lately she cloyed and demanded and her intemperate outbursts annoyed and drew unneeded attentions.

Outrage and anger seethed his neck. The bastard she carried, a woeful miscalculation, he would address without ambivalence. Her crass dalliance with Jacks, on full display the prior night in the tavern, sealed both their fates. Discipline mattered. Order and place mattered.

Thin lips creased and remorseless, he re-locked each trunk and carefully re-set the black threads.

He needed to get clean again. Despite a shave that morning he opened his razor kit at the bedside table, removed the small mirror and honed the blade along a folded leather strap. Cold basin water and the harsh scrape of the blade across his skin, always without lather, confirmed and enlivened him once more.

◑

Chickens rescued from the smoke house clucked, lunged and pecked each other for dried corn Dayne dribbled to the ground in the front portion of the cellar.

Thin daylight framed the outside windows and cold drifted stale air. Overhead, ceiling boards groaned as his father's familiar footsteps thudded along the upstairs hall. Once a sound of safety and comfort, the noise stirred intrusion and betrayal.

Dayne turned away, stopped. Lauch's coffin leered in the side alcove. Its askew lid lured him close and he peeked uneasy over the edge, unsure what hid past the dark opening. Despair, loneliness. No light, no air or being, a cruel box for forgotten bones and ceased memories. He did not want to think that way of Lauch or the kind man in black.

The taint of spoil, decay rankled Dayne's nose. Loss and empty sadness crawled his gut. He retreated from the misshapen wood.

Brace removed on the rear outside entrance, Dayne pulled open the door and harsh wind and snow scoured his hands and face. He heaved uncaring, grateful for unmarred air.

A small corner of blanket and bottom part of a shoe protruded from snow mounded along the basement wall. Sudden awareness sagged Dayne's shoulders. The kind man. No inner light lingered beneath, only absence and deep chill.

He felt his pocket for the colored bead retrieved from the mule's stall, upset he could not find it. Scalded by images of the body in the barn, he grimaced and swayed, heart squeezed by anger at his father's repeat cruelty to the dead.

Eyes closed, he receded into the cellar and tried to drain.

The faint creak of the drink room door disturbed the silence. Unable to reach the passage to the spring or rear cellar, Dayne crouched low along the floor behind crates and baskets stacked beside a corner shelf and peeked out.

Soft steps approached. The sad woman's shoes and skirt stopped opposite Dayne's face and she tapped anxious on the shelf above his hidden head. Chickens gathered at her feet for more feed from his hand.

Heavy footsteps came closer and the driver's imposing knee boots scattered the chickens.

The woman's voice wavered. "You follow me too quick. The others?"

"None noticed, none cared. The great man toilets upstairs."

"His eyes are cold and spiteful unlike before. His mind changes, hardens."

"He's always a rude, nasty look."

The woman turned and her skirt nudged a curious rooster toward Dayne's face. "This is different. Something goes amiss. He knows."

The driver stepped closer. "Showing scared will only make it worse. He thinks you weak, unaware. Your belly is a taunt, a broken frolic he no longer covets. You know his secret now. Take the money. Take all and show a lesson."

Her shoes moved away. "He would never abide that. He would hunt me. And you."

"Not if he loses the chance. Wait the storm and I'll take you to Albany myself."

"You short his wrath, his guile."

"He'll not catch us. I'll make it so."

The rooster pecked Dayne's hand for corn, drew blood and pecked harder. Pain welled but afraid to move, he grimaced and withstood.

"You had nerve for the trunk," the driver said. "A good first push. Follow it."

"You make it play easy. My choices are not so simple."

Circled behind, the driver's boots nudged the back of her shoes. "He leaves you. You know it. You've no future with him past this inn. Don't waste me."

The woman moved away. He pursued and she stepped further off.

"He hides a small belt pistol," she said. "You should know that."

"He is not the only one with a belly gun."

The woman rummaged a basket and a wooden clothes-pin rattled to the floor near Dayne. Her hand retrieved it.

"I will tell my mind when ready," she said. "Do not follow me so close again."

"Then give no more fetching looks."

The woman's shoes retreated toward the drink room door. The driver grumbled, spat pipe juice to the floor and removed the madeira bladder from its shelf nail.

"I was shorted the other night. Not again."

Head tilted back, he opened his mouth to gulp but the bladder was empty. He squeezed to make sure and angrily tossed it aside.

◑

In the common room Gert hung laundry on lines stretched between walls and across the main table and benches. Lingered among clean smells she breathed deep, a brief escape from the hot cookery of the hearth.

Her spinning wheel rested ready in pale light near the window, the best spot for afternoon sun. A necessary toil without the allure of her garden or plants, many hours alone at its bobbin and treadle deepened her broods, her distance. The wheel, fashioned from the metal band of a large barrel, always squeaked and waggled but she endured its pester. At times she wished for a younger sister to aid her hands and pass the chore to. Efforts to interest Dayne did not prosper.

Gert hung the boy's breeches over the wheel to dry and returned to the kitchen. At her chair beside the wash tub opposite the fire she hard scrubbed Silas' bloodied shirt with a thick lather of black lye soap. Undergarments and shifts placed to dry dotted the room.

"May I intrude?" The woman edged into the doorway.

Gert grunted.

The woman entered. "You are true to your word about the Moravian. Thank you. He deserves some basic human decency."

"No man had the courage to pull the knife," said Gert. "The cowards left it for a woman."

"I brought these if need." The woman set clothespins on the table and her eyes wandered the room.

"As a child I helped mother tend the house master's laundry and we often filled the dining room like you," she said. "On sunny days linen and clothes hung from every tree and bush in the yard. A pleasing sight and rare good memory."

"Reminders?"

"A less complicated life."

"But you were not happy when young."

"No. I still search."

The woman turned. "All your dresses are black, gray. Almost mournful."

"Practical. One hides char the other ash. Mud I deal with separate." Gert added more soap to the stubborn blood and continued her scrub.

The woman stepped beside her. "Who would kill so vicious and cruel? Was it the savage? He has wild eyes and the air of a madman."

"The tinker is too clever by half to be snared so easy."

"Do you believe the story about the wagons?"

"All on the road lie. I believe little."

Gert placed the shirt with other clothes in a sturdy bucking tub raised on wooden blocks. Wood ash spread on a coarse cloth across the tub, she poured hot water and drained the mix through a plug hole and back into a pot to reheat.

"You'll never rid that blood," said the woman.

"A night's soak in lye with apple wood and urine will help. Tomorrow it may yield."

Gert again spread ash on the tub cloth, poured another kettle and wiped blackened hands on her apron. She glanced at the woman's coarse, telltale hands.

"Lye never leaves a woman," she said. "The taint of hard work. Life's work."

The woman opened her palms. "Yes, my female blemish."

She moved closer to the hearth. "I cannot get warm and am already prisoner to the fire. Roasted on one side, frozen on the other."

"One reason I enjoy wash on winter days," Gert said. "Hot water always soothes."

"How do you manage in this wilderness without neighbors or other women close at hand? You must be terribly lonely."

Gert's mouth creased wry. "Alone here is no different than alone in town. Noise and numbers make no warmth, only gossip and covetousness. I have my plants, my quiet and the promise of spring. This inn and its hardships are all I know."

"Even the strong-backed get weary."

"I still have my angry days."

Gert filled the water kettle. "You eye danced with your man all afternoon. The harsh driver, too. An ill brew after last night."

The woman looked away. "I know I disappoint."

Kettle set over the fire Gert turned, voice blunt. "You risk much. Think, child. You'll get but one chance."

The woman folded the Moravian's black coat from a chair back. "My faith wanes and strands me bewildered. No choice seems clear."

Two small objects fell into her hand. Gert moved alongside.

Lemon seeds.

◑

In wall shelves behind the bar counter the Innkeeper placed small kegs of rum from freight piled in the tavern corner.

Dowd stumped on his stick between the window and outside door, metallic tap an annoying intermittance. "You wile my kegs as your own."

"I want no mice at the spigots."

The driver crossed from the hearth. "Had my eye on one of those kegs. The afternoon crawls, Keeper. Open the bar. I have money."

He placed a small silver coin on the bar. "If not rum then beer."

The Innkeeper closed and locked the shelves. His swollen right hand throbbed and his mood wanted no argument.

Jacks added another coin. "I'm no day drunk. Want to sluice my gob is all. Two bits, double your rate."

"No."

The driver stiffened. "I like my drink. Don't deny me."

The Innkeeper glanced at the coins. "Your bits are short."

Jacks dropped others on the bar. "Who hasn't passed shaved coin? A working man takes what comes and sugars the rest. No noise. No complaint."

"No drink."

"Indulge us," said Dowd. "I am also in habit of beer before supper. A small nick would satisfy."

"No beer, no drink. Not today, not tonight."

Dowd pursed. "I see no reason. Or do you beat your brew? Most tavern minders cheat the mix, especially in winter. Saves two bushels of malt in eight."

"An ill trick which fuddles many a stout man," the Innkeeper said. "One I do not abide."

Jacks replaced the coins with a fresh two dollar note. "Deny this. Yorker money, crisp and unspoiled. Worth a lone beer. Several."

"Do not ask again." The Innkeeper turned aside.

The driver slammed his fist on the counter. "A man just wants his beer."

The Innkeeper wheeled slow, voice restrained yet final. "A drunk who stumbles home is one matter. A pest who suffers me under roof is another."

"Your son was a drunk," Jacks said. "Is that it? You shutter the drink from yourself."

The gentleman descended the steps, approached and set his satchel on the floor. He glanced at the note without expression.

"A crowded counter bodes well for a public house," he said. "Yet none here seem content. Does Jacks foist jaundiced money again?"

"False bills are common on the road," said the Innkeeper. "The bar stays closed."

Dowd curtly pivoted toward the window. "Poor business, Keeper. A smarter man would do better."

"I apologize for my driver," said the gentleman. "Like all of us, the cold and tedium tilt him astray. That will change."

Shelf lock pulled on to make sure, the Innkeeper left the counter and hefted his rifle from the table.

Behind him the gentleman hissed at the counter. "Imbecile."

"Call me another name," said the driver. "Go on, do it. I dare you. Do it and I'll break your hands and empty that satchel."

The Innkeeper climbed the main floor steps. In the common room he lingered among the laundry, grateful for brief quiet and place to brood. Despite misgivings, he wished to avoid the unwanted mystery of the gentleman and his satchel. No good would come of it.

At the kitchen doorway he paused. Gert kneaded buttermilk from chunks of fresh butter set into a tub of water and knuckled remnant into a clay mold she salted, sprinkled with herb and sealed with stone atop a piece of wood. Set with others near the window, she placed holly sprigs on top of each.

The Innkeeper set his rifle against the wall and spooned stew from a pot over the fire.

"Cabbages and onions, new bread, some meat," said Gert. "Will serve for supper. The lambs were not happy with their prior feed."

"Let them bleat."

Gert poured hot water into a wash tub. "The missionary's bloodied shirt soaks the night. I will clean the body in the morning."

The Innkeeper waited, wary of her response. "He is already outside. Given to the snow."

Gert turned. "You gave no words, no final ritual for his soul?"

"He stays mounded where he is."

"You will burn for what you do, Keeper. Burn."

"My choice. Mine alone."

"You are wrong to see it so."

She poured more water and scrubbed hard over the tub. "What of the cripple? I did not believe his tale on the freight. He spouts innocence too hard."

"Those are not soldier weapons. No camp goods, no trinkets, only guns, powder, drink and blankets. Contraband. Brought for one purpose."

"His wagons stain," she said. "A bitter bait and poison, the same as what took Lauch. See you remember your first born. Like the missionary, he was killed for what he saw or heard."

"I do not forget, woman. That ghost yet haunts."

Gert re-filled the water kettle from a bucket and placed it over the fire. "Did the tinker do the missionary's murder?"

The Innkeeper set his spoon aside. "Claims he sank the knife only after. Yet you saw the body. A gypsy taunt, not an Indian kill."

"He is not un-clever. Why stay where he would first be sought?"

"He is bold, brazen and comes not innocent or at random. He stirs mischief and rift, confusion and upheaval. For reason."

The Innkeeper's hands flexed, restive in nettled warmth from the fire.

"Your rheumatoid worsens again," said Gert.

"The cold sharpens and runs it to the bone."

He added wood to the grate and poked the logs. "There is more. Moccasins marked the missionary's body but two other tracks went beside the barn and one toward the road. Maybe the gypsy, maybe not."

"The Iroquois make bold. The woman said a raided homestead burned not far up the mountain, the family killed. Her man wanted her quiet but she spoke to warn. The rumors come true. You can no longer deny the Beast."

"Aye. But which or what is he? Is he already here?"

The Innkeeper moved his rifle to the table, sat and dry fired the lock mechanisms on two pistols removed from coat pockets. Stiff fingers struggled to load powder from the horn and a dropped pistol ball rolled across the table.

Gert glanced from the tub. "What burdens do you hunt now?"

With a short rod he forced shot down the pistol barrels. "The moccasins will be back."

She wheeled to face him, concern measured with question. "We will live here as before, long after the lambs and wagons depart. Here, hard by the Nations, regardless the war. You know that. Do not lose your way now, Keeper."

"My barn, my task. No other."

"Give up the freight. Its lure draws too many snakes, too many ills."

"The valley will not survive its wrath."

"Consider this inn, this farm and these many years. Harsh struggle and survival, the two of us, alone against the wild. You risk all if you go against the tribes."

The Innkeeper returned the pistols to his pockets and took up the rifle. "It cannot stand."

Gert nodded slow. "You will end us."

He left the kitchen and went out the inn's front door head and hands uncovered. No new tracks approached from the road and he fought through the white mass down the side yard along the tavern windows and followed prior paths past the barn to the back fence. Fresh snow mostly obscured earlier prints toward the copse of trees beyond yet he guessed two or possibly three trespassers in the night.

Wind whipped and knifed by icy flakes, he stared into faded light and swirled haze for apparitions he could not see and haunts he did not understand. Purpose lurked the violations of his inn and barn, open personal affronts he could not ignore.

Turned into the wind, he crossed the barn yard and struggled up the hill to the thick snow blanket atop the buried road. White shrouded woods and mounded fields crept toward the bleak ominous rise of the mountain.

The bird call from a laurel thicket across the road drifted past on the wind. Its answer came somewhere in the middle distance to the right.

The watchers remained close.

Snow-crusted but unbowed, the Innkeeper confronted the storm and those behind it. With one hand he slowly arced the rifle toward the sky. The angry, defiant shot jolted his pained arm and briefly pierced the tumult until captured and swept away by wind.

The rifle settled across the crook of his opposite arm in blunt warning and stern promise.

He would defend his own.

CHAPTER FIFTEEN

No one noticed. No one cared.

Dayne held the heavy water bucket near the drink room bar, one shoulder pulled toward the floor like the drooped arm of a broken straw doll. Blood blocked him. He could not move, unable to step past the dark smear where the kind man's body lay earlier.

The room writhed. Gloom, smoke and ash crept rafters over the hearth and grownups sat huddled in blankets, unhappy lumps of field rock mired in the same soiled pasture.

Dayne hefted the bucket with both hands and willed his legs forward. Eyes closed until past the stain, he crossed toward the fireplace but his father and the long rifle came down the steps and cut his path. Dayne struggled the bucket to the floor and water sloshed.

Balance regained, he continued and passed the sad woman seated at a table opposite the fire. She sipped hot cider yet her worried face held no warmth. At the next table the gentleman read behind spectacles.

"You shaved again," she said.

"To fill the time."

"You only do that when you are angry."

The gentleman did not look up. "I regret I am so obvious."

Tired arms sagged, Dayne approached the hearth. Leg straightened from his stool in front of the fire, the driver idly peeled bark off a pine log and flipped it into the flames.

"I dare you to spill it again." The driver kept his leg in the way.

Dayne set the bucket down, did not fill the water kettle and retreated across the hearth to the wall wood pile.

The red hat man shivered in blankets on his chair nearby. Cough rasped his voice. "We foul the room and shrink the Keeper's stack. Precious heavy use for little warmth."

The cane walker paced the edge of firelight on his stick near the door. "A poor chimney. Weak draft and ill wood suffocate us all."

The red hat man coughed again. "At times I would be a dormouse and sleep away the winter cold, cozy in my little hole."

"Your ambition lacks, sir, if you wish to be a rodent," said the cane walker.

"A warm rodent."

Gert came down the steps and scraped uneaten food from trenchers into a tub.

Throat rumbled, the cane walker turned toward her. "Another modest meal, madam. A thin, unsavory kettle and old cheese. Better effort is required."

"You ate full enough," said Gert.

The red hat man looked up. "Mollify him with meat and johnny cakes on the morrow and end his mouth aches for all our benefit."

The cripple wheeled. "Mind your manner, sir. You accused me harsh this morning with the wagons. Harsh and unjust."

"The back wall speaks otherwise," said the hat man. "Your story does not persuade. The muskets do."

"Then we remain at odds."

The hat man pulled a kerchief from his pocket, noisily blew his nose and spilled coins to the floor.

"One measure of a man is oft his purse," the cripple said. "Pennies and pittance, I see."

He jabbed his stick at a halved silver coin rolled near his foot. "Another Dutch dollar. I was not aware bastard silver was so common."

The hat man bent unsteady and retrieved the coins. "The price of apostasy. Has always been so."

Dayne carried fresh wood to the fireplace. A spindly spider dropped from a log and he teased it along with a piece of bark, taken by its halting yet busy walk.

The driver's heavy boot stomped the spider as he rose over Dayne. "Spiders bite nasty. Not this one. No longer."

The dark man edged the bottom of his boot along the stone and with a wood coal lit his pipe.

Confused fury and hurt surged Dayne's spine and sputtered his mouth.

The driver grinned. "Almost got your words didn't I, boy?"

Dayne grimaced, shook his head and searched for help. His father bent over fixes to a lantern frame at a far table, intent with his pliers. Gert dried tankards from the dish tub at the rear counter, back turned. On his corner blanket the stranger sat eyes closed.

Isolated in the crowded room and surrounded by dislike, Dayne stiffened and shuttered all feeling. Turned away, he walked well wide of his father and escaped into the cellar.

Beside the spring Dayne licked small hand wounds from earlier hard chicken pecks and smoldered. He expected more from the blood bond of family but he and his father ruptured and Gert understood only parts of his fears. Neither seemed to care when needed. Stubborn silence, defiance blossomed deep.

Root removed from his pocket, Dayne's upset strokes with Lauch's pocket knife scraped the half carved wood. He wanted to end the slow fade of his brother's image but the twisted, hateful face he created reminded more of ugly spirits deep within his dreams. Restless, Dayne set the root beside the knife and followed the passage toward the front cellar.

Thick shadows lengthened recesses, dimmed corners and seeped insistent cold. Daylight faded too fast and darkness grew. Night fears already gnawed.

Footsteps approached the drink room door and Dayne hid among corner shelves.

Prodded by his father and the long rifle. The stranger and his pack entered. His father bound the wanderer's wrists with rope and shackled his legs to a ceiling post.

"These irons hoisted a hog," said his father. "Will hold you."

"The weakness of the strong. The end stays the end."

Fingers stiff, his father struggled to clasp and key the lock. "You scare me not, gypsy."

"An easy lie. You wear your hunt face. Your eyes gleam yet your hands tremble, shake. What haunts do you chase this night? Or do they chase you?"

"Ghosts are for fools."

His father tested the lock, rose and retrieved the rifle. He looked along the passage and Dayne crouched lower behind vegetable baskets, careful not to breathe.

"Dayne? Dayne? I know you hide. Chores, son. Pile more wood at the fire."

His father's footsteps continued toward the rear door. Storm noise from its open and hard shut dwindled into silence. Dayne waited, crawled to the corner and peered through a low crease in shelf boards. His father was gone and the stranger sat on the dirt floor.

Returned to the spring, Dayne brooded and wanted away. Gloom weighed heavy, a thick tar in the air he could not avoid. Twice he restarted his carve but set the root down, disturbed once more by its likeness. Instead he fingered the owl feather.

Metal clinks and drag of a foot came close along the passage. At its corner the stranger held the iron shackles piled in rope bound hands. The chain dangled loose.

"Life does not always run fair," he said. "The spider learned it hard. So did your brother and the round hat. So will you."

The stranger stared owl-eyed, stepped closer and offered the shackles. Dayne could not look away.

"You have seen such binds before," the wanderer said. "The hogs and the jail wagon. Trusses, fetters, hobbles bitter and contrary to all spirit and nature. Scourges."

Dayne had never touched the irons, refused. He waited, an unspoken question, and reached hesitant. Stark with anguish and hate, the cold chain rankled and curled his hand.

"You know what it is to be prey," the stranger said. "Remember it when you are the hunter."

Shackles and chain dropped loud, sudden to the ground, he sat cross-legged by the spring. "Your father's gift is not what it seems. A vain notion. He knows the better. None can still my itch."

From his mouth the stranger removed two slivered bones, one curved and one straight, and tapped the shackle lock. "Old animal bits from a roasting fire. Useful tools of our ancestors."

He reeked decay and deep forest, distant oldness. Faint white glimmers around his scaled head tugged and beguiled Dayne with wisps of nature, truth but also trickery, violence. Dayne glanced at the owl feather in his hand and the sharp flint arrowhead prickled his leg in a breeches pocket. Doubt, fear tugged one side of his face.

The stranger picked up Lauch's pocket knife. "A useful blade. A sturdy edge."

He jabbed the knife point into the ground and thumbed the unfinished tree root. "The wood is stubborn, a hard yield. And your hands are young, not yet suited to such work."

He continued to rub the wood. "For now the root stays angry, ill formed. Like your heart. Your brother's loss was real. You will get him back only by dreams."

The wanderer set the root on the dirt. Eyes lidded but not closed, he swayed tight circles.

Small red-veined river shells on a sinew cord looped the stranger's neck and Dayne leaned curious.

"Wampumpeag. Life simple, made splendid by nature."

Dayne lightly touched the necklace. The stranger grabbed his wrists tight.

"Watch the trap. Not the bait."

Released, Dayne shifted away unsettled.

"All things hold light and dark," said the wanderer. "Both fight the other with guise and ruse, without pity or regret. I am no different."

He rose over Dayne. "Tonight the dreams return. More visitors, some old, some new. Is up to you to hunt the meaning and seize its power. If not, others will. You saw the wolf. But the wolf also saw you."

The stranger gathered the irons and at the corner looked back. "Finish the root. Is your path. Your voice."

◐

Rifle poised, the Innkeeper listened in unsettled quiet of the darkened barn until satisfied no one lurked. He knelt and sparked a pocket flint into straw to light a small candle lantern.

The shadowed soul of the barn emerged slow. Deep gloom shrouded the corridor and stagnant animal smells stiffened the air.

The Innkeeper sought normalcy, routine and the pretense of control. None remained, only unwanted provocations. The enraged mule, the missionary's scalped corpse and the contraband weapons twisted and poked his mind. Disruptions, blights, cankers he could not shed. His hand traced the damaged wheel and side of the rear tandem, proof he did not dream.

The Innkeeper climbed the axles of all the freight wagons and unrolled their coverings to conceal the lack of cargo. Hay from the sled forked to restless coach horses, he entered the mule's empty stall in the lantern's dim puddle of light.

Streaks of dried blood remained in the dirt next to moccasin and shoe marks and the overturned feed bucket. From the rafter the sliced mule girth dangled limp. Signs, remnants, cold reminders. Death stench hovered insistent. Yet no clarity, no purpose.

He crossed the corridor to the cow's stall, opened the door and fed the Welsh Red a piece of stalk. "What did you see this morning? What do I miss?"

Her flank drew his strokes and he thought of the unborn calf. Winter again started hard but spring would yield different. Life's yearly test and renewal, his only reason to continue. The one religion he could believe.

Muffled, unexpected sound and presence intruded from darkness along the rear corridor. The Innkeeper lunged from the stall, grabbed his upright rifle and wheeled barrel poised.

The mule loomed in shadows at the edge of the lantern light, eyes blunt, a question the Innkeeper could not answer.

"You guilt me like the boy. Unforgiving. Unfair."

The Innkeeper stepped forward but the mule's taut neck countered and swayed. He retreated.

Leftover blankets gathered beside a wagon, the Innkeeper climbed the loft ladder with the lantern and huddled near its opening. Night bloomed quick. Cold slithered his coat and wound his neck but he pushed it away stubborn, unmoved.

His hand followed a rough-hewn ceiling post. The barn and inn consumed his life, lonely testaments to hard won survival. Pride swelled brief but Lauch nor Dayne were farmers despite his tries. Neither son understood the harsh demands of the fields.

He sensed no future, no permanence. One day the barn would end. Only the land might endure. Slow decline and void awaited him patient, certain. Blood weakness. The bitter ire of human finality.

Willful anger flared, girded. Irksome strangers and events trespassed his life, unyielding threats which ended all further avoidance or denial. Indignant at loss of dominion, the Innkeeper saw no choice in his plan.

Pistols set beside the rifle, beneath blankets he settled on his stomach at the loft opening and reluctantly pinched out the lantern. Swallowed whole into night's black clutch, he rued the lost light.

Wind moaned rafters, the overhead pulley creaked and nervous birds fluttered and chirped the dark. Deep cold soon choked his lungs, chafed his face and crept tight his spine. Stubborn defiance failed to stop unwanted shivers.

Blackness ruled rampant, relentless. The Innkeeper's hand sought the comfort and bitter delusion of the pocket flagon. Briefly taken, he pulled clenched fingers free of the poison and with a kerchief blindly tied his wrist to the rifle stock.

Dread night continued. Besieged by awful apparitions and the cruel beckon of temptation, the Innkeeper waited.

◗

Dayne extended Lauch's pocket knife in his hand.

"Are you sure?" The stranger looked up from the ground beside his pack in the front cellar.

Dayne hesitated. Fear fluttered his chest. He was not sure. Yet the rope and irons galled, angered. Unneeded binds, undeserved pain. He cut the tie from the wanderer's wrists.

"The others will speak harsh," said the stranger. "And your father. Know that."

Dayne nodded. Unplanned, his choice seemed true even if he could not see its end. Two outcasts, each misunderstood, defiant toward those who ignored. Escape for both, however brief.

Shackles gathered, the stranger stood and hefted his pack toward the drink room door.

Dayne followed and placed the knife in a corn silk he set unnoticed in the pack. The wanderer might need it again.

Near the edge of firelight past the bar counter they stopped. Back turned at the hearth, Gert filled the cider kettle. The cane walker warmed his front alongside and squat on the stool the driver scraped his pipe. The sad woman and squint gentleman sat separate tables and the red hat man huddled beneath blankets across the fireplace. None noticed.

Dayne and the stranger waited.

The cane walker turned and raised his stick in alarm. "The wild savage runs free! Defend yourselves!"

The stranger handed the severed tie rope to Dayne, stepped into the light and lifted high the open irons. "Nature's grace come early. The courage of a boy."

Dayne edged forward, rope loose in his hand. His eyes sought Gert, an explanation. She started forward but stopped.

"Where is the Keeper? We are unsafe." The cane walker wielded a piece of firewood.

The red hat man peered over the kerchief at his nose and stood. "I think not. No harm is intended. Neither he nor the lad."

Up from his stool the driver strode forward, hand on a pistol butt inside his great coat. "The Keeper wanted you chained, Indian."

The stranger dropped the irons to the floor. "I suffer no more shackles."

Gert gestured the driver to hold, approached and knelt beside Dayne. Her hand traced his forehead and chin, touched his hair. Concerned eyes questioned but did not accuse.

"You hold a different soul to do this," she said. "Chores now, son."

Dayne curled the rope around his wrist, moved to the hearth and scraped piled embers from the grate into the ash bucket. Heat bristled his cheeks and hands, penance for the brief thrill of small triumph.

Across the fireplace the dark driver lowered to his stool. "Fool for a boy. Like as not the half breed will choke you with that twist tonight."

The cane walker turned on Gert. "You cannot accept such heathen insolence, madam."

"He stays for now. The Keeper will sort it." She moved past him.

The wanderer crossed between tables, placed his pack on the blanket beside the steps and sat.

The driver scowled. "This smells a gypsy trick. Leg irons do not go easy. He guiled the boy. Black magic."

One hand on his satchel, the gentleman shifted on his chair. "Indeed, he proves a difficult tinker. What next?"

The stranger blinked slow and picked teeth with a bone sliver. "The pot is not ready. So I stir some more."

Gert moved beside the wanderer, voice quiet. "Why do this?"

"The boy finds himself."

"And the Keeper will find you."

"Is the same."

Face pinched by spasm, the cane walker paced on his stick near the window. "Grievous folly to let him remain. The brute but waits to kill us all."

The red hat man blew his nose and dried the kerchief at the fire. "It appears we weather the moment. Let quiet return."

Dayne finished the ash bucket and sat the corner hearthstone, knees to chest. Tired and empty of emotion, he yielded to the fire's warm burn. His fingers lingered in the coarse feel of cut rope and he glanced toward the corner.

The stranger hissed soft and extended folded white linen from his pack toward the sad woman at the near table. She smiled faint, uneasy and looked away.

"You affirm life," said the wanderer. "A gift."

"Please, no."

"Is meant for you."

Reluctant, she opened an infant's cap with lace drawstrings. Three pale red blots marked its edge. "Thank—"

She dropped the cap to the floor and turned abrupt. "How dare you."

Linen retrieved by a boot heel, the gentleman squinted over his spectacles. "Blood stains."

"An old Mohawk witch cast spells with it," said the stranger. "I but return it to a happier home. Small heads seek calm and comfort."

Gert turned from the kettle. "And the child who wore it?"

The wanderer's long-nailed finger lightly clattered a cord of small bird claws and beaks on his pack. "He had no more need."

"Liar," said the driver. "A white bairn was tomahawked in that wrap."

Gert examined the cap. Rippled by surprise and anger, she glared at the wanderer. "You brew new trouble. Needless shame and hurt."

"I am disorder," he said. "Disarray."

"Outrage, insult," said the cane walker.

The gentleman stood. "I find no amusement in this."

"Nor does your woman," the stranger said. "Yet your bastard grows snug within, warm despite your cold."

The woman groaned and curled, hands clutched across her abdomen as if struck. "Dear God—"

Gert moved alongside and gently squeezed the woman's hand. "Men are fools. Women the unfortunate vessels of their spew."

At the hearth Dayne tightened, head up. The room shifted, pained by the sudden bite of hard emotions.

The red hat man peered over the gentleman's shoulder at the wrap. "He accuses without cause, surely."

"Vile insinuation for any decent man," said the cane walker. "Unjust, wicked. Such bald affront must be hotly refuted, sir. I do not hear you."

Fury twisted the gentleman's face. His creased mouth twitched hateful, silent.

"Nor will you." The woman's words lingered quiet, unexpected.

Gert wiped hands on her apron and returned to the hearth. "The bitter truth of it."

The cane walker followed her. "This inn is a poisonous den, madam. Soiled. Lecherous."

Poker thrust into the fire, the driver approached the wanderer's pack. "I'll end this farce since no other here will."

"My pack is not for you," said the stranger.

The driver tapped its top with the poker. "What if I say it is?"

With sudden force the wanderer rose, twisted the poker free and pressed its point under the driver's chin.

The dark man grinned and cocked a small pistol from his hip against the stranger's stomach. "I'm ready for you this time, canter. Move untoward and my dog will bark your belly."

He slowly took back the poker and again tapped the top of the pack. "Time we saw what spoil you carry. What else have you stole?"

Gert turned. "Must there be more of this spectacle?"

"I want to know what he's stole," said the driver. "He's an Indian."

The cane walker approached the driver. "Be bold, man. Unmask this thief and murderer."

The red hat man snuffled his kerchief. "I want no part in this."

"You'll stay and gawk all the same," said the cripple.

Eyes barely slit and palms open at his sides, the wanderer stood motionless. Dayne expected fight, strength and cleverness. Confused, he did not know how to help.

Different colored animal skins stitched around a crooked limb frame formed the back-length pack. The driver opened its top and bent back from a snakeskin poised within, fangs exposed.

"You're a craven devil," he said.

"More possum, I think," said the cane walker . "An odious charlatan."

The driver toppled the pack with the poker. Trinkets and strings of claws, bones and beads spilled and clattered the floor along with eyeless small bird carcasses, squirrel tails, crystals, ochre-painted rocks and gnawed roots and nuts.

From a cloth the driver unwrapped a honey comb filled by dead bees. "Such filth suits you."

With his stick the cane walker lifted a woven sash marked by arrow shaped purple and white river shells. "How did a beggar get such a wampum belt?"

"Safe passage through the Nations," said the red hat man.

"No more." The cripple set the sash behind on a chair.

Gert stepped forward "You have no cause to thieve, either of you."

The cane walker's stick blocked her further advance. "Stand back, madam."

"I'll not stand anywhere for you."

"This is not a woman's task."

"Nor a traitor's."

"Regardless of your fervor, you are not involved."

"You go too far."

The wanderer fingered a small fur pouch corded around his neck. "Let them poach. Empty gourds hold no seeds."

Gert waited but stepped back. The driver picked up a tied bundle of oblong objects.

The cane walker took and unbound the find. "No seeds indeed. Proof of his crimes. Six white scalps. Add the dead Quaker to the list, at least."

Dayne rose and angled to see. He knew Lauch and his father deeply feared and detested scalps but had no notion what one looked like.

Rolled and tightly braided by colored beads, the tanned skins looked unnatural, too neat to be what they were. Black stick figures and curious symbols marked each and gray, red, black and brown hair tufts, male and female, echoed pain and anguish. Upset, Dayne's eyes confronted the stranger but his blank gaze refused answer.

"Merchants gossip half of London's parlors are papered by such trophies," the gentleman said. "I did not think the stories true. Brutish incivility in such a proper, mannered society."

"The light and dark of all men," said the wanderer. "Is a hangman's noose any better?"

"Why the symbols?" The cripple fingered the scalps.

The red hat man moved close at his side. "Man or woman, sun or moon, location and weapon, whether rifle, tomahawk or knife. A deadly almanac."

"I said you would join." The cane walker sniffed.

Dayne looked at Gert, question and regret. Once so clear and purposed, his choice to free the wanderer and his pack melted into mistake he could not change. More trouble would follow.

With both hands Dayne pulled the heavy ash tub across the floor in small starts and stops toward the rear bar. He wanted distance, an end to the disquiet.

Scalps re-bundled, the cripple turned to the others. "What else is needed to condemn this miscreant as the murderer he is?"

The driver shook a hand drum of hide and hollowed tree limb removed from the pack. "He throws bones. All Reds do. Human ivories, I'll wager."

He pried the drum skin loose. Pine knots and cones, sliced birch and irregular chunks of wood filled his hands. Red streaks marked two rough carved pieces.

"Naught but fire chips," said the driver.

The cane walker looked closer. "More figures of a sort. The dark hickory is shaped much like the Quaker's round hat. The red cedar an apple."

"As a boy the Keeper's older son was called Apple," said Gert. "He climbed trees to eat and brought nuisance at harvest."

"This looks a boot and heel," the driver said of a pine knot.

The cane walker fingered a snapped white birch twig shaped like a crude rifle. "He carves each of us. Personal affronts. Impertinent, despicable."

"A canter's cheap spells. More black art." The driver dropped the pieces to the table.

The gentleman and red hat man approached to look.

"Crude but deft, not unskilled," said the gentleman. He studied an eye misshapen like ruptured egg yolk framed by a portion of spectacle.

"There is true purpose here," said the red hat man.

"Mementos of those he means to kill," said the cane walker. "The two marked in red were but the first."

The woman refused a pine cone shaped into an infant profile and turned away. "Please, no further with this."

"But one taunt remains." Gert picked up a forked juniper twig and wheeled to confront the wanderer.

"You used the boy," she said.

He licked his long finger and nail. "I play not fair."

Gert placed the twig on a table and turned. "The forest has peculiar ways. Give the wood no feel, no touch and mind no questions. Fear and weakness are what he wants."

"I like none of this." The red hat man tossed his daggered sliver of rotted oak to the fire.

"That will not aid," said the wanderer.

The driver circled his pistol around a fur pouch on a sinew cord from the stranger's neck. "He hides more."

"Yes, his medicine bag," said the cane walker. "Holds his spirit or so he believes. Open it."

The driver pulled the pouch loose and on a table emptied a shrunken lizard head, animal bone charms, feathers, jagged deer antler tip and small turtle shell.

"Meager," said the cripple. "No magic here. Only an unctuous, ungrateful toad."

The driver leaned close to the wanderer. "Got most all of you, didn't we?"

The wanderer slow blinked. "Is I who have you."

Pistol pressed against the stranger's gut, the driver leered. "My dog says other—"

Two fingers jammed between the gun's cocked flintlock and powder pan, the wanderer pressed the sharp tip of the antler under the driver's chin with his other hand. The gentleman and red hat man stepped forward but retreated from the wayward pistol barrel.

Rage and exertion bulged the driver's surprised eyes and trembled his arm. He tried to pull the pistol free but the stranger's grip refused.

"You quail," said the wanderer. "I smell stink, fear. Betrayal."

Thrust deeper, the antler forced the driver's head back and exposed his grizzled throat.

"Bark," the stranger said. "Bark like a dog."

Defiant, the driver snarled and shook his head.

The wanderer pressed the antler tighter and rapidly clicked his teeth. "Bark or I will chew your tongue."

A strangled, grudging sound escaped the driver.

"Again," said the stranger.

Face mangled by fear and fury, the driver emitted a second hoarse cough noise.

Head cocked slight, the wanderer rumbled and exhaled slow. "You are not worthy to be called a dog."

He ripped the pistol free of the driver's hand, pushed him away and threw the weapon into the fire. Its shot edged a table leg and thudded into the rear outside wall.

Dayne lunged away but stared back, taken by the abrupt fury. The gun's discharge hovered the room over the cowered grownups.

The wanderer roughly scattered the wood chips from the table. "I come not at random, only from deed. Each of you retches life, rotted and unhealthy. Who will next gag on it?"

◗

The Innkeeper seldom recalled dreams. Often stark images or raw emotions frayed edges of his thoughts, teases and goads, reminders of his darker self. Too real to be dreams.

Adrift within the frozen black of the barn loft, his mind danced. Lauch's dim figure lingered before him. Ghost or perhaps a wish, his son blended various childhood ages and forgotten events, cried and laughed, accused and acquitted, cajoled and listened, sought and avoided.

The Innkeeper's hand reached to touch, to make sure but Lauch's face melted into a drunken grotesque grin flooded by hideous smells of rum and ale. The tavern steps loomed large, sudden behind and his son's evil sneer mocked and shamed.

Confused clouds of rage, guilt and yearning rebuked and lashed the Innkeeper even as his heart pleaded for Lauch to overcome the void of surrender. The image vanished.

Unknown intrusion stirred. The Innkeeper strained to see in total dark and hear through constant storm sound. Soft rolls of the cow's bell wafted below, idle movement or warning, and nervous flutter of birds overhead pricked his ears. He set the blankets aside and inched over the ladder opening.

Wisps of disturbed air in heavy stillness hinted at other presence or an open door.

Possible movement across the corridor shifted his eye. Closer in a rustle floated upward, perhaps bare whisper or footstep on straw.

The Innkeeper untied his hand and brought it alongside the rifle. The bell sounded again, sharper and more pronounced, and the cow grunted.

The Innkeeper lifted the rifle. Knocked askew, the unlit lantern loudly clattered down the ladder.

He fired into blackness near the stall and recoiled, briefly blinded by the blast. Part way down the ladder he discharged one pistol toward deeper darkness near the barn door and on the ground wheeled and fired the second pistol at muffled sound in the corridor.

Crack of firearms loud in his head, he crouched between freight wagons to reload by feel. Cold stiff hands awkward and slow, he finished the first pistol but fumbled round shot past the barrel of the second and vainly searched the dirt beneath. Afraid of further delay, he cocked the loaded pistol and unleashed the tomahawk from his belt.

Weapons poised, he advanced toward the main door.

Blur in blackness to one side drew his aim. The pistol pan flashed but misfired and he lunged, threw the tomahawk at the unseen foe and sliced ready with the knife.

His ragged breaths punctuated fractured stillness. The soft bell and heavy gait of the cow lumbered close and he touched her thick hide and waited. No other sound. No other movement.

The Innkeeper's foot blindly probed the ground. The trespassers escaped.

Barn door slightly ajar, he forced it open and lunged awkward into deep snow and savage wind. Twice he fell forward but cornered the barn front by feel and repeatedly cocked and clicked the fouled pistol toward the pasture fence.

His rage and defiance screamed unheard against the fury of the storm.

CHAPTER SIXTEEN

DAYNE WORRIED.

Knee to chin on the floor beside the drink room bar, he stared over his coat sleeve at both shoes, body tight and unwilling. Tension, turmoil burdened the room's thick grit and rankled the grownups. He knew not what to expect and in part wished his father would return.

Gert gathered the stranger's carvings in a bucket she filled with cold ash and rags. She turned on the wanderer, face grim and disturbed. "What you did was inhuman, cruel. The cuttings and head cap both."

"Every fire needs a spark."

"And why such scalps?"

"You cannot make me white."

The sad woman rose beside Gert. "I should have said my mind open prior but do so now. Know I felt full the disgrace and disgust you intended."

The wanderer straightened dangles of shells and trinkets on his pack. "My words were true. I am not the cause. Only the voice."

"Many things are true," said Gert. "Not all are right."

Angry new cold clawed the back of Dayne's neck. He scratched uneasy and pulled his coat collar close. A floor board creaked behind and presence loomed shadows in the cellar door.

Imposing dark outlines of his father and the long rifle widened Dayne's eyes. He curled further within, lessened and turned away.

The Innkeeper moved past his son and lingered apart, separate among rear tables. Sight clouded by thin veils, deep chills throbbed his body and snow crusted his face and clothes. He stepped rigid into the firelight.

The surveyor turned and paused the nervous gnaw of his peel. "A spiteful winter spirit. More stern than the cold."

Gert approached but stopped, unsure. "What happens?"

The Innkeeper stared, disconnected. Ragged breaths slowed and quieted his voice. "Mice. In the barn."

"Raiders, after my wagons," said Dowd. "You followed tracks in the snow at the barn this morning. I saw."

"Gypsy trick," the Innkeeper said. "The tinker loosed the cellar and roamed the yard in the night."

Dowd jabbed his stick against the floor. "For what purpose? You warned not of this."

"Will not happen again."

The driver removed the pipe from his mouth. "So was the savage who sliced the Quaker."

On a stool at the hearth the Innkeeper pried stiff reddened hands from the rifle across his knees. Flames danced curious before him but yielded no warmth, only needled scourges and pricks.

Gert knelt alongside and lightly touched his face. "The cold cocoons you."

She motioned Dayne forward. "Quick, aid your father. More wood for the fire. Pile it."

The Innkeeper's glance drifted toward his son. Dayne skirted the fire glow to the wood stack along the outside wall and did not look at him.

The woman approached. "Can I help?"

"The kettle." Gert pulled snow from the Innkeeper's beard, hair and brow, removed his iced great coat and brushed clear his breeches and leggings.

He shivered, stiff and remote. Both women wrapped shawls around his shoulders and Gert soaked a cloth in hot cider and gently rubbed ice crystals from his face.

She covered his quivered fingers with a second cloth. "You scour. Here is warmth. Use it."

The Innkeeper drifted distant, separate from himself. The others' movements and words slowed, dim noise behind cold shrouds. Dayne placed wood on the fire and he knew he should speak but words rumbled his throat unspoken and his hands did not move. His son turned away and left only the empty flutter of disappointment.

Body gradually loosened and quakes quelled, the Innkeeper sat quiet for a time. Cider eased his wind and his hands cradled the warm tankard. He recalled only thickened blackness in the barn, sudden bursts of noise and bright flashes, rage and unsettled confusion. He wondered if he mistook, knew he did not.

The Innkeeper rose stiff with his rifle, turned toward the steps and stopped beside pack debris on the floor. "Why this?"

"The tinker drew ire," said Gert. "The cripple and driver pillaged his pack. They would not cease."

"I am not a cripple, madam." Dowd caned closer and displayed the bundled scalps.

"The savage carried these heinous peels," he said. "An entire family, possibly valley neighbors, murdered for their hair."

The Innkeeper fingered a scalp on his open palm. "Seneca beads. The Nations use scalps as barter and bribes among each other. A gruesome trade but well known. He is not Seneca."

"He carried such trophies nonetheless," said Dowd. "We know he is a scalper. Ask the Quaker."

"The canter also brought blocks of wood and tree cones," said the driver. "Tokens hacked to bedevil all of us."

"Except you and the young boy," said Cotswold. "An oddity."

"Gypsy tricks hold no power unless you grant it," said the Innkeeper.

From the floor the driver retrieved a piece of folded corn silk and opened the pocket knife within. "Now this. A right bold nicker he is. Caught clean."

The Innkeeper thumbed the single initial carved in the knife's plain wood handle. A gift from his father years earlier, he passed it to Lauch on his older son's fifteenth birthday. Core rage surged his spine and burst his shoulders. He shuddered once, a loaded reflex.

The Peddler stood arms wide. "So it begins. Do it my brother."

Knife point furiously driven into the table, the Innkeeper wheeled and slammed the rifle butt into the tinker's abdomen and doubled him to the floor with a second blow to the chin. He raised up for a final strike but Dayne straddled the Peddler's body.

Rifle cocked, the Innkeeper pointed its barrel close at the Peddler's head beside his son's back-turned face. Dayne grunted, guttural and anguished, and winced at the sudden metallic snap of the flintlock.

The Innkeeper kept the unloaded rifle poised. Finality and futility lowered the weapon.

"See now the truth of it," he said. "All of you."

◑

On a stool at the kitchen fire Gert mumbled dark. Short, fierce knife cuts sliced dried candle nubs into a simmer pot of tallow.

Threats to her house loomed large, real and her choices on the tinker and sick surveyor turned ill. The future dimmed unwanted, unplanned.

"Do I intrude?" Quayland coughed and fidgeted in the doorway.

Pale and fevered, he shuffled closer to the hearth despite her bothered glance. "I like your fire better. Less commotion makes it the warmer. Yet that awful smell always taints."

Gert spooned char and burned wicks from the pot and stirred the thickened fat. "Hog grease is a farm woman's constant lament. Hard stench, heavy smoke and dim light. Aids the cooking, though."

"Whale fat—blubber—burns longer, brighter."

"I've heard that said. But there be no whales in the river."

Gert tied pebbles on ends of long wicks draped across a short lug pole, dipped each three times and lifted the wicks to cool and harden.

Quayland scratched under his neck kerchief, crossed to the window work table and bent over but did not touch her small pots, roots and cuttings.

"I share your fondness for plants," he said. "In dark woods they are often an only friend, a needed companion. Regrettably I stay not in one place long enough to grow any of note."

Gert dipped and lifted the wicks three more times.

"Candles are a tedious chore," said Quayland.

"No different than another. The tallow sets quick in this cold."

She dipped the wicks deeper to neck the candles, set the pole across a table edge to let the candles shape a final time and cut more wicks.

The surveyor trifled pots on the hearth mantel. "The young son is beset."

"He learns too hard, too fast."

"I do not like to see children so burdened."

"You have woes of your own. You do not mend."

"No. I—No, I do not."

"You come restless. Speak it."

He turned. "Our work grows stronger, more needed. Now, after the tinker's crude display and the adventures in the barn."

"The house spins uneasy. All here bring purpose, dislike. And you are no innocent."

From an apron pocket Gert removed three lemon seeds she displayed on her palm. "The missionary hunted you."

The surveyor looked at the seeds and forced away his cough. "Perhaps we hunted each other."

"And?"

He wavered , hand against the hearth. "God's judgment comes soon. Convince the Keeper what he must do. No more delay."

Gert tested the hardness of the candles, cut loose the pebbles and trimmed the wicks to length. "He will not be pushed. You know that."

The surveyor looked back, bleary eyes intent. "The danger is already here. Not just I. You see it plain. Help—"

The Innkeeper entered the kitchen and set his rifle upright at the wall beside the door.

The surveyor moved further from the fire light, fingers on his neck kerchief. "The storm leathered you. An unsettling change. We worried."

"Will pass," the Innkeeper said.

"Indeed. You have a brave son. A defiant root, like his father. Did you know the rifle was unloaded?"

The Innkeeper flexed stiff hands at the fire. "Let the gypsy ponder it."

"He finally goes astray," said Quayland. "Little of what he does is mannered, including the dark carvings. I do not envy you this houseful. But now I will retire."

At the door the surveyor glanced back. "Will you return to the barn in the morning?"

"I tend the barn each day regardless."

"Then likely you will see more mice." Quayland left.

Gert dipped new wicks. "What did you shoot at in the barn?"

Ice pulled from his beard, the Innkeeper stared grim at the fire. "Trespassers. Or shadows. I know not which."

"Perhaps you look too keen. Or perhaps tis true. The Beast comes for the freight."

He twisted a drying candle on the pole. Slowly unwound, its tallow dripped forbidding and unrepentant to the floor. "We both of us know it goes deeper than that."

Gert removed the lug pole from the pot and set the candles to firm. "I cut some pie for Dayne. He likes to finger and lick the molasses. You give it to him."

"Why?"

"So you do not lose your son."

"Maybe he loses me."

"He is not you. Yet he saved your lapse."

"The rifle was no mistake. You saw the hand knife."

The Innkeeper stilled the candle but kept his eyes away. "Did Dayne give it to him?"

"The boy meant no harm. Was the others what did that."

"He smells himself. Too much."

"He searches for his root. Give him one." Gert turned.

Dayne tilted stiff in doorway shadows. Caught and confused yet unwilling to approach, he glanced nervous back and forth between her and his father.

She rose and started toward him but stopped and handed the Innkeeper a wood bowl of pie he held unsure, an unwanted chore.

The Innkeeper stood, waited awkward and offered the bowl. "Saved for you. The pie you like."

Dayne looked away. Head shaken, he refused his father's eyes.

Gert nudged the Innkeeper. He stepped closer to the door and extended the bowl again but Dayne placed both arms behind his back.

"Take it." The Innkeeper's voice hardened and he pushed the bowl against his son's coat.

Dayne cupped the bottom of the bowl and let it drop. Bold clatter. Gert winced.

Confused fury and disappointment clouded the Innkeeper's face. "Ungrateful. Is yourself you shame, not me."

Dayne backed defiant into the shadows and fled.

◑

Disturbed darkness.

Dayne shivered uneasy, crouched on the ground between Lauch's death box and earthen wall in a dank cellar side passage. His father would not look to find him there. He wished for the kitten, some source of warmth or life, empty at its absence.

He regretted the bowl but his anger wanted no truce. The unexpected rebellion surged unwanted emotions, choices he could not yet make.

When all sounds in the drink room ended he crawled to the cellar entrance, pushed open the door and waited at the bar corner. The grownups slept bundled in blankets around the hearth and the stranger sat cross legged, eyes slit, chained to the post beside the steps.

Dayne crept careful among tables and in shifting firelight looked down at the wanderer.

Odd remnants of his clutch with the stranger on the floor beneath his father's angry rifle stirred. Deep fire yet cruel cold. No life throb yet strong alive. Scaled and scarred yet slippery. Old and weathered yet endless. Dayne thought of frogs or newts he sometimes helped Lauch catch in chill creeks or from rotted tree limbs.

He brooded about the pocket knife. His brother's gift to him became a gift from him. His choice, like the cut rope. The others should have understood. Dayne did not know if he would get the knife back. More resentment, more anger between he and his father.

The wanderer blew deep, a low whistle like wind but made no movement.

Dayne passed up the steps and crouched in the doorway. The entrance hall candle burned dim and he listened in thick shadows for sounds of his father. At the common room the welcome yellow light of the kitchen door beckoned and he peeked around its edge.

The sad woman combed long hair undone down her front on a chair opposite the hearth. Gert kneaded dough at the work table, hunched shadow oversized along the wall, face reddened by fire.

"The Keeper frightened me earlier with his deep cold," said the woman. "It is never good to see a strong man weak. Even more so now."

"He is no longer young and knows the better. Still, an odd happening."

"No one believed his answer of mice. We know there are Indians about. Is it the Beast?"

Gert turned, grim. "Morning will tell more."

She set the dough in a covered bowl near the oven, stoked wood on the grate and glanced back at Dayne. "Is safe here, child. Come to the fire."

He entered, gathered the sleeping kitten from the hearth stone and thumbed its chin. The annoyed cat squirmed free.

"The Keeper stays his room," said Gert. "Best you keep here."

Dayne sat the stool near the fireplace. The woman smiled, brief and unsure, and let the kitten sniff her comb. Gert offered Dayne blankets and a small piece of bread.

He pulled his knees close and tried to settle yet rooted chill seeped his bones and wrestled his mind despite the fire.

Gert knelt alongside and moved hot embers under a simmering pot of cedar sprigs. "A bitter day, long and harsh. I thought your anger might speak tonight. Soon it must for all our sakes. But leave it now. Rest."

She lifted sprigs for him to smell. "The scent will ease your dreams."

Gert searched his face, curious but reluctant. "Did you give the tinker Lauch's hand knife? Tell me true."

Dayne nodded.

Gert gently tugged a forelock of his hair. "You wanted him free. Yet be careful. He has many faces, some ill. And hate not your father. He wants well for you in his heart."

Dayne looked away.

Gert readied blankets on her chair and sat near the woman. Bundled under thick layers of wool, tiredness gradually softened their faces and narrowed their eyes.

The kitten cried lonely in a corner and returned near the stool but Dayne paid no heed. His thoughts jumped jagged, disturbed. The deadly click of his father's rifle echoed. An easy, simple sound. Beguiling, brutal. He did not like guns.

Footsteps came from the main hall into the meal room. Dayne tensed and hoped his father would not enter the kitchen. The steps paused unsure and went away.

Rest perched unlikely. Instead Dayne watched the fire, adrift in soft crackles of wood and curled wisps of flame, and pretended to be warm. Night's thick shadows and surround edged close as the hearth waned.

Eyes closed in failed wish of forgetfulness, Dayne wandered the fitful mists of almost sleep. Teases and taunts disturbed, odd shapes and lights watched curious, strange memories long forgotten or never known swirled.

Sometime later the first dream came, a slow awakening.

He walked a narrow trail through dense wilderness, bathed in shared life rhythms and sounds. Raw earth and strong plant scents filled his nose. A bobcat with a squirrel's body paused to watch him pass, large flying ants swarmed an old stump like bees and birds without wings hopped branches overhead.

The woods thinned and a spring pooled downhill into a small clearing. Odd symbols on ringed stones and forgotten bones told of an ancient campsite, prior passage and vague memory.

Dayne gathered red berries and gorged in lush grass and warm sunlight at the clearing edge. Minutes or hours passed unmarked, uncared. Pleasant tired, soon he dozed and drifted in and out of himself, content.

Leaves rustled. Brief flutter, vague intrusion.

Alarm exploded sudden and Dayne's eyes burst open. Ruptured quiet wafted the forest, an uneasy chill. Hidden menace scraped his spine.

Fear seized before he saw its source.

Masked among trees across the clearing, the wolf's intense yellow eyes stared shameless. Grisly snout a bloodied taunt, the wolf crept forward poised, face blended with those of the young cabin boy, his lost brother, the painted Indian chieftain and dark spirits Dayne did not recognize. Cruel hate slithered the ground in front.

Another presence lurked behind Dayne. Evil, covetous and greedy for his flesh, its low rumble and foul stench bored and soiled his being and Dayne dared not turn. Urge to flee rippled his throat and twitched his arms but he could not move, held fast by coiled vines which sprouted at his feet and blistered his skin. Silent screams of terror and agony smothered his lungs, echoes long lost in time.

The wolf crouched close, certain and unhurried.

Twisted, tangled colored lights rose from the earth in front and whirled at great speed, the history of ages blurred into seconds, thunderclaps of countless lives, ends and renewals. Ancient words stirred ancient emotions, old wounds gushed raw and stained ones yet to come. Guilt and forgiveness, reckoning and redemption, darkness and light raged within.

Unseen claws behind Dayne rended and ripped at his being. Final instinct thrust his hands forward, desperate outstretched fingers. Just beyond, the wolf snarled bared teeth and leapt. There was no escape.

Inner self offered up to the light, Dayne closed his eyes.

He awoke opposite the dwindled kitchen fire, strained breaths cold wisps. Sullied and spent, he gulped cold sweet air and rubbed at a sense of rawed, peeled skin on his back. Yet the room remained as before. Across the hearth Gert slept rigid and stone-like, the woman curled and bundled in her chair alongside.

Dayne lifted the sleeping kitten from the floor and held its warmth to his neck. He shifted tense and stiff, expectant. Around him night swelled full, brooded stillness.

In his coat pocket the sharp arrowhead hummed and sliced at his grasp. Dayne stared at the finger mark of blood ooze.

The Beast was real and came for him.

Dayne huddled inside his blanket. Time passed slow, unyielding, and gradually weighted his sight. Several times he startled himself awake, scared to sleep, before tiredness again pulled him into darkness.

The second dream came quickly.

Dayne followed fresh bear tracks along a trail through dense fir forests, rock slides and jagged tree falls deep into unknown mountains.

Ahead in a ravine two young black bears foraged berries, pawed grubs and scratched backs against trunks of trees. The larger bear occasionally glanced back, rounded face careful and calculated, and plodded on. Dayne got close.

The larger bear brushed the smaller aside and took food finds with aggressive snarls and feints. Playful but purposed, the encounters often became fits of challenge the smaller bear always lost.

Near the top of the ravine the bears stopped and rose tall on hind legs, cupped ears active, and sifted the breeze. Both grunted and raced forward with startling power and speed. A lame mountain goat on the slope ahead reacted to the rush of movement and fled for its life.

Dayne struggled to keep up. Cold air ravaged his lungs yet he continued, enthralled and driven by raw ferocity and force of the chase.

The bears crashed undergrowth and with long purposed strides hurtled over open ground to narrow the gap. The exhausted goat sought refuge in a small pond and uttered a trapped prey's cries of anguish and defiance.

Heads low and snouts gorged with fear scent, the bears moved back and forth on opposite sides of the pond. Each arc lessened the final distance and the goat turned to confront the nearest foe only to have the other creep closer.

The larger bear grunted and splashed forward for the kill. Dayne turned away, jarred by brutal reality. Thick, sickly sweet smells of fresh meat and organs on cold wind reminded of slaughtered pigs.

For two days the larger bear fed alone on the carcass. Chased away, the smaller bear waited hungry and deprived, bitter grumbles ignored. Scavenger animals and birds gathered and taunted the smaller bear's weakness. Angered and spiteful, it ran at and scurried the intruders.

Dayne foraged nuts among the woods, tasted a small salt lick and uncovered colored stones along a creek. Baby birds chirped lonely, exposed somewhere in the trees and tension tainted the air.

On the far bank a squint-eyed possum shredded a crayfish. The guileful hunter licked its claws and looked up, small dark eyes behind a cruel curved mouth. Unafraid, it watched Dayne then moved toward the forest.

Stopped beside a tree, sudden and quick it climbed the trunk and sat beside the bird nest. Slow and unhurried it ripped and ate the frightened birds as the agitated parents shrieked and flew past.

The possum glanced back. The stranger's face leered mean, grinned and chewed. Dayne turned away. He left the creek and sat sickened and alone, cold.

At dusk the larger bear left the kill and wandered further up the slope. The smaller bear approached the remnant, waited to make sure and ate eager.

CHAPTER SEVENTEEN

HUDDLED SMALL in his coat and scarf on the top step down to the drink room, Dayne awaited dawn in the thick gray haze of first light. He knew no other place to escape the dark dreams.

Belief. He wanted to trust in the new day's promise of warmth and being but was no longer sure he did. Change came to the inn, to him. For the first time, faith in continuance of the farm and his life wavered. The harsh spoil of doubt intruded.

Milk pail and curled kitten close alongside, Dayne shivered in stubborn cold. Shadowed veils of unsettled stillness drifted the room below.

Shifted to the lower steps where Lauch died, his hand searched but no remnant or life throb stirred the wood. His brother faded too soon.

At a table on the edge of faint firelight his father slept slumped head across one arm, fist tight around the rifle beside a burned down candle, face troubled and unrested.

The stranger sat the floor in shadows beside the steps, palms on knees and eyes slit, leg shackled to his father's chair by double lengths of chain.

"The visions come hard, full," he said. "The bear and the wolf, the wolf and the bear. Both deceivers hungry for your spirit. Be careful which path you follow."

That the wanderer knew his dreams did not surprise Dayne. The stranger's face on the awful possum atop the small birds' nest still weighed sharp, fresh. More doubt and confusion, more puzzle and fear to endure.

Dayne stepped careful past the chains and continued to the hearth. Wrapped in blankets on the floor at its side the driver rolled over, one eye partly open, and grunted. Dayne jerked still, rigid until sure the eye slept unseeing.

Across the fireplace the red hat man lay back turned on three chairs, empty fingers curled above his tricorn dropped on the floor. Walking stick upright between his knees, the cripple sat nearby head back, mouth open, and snored unhappy.

Dayne knelt in front of the grate. The fire burned low, creases of orange and red amid shrunken black logs over mounded ash. Two fingers reached to trace small darts and ripples of color, he yielded to pretend memories of warmth and drifted dreamless, unaware.

"Only an ornery, lazy boy lets the fire wane."

Dayne blinked awake.

Face pinched and knotted, the cripple peered stern overhead and dropped a new log on the fire. Throat rumbled clear, he wheezed cold wisps. "More wood."

Eager to move away, Dayne gathered logs from the stack along the wall and lumped wood on the grate. With both hands he poked the fresh pieces but stirred only crackled pops and smoke.

The cripple snatched the poker from him. "Pay attention. There's a proper way to spirit a fire."

He roughly jabbed the logs and stirred flurries of embers and sparks. "Youth cannot be an excuse."

Dim puddles of yellow light came down the steps. Behind smoky candles the sad woman and Gert carried kettles of cider and porridge to the hearth.

The cripple pulled his blankets close and turned his back to the fire, walking stick upright alongside. "You come early with the gruel, madam."

"A hot bowl will ease the cold," said Gert. "And lessen the bleats."

"Yes, I am told you and the Keeper call us lambs in privy." The man threw off his outer blanket and stomped flared embers caught along its edge.

Startled, Dayne stepped back and knocked the walking stick to the floor beside the fallen hat. Lower part of his face shielded with his hand, he barely breathed and hoped to be ignored.

The cripple glared. "No manners for your clumsy? Pick it up."

Dayne lifted the stick and offered it with the hat. The cripple curtly waved off the tricorn, took the cane and turned away but looked back. He peered closer at the hat and shifted to allow more light from the fire.

White specks and fine black dust covered inside the hat and marred Dayne's fingers.

"Louses," muttered the man.

Stick loudly slammed across a table the cripple pointed at the tricorn. "Typhus! Typhus!"

Dayne did not understand the word. Confused by the outburst he continued to hold the hat and glanced across the room.

His father bolted upright, rifle poised in uncertain alarm. The wanderer popped his mouth fish-like and wrinkled a small grin.

Bleary and disoriented, the hat man rolled over and struggled upright. Specks covered his unwashed hair and reddened, scabbed scalp.

"Why shout so?" He adjusted loose neck kerchiefs and fingered for his hat until he saw Dayne held it.

The cripple stepped back in disgust. "Your disease seen true at last. Head and hat both. You have the typhus."

Gert approached Dayne, voice calm. "Give him the hat, son."

Upset by the commotion and unsure of his blame, Dayne trembled as he extended the hat. The hat man held the tricorn upside down, face sagged by hopeless guilt.

Dayne looked away. He knew the cold hurts and shame of others' quick scorn. Gert covered his hands with a cloth and firmly took his wrists.

"Touch nothing else." She whispered. "Not clothes nor yourself."

He willed himself not to move or look up. His father strode past to the fire, welcome strength and presence to quell the room.

"Stand back."

The Innkeeper stared grim at the surveyor's tricorn and exposed sores.

Dowd pointed his stick. "He has the typhus. See the scourge yourself. Tell him to say it."

Risen from his chair, the gentleman squinted over spectacles and retreated satchel in hand. "Rank disease. Vile. You are reckless, sir, and lower yourself."

"Yes," said the surveyor. "Yes to each parry and thrust."

He returned the hat to his head. "So then. You have unmasked me."

The Peddler chortled, mouth cornered by his long fingernail. "Another mouse come to chew, Keeper. And only the dawn passes. What other joy brings the day?"

Dismay and resentment rounded the Innkeeper's shoulders, gripped tight his hands. More rot inside his house. More unwanted involvement, more unneeded complication.

He turned on the surveyor. "How long?"

"A fortnight. Perhaps more."

"What cause?"

Quayland coughed, waited. "A woodland swamp, sharp hillsides, dusk and loose footing. My boot edged a fallen tree. I stumbled in brackish water and took chill. Family at a small cabin offered roof and bedding. I discovered too late it was soiled."

"An unlikely tale," said Dowd.

The surveyor wheeled, diminished but defiant. "True enough to admit. Unlike you and your wagons."

Dowd stepped closer to object, realized his mistake and retreated. "Do not evade."

"You advised nothing," said the Innkeeper. "No mention, no warning."

"I weakened and could not go without shelter," said the surveyor. "Not in this cold, not in this storm. I did not expect it to worsen so."

"In close quarters you risked us all," said Dowd. "We played a game board at your ask and shared fires, meal tables."

Quayland nodded. "Yes, I am guilty of all that. But I touched you not and took only your coppers. You are the liar here."

The driver spit into the fire. "Jail filth. He and the Indian both."

Dowd sniffed. "You betray all decency and deserve your disease."

The woman clutched her heavy shawl close. "Is the taint which distastes. Here among us. That and the lie of it."

The gentleman turned. "What say you, Keeper? This be your house."

Gert stepped beside the Innkeeper. "He has no other place."

"The barn," Dowd said. "Like the rodent he is."

"He will not survive there," said Gert.

Fury and disgust crawled the Innkeeper's skin. Instincts to defy, confront and overwhelm, always strong and vital, slowly yielded to question, unknown purpose.

He spoke without emotion, unsure of his answer before he heard it. "He stays his room, separate and apart. We burn his blankets and clothes, his kit. All of it."

"More remedy is needed," said Dowd.

"There is no answer but fire," Gert said. "Each should clean their skin, clothes and hair. I will heat water for it."

Quayland sagged, relieved. "I am in your debt, Keeper."

"Expect no further. Make it worse and I shall do worse."

The surveyor edged the neck kerchiefs higher over his sores, straightened his skewed hat and turned to the others.

"You stare at me, all of you, even the boy," he said. "Safe in your distance and righteous in your indignation. Burn my clothes if you must. I will not fault you."

"Indeed you will not," said Dowd. "You insinuated among us diseased and unwashed, a poison affable to some but still a poison. Rude. Intolerable. Heinous."

"Enough," the Innkeeper said.

Dowd stepped back, stick handle a vindictive pointer. "Yesterday he rode high-stirruped on me. Now he is the one who dangles, alone and outcast. Justice, I say. Retribution."

◑

Small. Unmoving.

Two white worms on top of Dayne's extended first finger seemed harmless. He wondered why the grownups feared them.

Beside him Gert added new wood to the kitchen grate and filled large water pots placed over the fire to boil. Upset, she snared the worms in an apron rag and threw it into the flames.

"Louses are unclean and bring ill sickness. Let none linger on you."

Open alarm edged her voice and she held his chin but her face softened. "I will look for others. Sit the stool."

Gert searched his hair, ears, neck, coat and scarf. Dayne yielded to her coarse hands, eager for any connection, any care.

"Stay still," she said. "Mind where you sit, what you touch. And take nothing from any hand."

Her fingers stopped. She hissed, pinched his neck and threw another worm to the grate. "Take off the coat."

Already cold, Dayne hesitated.

Impatient, Gert unwound his scarf and tugged his collar. "Take it off, child."

He removed the coat but retrieved the black arrowhead and placed it in his breeches pocket. Gert's scarred hand probed his shoulders and she set the coat and scarf on the fire.

Dayne frowned, another unexpected loss. His outer shells and winter companions resisted the flames at first but curled and gave way. Harsh smells of burned animal skin and wool tainted his nose. Unguarded and exposed, he shivered.

Gert knelt in front. "You dreamed much last night. Fears and questions burden your eyes, your face. Tell me what and why. None can help if none are told."

No words came and Dayne wanted none. He shook his head slow.

"One day you must make a different choice," she said. "Life cannot always be silent."

Gert ruffled his hair and stood. "Lauch had a smallish coat when young. You shall have it."

His father carried the milk pail through the doorway. "Dayne left his chore in the drink room. See he does not forget—"

Stopped, his father gestured at the coat and scarf on the fire. "Why this burn?"

"Dayne was soiled both hand and neck." Gert said. "I take no chance."

His father strode forward. Cold, demanding fingers roughed Dayne's shirt collar, neck and head. He squirmed away.

"Are you also befouled?" His father turned on Gert.

She bristled, unyielding. "What mean you?"

The abrupt words crackled Dayne's ears and lowered his eyes. Once more resentments, angers trapped him between the only family he knew. Icy coils snaked his gut.

His father set the milk pail aside. "You comforted the surveyor with potions, teas and spoke quiet with him. Are you befouled?"

Gert turned away. His father took her wrists and thumbed her sleeves.

She pulled free, furious. "Never touch me rude again."

"Was you who brought these curses here. The gypsy beguiles us all and now this filth."

Dayne's grimace welled with the insistent boil and hiss of water on the fire. He edged past his father, took the pail and moved to the doorway. Afraid to stay, afraid to leave, he looked back.

Gert angled trammeled pots from over the grate. "Mind your son. He sees and hears your anger, your lashes. He is different and bruises easy. Be his father, not his whip."

"Words, woman. Excuses."

"Reasons. Long unsaid."

She approached Dayne and touched his shoulder. "To your room. Is alright. Fret not."

◑

Sybil rubbed soft black soap into a soaked cloth at the small table beside her bed. Hair bundled in one hand she wiped her neck, ears and throat.

The door opened and Cotswold observed, hands filled by his satchel and book. "You have the lye."

"Yes, to wash twice. I feel horribly unclean."

Unsure whether to continue she stopped. "You come unexpected."

"None are upstairs."

Sybil dipped the cloth and resumed. "I pity the surveyor. He endures much in many ways."

"Scorn well deserved."

"I am not sure he intended it so."

"How could he mean other? He endangers us all. A lascivious house, this inn. Burgeoned, plagued, unsavory."

"At least we have shelter, fire and are not stranded chill in the coach."

She half turned, belly profile briefly exposed, and extended the cloth. Her voice wavered more than she wanted. "I will share the soap."

Cotswold released the satchel beside the bed. Book and glasses set neatly on top of the quilt, he stepped close and took the cloth from Sybil's hand. She did not move away and he stiffly wiped the nape of her neck and exposed top of her shoulders.

She reached to cover his hand but he turned to the bowl and soaked the cloth. The missed chance swayed her fear.

"Your touch is cold, indifferent," Sybil said. "Your hand too long absent."

"Hardly a time for intimacy."

"Simple emotion and care would serve."

Cotswold minced, dropped the cloth on the table and stepped back. "Do not cloy."

Regret and disappointment tightened Sybil's frown. She covered her shoulders and neck with the shawl. "What do you intend?"

"To survive. Intact and unconstrained."

"You know my question."

Sybil waited. "Only silence? The truth should come easier."

Cotswold retrieved his book and glasses. "An unfinished chapter. Why complicate it?"

She searched his cold, pocked face and turned away. "Your mind is already set, closed."

"I did not mislead."

"There is no warmth, no humanity in you."

"I pretended no other."

Sybil nodded. "Was I who overlooked and avoided all wisps of a child these long years for reason. I embody no mother and hold no delusion of you as father."

"No. I am not so inclined."

She pivoted, face averted. "This change was not my choice. It comes a harsh cruelty of nature, the unfair join of chance and God's grace."

"Yet your mistake. Bitter, foolish."

"Not bitter. A new life cannot be that. I will not let it."

Cotswold gathered the handle of his satchel.

"I found the false money," said Sybil. "You are a rank criminal. An impostor."

His crooked smile mocked her. "More an artist, craftsman. A difficult trade, long studied and honed. And your means, your comfort, my dear. Oft used and enjoyed."

"Our precious life bloods. Frauds, both."

Cotswold hefted his satchel to the bed. "I smelled Jacks' taint on the bills. Is that your plan? Take the money and flee, you and he together? Would you demean yourself so?"

"His notion. I did not—"

"He would steal it all and do you no favor in the woods."

Cotswold extended an open palm. "The trunk key."

Sybil shook her head, angered by the curt demand for obedience which so often girded their past. "No."

"I do not bargain."

"And I will not be without what is mine."

"But is not yours."

"Leave."

Bemused, Cotswold openly smile weighed her defiance. "An unwieldy impasse."

"I said leave."

He stepped into the hall with his satchel and book. Sybil closed the door behind him.

Gert carried a kettle, tray, empty sacks and bandages around the corner from the steps. She ignored Cotswold's false nod and passed toward the end of the hall.

"You walk a woman on a purpose," he said. "Why tend the diseased surveyor?"

Gert paused, glanced back. "Small kindness. He suffers hard for his deeds."

"We all do." The gentleman descended the stairs.

Misgiving slowed Gert at the room door. Her choices on the tinker and surveyor went astray. Their deceit rankled, disappointed and worried her further path. The presence of lice on Dayne and foul, unwanted sickness inside her house pushed deeper anger, resolve. Her response loomed, unkind or not. Poke weed from her garden. A useful remedy.

She knocked on the door and entered.

Dejected on his bed, Quayland unwrapped soiled neck kerchiefs and removed his hat. "You do not forsake me like the others. See me as God does. Meager, blighted."

Gert hardened but did not look away. "You hid the truth. None will overlook it."

"And you?"

"A selfish act, unneeded. Earns no loyalty."

Cough ravaged Quayland's lungs and strained his voice. "Yet keep me alive. Our work goes unfinished."

Gert remained blunt, distant. "I made no promise. The typhus grips tight."

She set the sacks on the floor and the kettle tray on a table. "All must burn. Clothes and bedding both."

"Let me lay the bed a while at least," he said. "I totter and have nowhere else."

"Will still burn."

"Oh, yes. The hellfire of damnation."

His thumb flicked lice from fingers reddened by angry scratches. "I itch fierce and so claw. Unwise, I know."

Gert bent closer. Lice and black residue mottled his neck and scalp and her hand fluttered near open sores but withdrew. She crushed dried sage and honeysuckle into the bowl and added hot water. Careful not to again extend her hand she shifted the bowl to the table corner.

"This balm will help soothe your fevers for now," Gert said. "A special brew. I will bring mistletoe later. Its paste may slow the typhus."

Quayland's fingers quivered as he lifted the bowl and he tongued cracked, swollen lips. "A true apothecary. I did not expect but welcome your continued aid."

"I have seen louses before."

He greedily licked the bowl. "Strong bitter even with the bee nectar. More."

The surveyor set the bowl on the table and Gert poured more water. He rubbed the mix across his teeth and gums. Excess dribbled his chin.

"The sick have no dignity," said Quayland. "Only misery. I wanted none of this. Surely not now. Yet fate binds me so."

"We bind ourselves. All sin is ours. Who else?"

He looked at her, curious. "Why so harsh, so unwilling for grace?"

Gert placed sacks on the bed. "Only fools chase winter mist. God never promised to save us from ourselves. We each make our choices and suffer what follows."

"You render the mysteries of divine providence simple. They are not."

He picked another louse and pinched it in two. "Fate is not choice but God's will. No man acts free."

Gert gestured at his sores. "And this?"

"Somewhere I failed God."

◗

Fire and cold.

The drink room grate crackled and gorged. Hungry flames seared and withered the sick man's great coat and clothes. Coils of thick smoke leaked the fireplace.

Dayne shivered on the hearth corner, arms pulled tight against his sides. Lauch's too big coat ill fit his arms and shoulders but its worn touch brought welcome reminders of his brother.

Gert nudged him further from the fire. "Not too close. Breathe none of the smoke."

Hands protected by rags, his father set the large reddish hat on top of the blaze. Charred yet stubborn, it yielded slow under two new logs.

"Roar the fire, Keeper," said the driver. "Make it hot. Burn the filth and stench out."

At his table, satchel close on the floor, the gentleman looked over his spectacles. "The bedding must also burn. The sacks as well. Best be thorough."

The sad woman sat nearby. "I hate to admit but I feel better to see it consumed."

"Riddance at last," said the cane walker. "A grave repugnance to all."

The stranger bleated twice from his corner blanket and flicked his chin. "Most sheep go dumb before the blade. Each of you go loud, boastful. Unaware."

Dayne's father turned. "You have no say here, gypsy."

The sick man's voice came from the steps. "I still deserve my place among you. Ill or not."

Wrapped in blankets he leaned unsteady against a post. Bandages drooped his head, a failed cap, and plant paste smeared his hands and neck.

He slumped weak in a chair. "I crave the fire's warmth. The blankets are my own."

Face pinched in disgust, the cane walker stepped back. "You were banished. I say it again, sir. You were banished."

The sick man's fevered eyes girded, angry. "I am not a wretch. Despite your glee."

"Indeed, you are worse. An ingrate wormer." The cripple turned away.

The driver spat into the fire. "Pond scum. Said it plain yourself. Your own words."

"This display is unneeded, Keeper," said the gentleman. "A diseased outcast should sit his room or the kitchen hearth, alone and apart."

"Not the kitchen, not the food," said Gert.

Dayne's father irritably poked the fire. "He is one of you. Sort it."

The sad woman stood. "I want no illness but what of simple decency? Have we none?"

"No," said the gentleman.

The cane walker waggled his stick in agreement. "Such vileness earns no mercy."

Hands bound, the stranger stood close over the sick man and fingered the head cloths. "Nature leaves its mark. Unhappy times."

"One day I will heal, tinker," said the sick man. "You hold no such hope."

The stranger grinned. "A fine bold answer. Proud, certain. False. Your lies are known deep in the forest."

Grin dissolved and eyes hard, he picked rotten teeth with a bone sliver. "The ravenous wolf always finds the abandoned lamb. Feel the harsh result."

"Enough." His father handed Dayne the milk pail.

"Stack more wood from the outside pile," he said. "No green to save the smoke. Then to the barn and the animals. I will follow shortly and bring the Welsh Red back from the barn."

Dayne rose and flipped up his coat collar reluctant. Already cold, he did not welcome the angry winds and deep snow outside.

"The storm yet blows," said Gert. "There is no need for the barn."

"Chores are chores for a reason. A lesson regardless the day. Do as I ask, son." Rifle retrieved, his father crossed toward the cellar.

The cane walker dropped the tip of his stick to the floor. "You flee, Keeper, stubborn as ever and leave us disagreeably to each other."

Dayne approached the outside door but glanced back. The stranger stared intent at him, an odd sadness.

He undid the cross brace and pulled but the cold rigid wood refused to give. Pail set aside, he struggled with both hands and forced the door open.

Wedged deep, the dagger end of the stranger's tomahawk nailed the swollen body of the kind man in black to the door by the coat. The round hat hung from the cruel weapon in bold taunt and humiliation.

Dayne blinked. He could not move, stunned and overwhelmed, snared to the floor by the kind man's empty unseeing eye and contorted awful scream.

"Keep-er!" Gert's shout floated dim somewhere behind.

Dayne shuddered. Dwindled and numbed, he drained away. Eyes closed, he separated. Deep silence. Blackness. Nothing.

CHAPTER EIGHTEEN

GERT'S ALARM EXPLODED the Innkeeper's chest, an unexpected ax cleave. Sudden disruption and dread blistered beneath his beard. He wheeled back into the tavern.

Dowd retreated awkward against chairs near the door. "We are attacked!"

"Savages!" bellowed the driver.

The woman's wrenched scream stymied into curdled, fitful moans.

The Innkeeper hurried past Dayne and through the outside door to the rear yard. Rifle raised, he pivoted into the blur of bitter wind and driven snow.

Gouges in the white mass along the tavern wall marked the drag path of the body from the rear door. Tracks also crossed to and from the barn and led up the rise toward the front road. Bald intrusion, trespass.

Mingled in icy hiss and angry gusts, a single fleeting bird call pricked. Close or far, real or imagined, the Innkeeper could not tell. No answer came.

He lowered the rifle and turned toward the door. The missionary's body gawked and mocked, accused and shamed, the awful revenge of the unquiet dead. Harsh dismay from its hasty burial bludgeoned, assailed.

The Innkeeper stepped past into the tavern and pulled the door but the corpse wedged in the snow and did not shut until shouldered hard. Forehead dipped against the wood, he gathered and re-set both braces. Across at the cellar entrance he pushed open the door with his raised rifle barrel and entered, wary eyes active.

Disturbance swirled. Laden fears and cold gloom crowded narrow passages and shelves. Lauch's burial box yawned empty, unmoved and no breach bothered either window or the rear entrance.

Yet the cellar struggled, burdened and unbalanced. The debris of the Innkeeper's life circled close. Reminders, false comforts. Objects familiar, each a use or need, turned weights and goads which strangled and writhed his gut.

He lost his inn and himself.

Propped upright on the window sill near the back door the broken corn cob figure leered. Rage and confusion clamped the Innkeeper's jaw. The gypsy's relentless taunt, purposed and clever.

He left the cellar, tied its door latch to the bar and crossed to the hearth.

Gert cradled Dayne against her front and gently rubbed his empty face. "Stay with us, child. Do not bend to the shadows and cold."

The Innkeeper knelt. His son looked abandoned, taken, alone. He tugged Dayne's coat collar and his fingers lingered unsure over young hands still clenched around the milk pail handle. He reached to touch Dayne's face but hesitated.

"The boy goes dormant," said the Peddler. "Let him."

The Innkeeper glared. "Speak no word, tinker. He is mine, not yours."

"I will mind Dayne till the faint ends," said Gert. "You have other worries now. Do you intend to leave the missionary on the door? He was put there for reason."

"And he stays for reason."

The Peddler slow jangled the shackles. "The mice play hard this morning, Keeper."

Black anger squeezed the Innkeeper's throat and he turned. "Is your shadow what haunts. Your goad in the back window. Your blade on the door."

"Who left it stay the barn?"

The Innkeeper peered at the tinker. "You hold no mark or bruise yet I hit you square with the rifle last night. More gypsy mischief, black art."

"Were not righteous blows."

"Each had purpose. The third would have finished it."

"No. And the trigger pull only upset the boy. Our time yet comes."

The Innkeeper stared blunt. "I will kill you. You know that."

A faint smile, almost sad, cornered the Peddler's mouth. "I have been dead before."

The woman turned in her chair. "In the name of God must we fight each other? Are two killings not enough?"

◑

Her life disarrayed.

Open trunks and fine dresses littered the floor and bed quilt in Sybil's room. The green satin favorite clutched close, she searched distant memories for compliments it once brought but the words echoed empty. Plans and dreams of many years withered around her, misguided and unfinished, the harsh cost of vanity, selfishness. Regret deepened her frown.

Eyes closed, she heaved a plea for hope. Instead fear crawled her neck and imagined flames of wrath seared her skin. She dropped the dress, unwilling to be furthered stained or taken and burned alive.

Escaped from the room, Sybil moved quiet along the hall past Cotswold's door and went downstairs to the main entrance. She paused uneasy, afraid of what lurked beyond heavy cross braces on the front door.

Jacks hissed within the open doorway to the tavern and motioned her to approach.

Wary, Sybil took the first step down and shut the door behind. "Where are the others?"

Shadows distorted the driver's. "Upstairs. Scared and too proud to piss in public."

She bent low to look across the tavern and make sure. "What is it you want?"

"To tie our bargain, finish what we start. I need know where lays my ground."

Grin lopsided, Jacks stepped close and his hand clutched her front. "Perhaps this be it."

Sybil edged from his touch and crowded the wall but he lingered, presence and great coat an unclean, unwanted cascade. "We have no bargain."

The driver stiffened, frown unhappy. "You lied."

"No. I never said it. You took matters too fast, too far."

"My fault is it? What of the looks, the easy touches?"

She could not meet his demanding eyes. "Mistakes. An unfortunate misunderstanding."

"Word patter."

Jacks leaned tight, stubble and breaths rude scrapes against her cheek and ear. "I don't believe you."

Sybil moved up a stair. "You must. You will. My decision is made."

"Unmake it."

She opened the door but his hand covered hers and stopped its swing.

"I'll end him," said the driver. "If you ask me nice. Quick. Neat. Gone."

Sybil closed the door. "No. Why would you think—"

"Done it before. To those who troubled my way."

Jacks gestured down the steps. "The Keeper's older boy. Riled my plans, my bottle, here and the barn both. Turned nuisance and mouth. So I roughed him. Hard. But simple enough."

Disbelief confused Sybil. "An accident, surely."

The driver shrugged. "Comes the same difference for him. Will you tell the shrew cook or the Keeper?"

She partly opened the door. "Someone must know the truth."

"Why? Changes naught. Did one, can do two. The toothless bastard deserves it for his ways, his airs."

Hand on the knob, Sybil closed the door and glanced back. "That is not my plan."

"It should be. He will do the same to you. You and the bump."

Cold truth gripped her lower back. "Then I will stay here and go no further."

"What if they won't have you?"

She left the steps into the hall, shut the door and turned toward the main entrance.

Satchel in hand, Cotswold stood in her path. His half smirk and cruel eyes bored disdain, displeasure but his voice held flat.

"You wander unwise," he said. "Especially now."

Cotswold moved past and opened the door. The steps gaped empty and he went down.

Sybil continued into the common room toward the kitchen door but stopped, unsure what to do. She dared not repeat Jacks' boast, afraid of pain and recrimination if she misspoke. The driver often goaded for attention and his deed with the Innkeeper's son would end any chance to remain at the inn.

Sybil glanced toward the kitchen doorway. Comfort smells and the pretense of honesty beckoned yet she hesitated, concerned her life warped so uneven. Shame nervoused her hands and dire thoughts rippled her mind.

Fearsome savages waited the storm without. Disease and no better choice existed within. The poisoned house already teemed unexpected treachery, death.

Doubt struck fear but survival ruled. Another secret, another pretend mattered little. Nor did her silence. She edged into the kitchen doorway.

Gert mumbled and scoured inside two large stew pots with sandstone and black lye soap.

Sybil waited, hands clasped and unclasped, unsure how to begin.

"Speak free child," said Gert. "Save the wait of it."

Sybil tried to smile. "Indeed. My tongue, my one strength, abandons when needed most. So I will say it straight. Is there a place for me—?"

Her hand briefly crossed her abdomen. "For me and mine. Here, if I stay?"

Gert rinsed and emptied the pots but did not turn.

"Forgive my abruptness," said Sybil. "But there are—I need know."

"You are not too proud to ask."

"More humbled."

Gert dried hands on her apron. "Your skills need learning but have use. And Dayne is not young much longer, especially now. A farm always needs its spring."

Hope fluttered Sybil's heart. "Then it could be so?"

Gert turned, grim and blunt. "This be no house for outsiders. You, here but a few days, know that."

"There is no other place. I thought—" Sybil sagged and looked away.

Suspicion tinged Gert's voice. "What is it you do not say?"

Sybil shook her head. The truth would not come, could not work. "Is my embarrassment not enough?"

Hammer bangs and scrape of a shifted table from the common room creased the air and she flinched. "I am afraid. And hearing that sound I feel no better. You are right. This house splinters itself, and us, dark with secrets, lies, death. I tell myself the rancor and the cold must end. I tell myself."

"Withstand," said Gert. "Survive. Dawn always comes."

"Is it true what they say? About Indians and white women?"

"You are not yet old. Likely they would keep you a captive, maybe for ransom. But I would not envy it."

"And my baby?"

"The child would not be wanted."

"Then I am already a hostage. What of you?"

Gert revealed a pistol butt in her apron pocket. "The tribes have no use for stubborn and old. So I go ready."

"Will Indians truly burn us alive?"

"This house is hard stone for a reason. But best to prepare. Keep water in your room. As much as can be had."

More hammer blows from the common room twisted Sybil aside. "Another horror. This cannot be true. This trip. This storm. This Beast. None of it."

◑

Dayne awoke.

Emptied, he sifted for memory or dream, grateful for neither. For a time he floated free, unburdened, content in being.

Winded snow pricked the window and cold quiet drifted his room. Hid safe beneath bed blankets, he eased open hard clenched hands and stretched stiff limbs, small tests. He returned slow and recalled only the downstairs fire, unhappy lambs and clutched milk pail. No emotion, no event. No reason for his blankness.

The kitten peeped lonely at his feet and he sat upright, shoulders wedged in the corner. Wiggled fingers calmed the cat and he set the unfinished root carving on the quilt. Misshapen and frightful, it kept his eyes.

The kitten turned, ears cupped at footsteps stopped in the hall outside the door. Dayne hid the root in his coat pocket. His father entered with wood slats and a hammer. They stared, both confronted, both muted, neither willing.

Slats dropped on Lauch's bed, his father rummaged a pocket for nails and waited. Above the thick mask of dark beard his eyes spoke concern, unease, question.

Dayne searched for an outward bond, some resemblance or connection, but saw none. He could not picture his father young, as a brother or part of himself. Their barren silence stayed as ever. He gathered the kitten and slid off the bed.

His father placed slats across the window and drove nails. Ears jolted by the harsh sound, Dayne winced. His room went unsafe. He had nowhere else to go.

Indians. Terrible painted faces in his dreams. Dark unfamiliar enemies from the forest, whispered about and deeply feared. He heard stories of killings, kidnappings and burnings and so shared the hatred of others, the gut dread of capture and torture. He fingered the violent edge of the arrowhead in his breeches and images of the horrible dead body of the kind man tightened his spine.

Yet he knew little. The always watchful eyes of the giant stone face at the waterfall, brief sightings of fierce-looking men in river canoes, strange signs of passage across farm borders and foreboding figures on distant ridgelines caused alarm but also curiosity.

The prior summer on a wagon trip to town with his father he walked among Indians in colorful clothes camped in fields to barter crops and trinkets for local goods. Although children on both sides mixed and played games, he sensed careful suspicions and quiet unease. Dayne guessed he would run if confronted by Indians on the farm. Lauch and his father told him to.

He left into the hall. The pound of nails chased him toward the main entrance.

At the table in the meal room the sick man chewed bread and spooned porridge, red hat askew on his head.

"Do not be afraid," he said. "Please. You know what it is to be unwanted."

Dirtied neck kerchiefs, leaky eyes and fevered face dwindled the man. His light dimmed, faded yellow pushed away by brown shroud. Dayne did not know how to help, approached slow and waited, careful not to touch.

The man set aside his spoon. "I know you miss the kind man in black. He showed his playful side and earned your trust. I shall do the same."

He leaned forward. "So a rhyme for your ears if not your tongue. The skunk sat on a stump and thunk the stump stunk. But the stump knew better and thunk the skunk stunk."

He pinched Dayne's belly. "Almost a smile. Reward for us both."

The man slid a glass covered wood box to the table corner. "I wanted you to see this. A chance to learn new."

Dayne edged closer. Inside the box strange marks covered a shiny brass circle.

"A circumferentor," said the man. "Survey compass. Tells which way the land moves and which direction to go."

He turned the box and a metal needle on the circle moved. "The needle points north no matter which way you turn. Here, you try."

Dayne glanced at the man's scratch marred fingers but grasped the box.

"Move it back and forth and in circles. Watch the needle."

Dayne slid and turned the compass. The needle bounced and jiggled but settled dogged in the same direction.

"The needle tracks the earth and always tells true," the man said. "So you will not get lost in the forest."

On opposite sides of the circle the man raised shiny pieces of metal with centers missing. "I look through these sights to make sure my chains are straight and the measures correct."

Dayne bent and peeked through the sight.

Gert's alarmed voice intruded from the kitchen door. "Unhand the box, Dayne, and step back."

Confused, Dayne frowned and did not move. Ire grew. He did not want Gert to interfere.

She strode forward and took his fingers from the box.

"A simple lesson," said the sick man.

"Dayne already knows how to bear from the sun's path. The Keeper taught him that."

Disappointment mixed the man's voice. "I meant no harm. You frighten without cause."

"And you go too far," said Gert. "Unasked, unneeded."

Throat rumbled, the sick man gagged and puffed cheeks. His handkerchief rose too late and reddish spit dribbled his chin.

He swallowed, hard distaste. "Forgive me. A sudden urge."

Gert pulled Dayne from the table. "Fetch the water bucket from the kitchen. Fill it full in the cellar. Now."

◗

The unfilled water bucket sat beside the cellar spring.

Dayne brooded alongside. Thoughts blurred, too quick and uncertain, he pulled the tree root and black flint from his pocket and carved.

The sharp arrowhead trembled his fingers yet he gouged and scraped the stubborn root, unsure what he made but compelled to finish. The wood gave grudging and blood stained the flint's edges and trickled his hands. He thumbed the red ooze into the grain and beheld.

The awful face stared back. Dark, deformed, evil.

An image from his dreams, him yet not. Angry truths, secrets old and hurts un-mended swirled. Distant sounds, birth cries and wails, cackles of a woman's voice. Sudden unease.

He hid the root in his pocket, dunked the water bucket and fled.

Dayne entered the cold stir of the drink room. Besieged by slivers of unclear memory, he stood near the bar counter both shoulders sagged by the bucket. A dark stain on the floor in front screamed rage and violence and he glanced back and forth to the outside door. Strong urge to yield once more and shut down rushed his chest but he refused.

Dayne struggled the heavy bucket to the hearth. Pieces of burned bedding and clothes strayed the fireplace and charred coat buttons collected under the grate. He did not know why.

From his stool the driver roused flames with the poker. "Back are we? You folded tight, easy the first time. Dead-eyed, a day old stew rabbit ready for the pot."

The words washed past Dayne. Unsure why the man spoke he stared blank at the fire, upset his body tightened despite his will.

The driver shifted near. "Now you gawk quiet and dumb. I think you remember. The door blade. The lump of dead meat stuck on it."

Rough face unfriendly, the dark man leaned in and pinched Dayne's shoulder. "He's still there. On the door like a kilt bird. Your daddy left him for you to find again. Go look."

The stranger rose from his floor blanket and his post chain clinked the floor. Approached beside the driver, he picked white specks from the hearth. Dayne thought them ice or apple worms.

The driver did not look up. "I smell you, savage."

"And I you. My nose is bigger."

The wanderer stirred the worms on his palm. "A curiosity of nature. Such small things. Such large events."

He pinched a worm in half, tossed it to the fire and blew others from his hand like snow. The driver recoiled, scraped his stool sideways and bolted upright. He swiped the brim of his hat in disgust and stomped angry at fallen worms with his boot.

The gentleman looked up from his book and spectacles. "Rude recompense well earned. You go unclean. Remove yourself."

"Is the half breed," said the driver. "Dropped the louses to nettle me."

"Remove yourself."

The driver bristled and resumed his stool. "I'll not leave this fire. No use to try."

Dayne shuttered the noise and turned toward the outside door. Hateful images and deep sadness filled his mind, tensed his bones.

He remembered what waited on the other side.

◑

The Innkeeper stared tired and forlorn at the kitchen fire. Swollen hands ached and his mind swirled too quick, unclear. Fears and haunts, questions without answer. Instinct said the gypsy played some role in the missionary's stake on the tavern door yet shackles, foot tracks and events in the barn showed other.

He gulped cider from a corner barrel. Spill beaded his beard.

Gert cut gourds at the window table. "You fret unneeded. Give up the wagon goods. Let the storm pass."

"I can bring no further death to this valley."

"Is not like you to worry about others. What of the farm? Of us? Dayne?"

"It cannot stand."

She grumbled. "You and your pride."

He turned, insistent. "I will not yield."

"Even when you should. Your sin of sins. Was always so."

Knife set aside, Gert busied with trivets and ash piles at the hearth. "You are hardened, changed. Perhaps too much."

"And you not enough."

She glanced sharp. "Do not misjudge. Will be long before I forget Lauch and the parlor door."

The Innkeeper nodded. "Was best. Regardless of it."

Her stare lingered. "For who?"

She rinsed trenchers and bowls in the wash tub. He tossed unfinished cider into the fire and dropped the cup back to the barrel. Neither looked at the other.

"Dayne punishes me unjust," said the Innkeeper. "No matter my mind or my heart, whatever I say or do fails him. Fails me."

"His silence is lonely, unsure. And he is young, different than you. There is yet time. If we last."

The Innkeeper shook his head. "I see not the end of this, only darkness. Festers hard."

He rose stiff. "There is work for doing. The morrow will not come kind."

Rifle retrieved from beside the doorway he went into the common room and probed the window slats. Gloom and shadow crept corners, eager for dread night.

In the main hall the Innkeeper removed cross braces and wedged open the front door. Snow mass piled the entrance and chill flakes and gusts invaded. Traces of foot tracks led from the door along the side of the house and across the yard toward the road.

The storm and its ghosts showed no quarter.

Gert stood alongside him. "We are jailed within and without. No different than Thaler's prison wagon."

"This is not of us."

"Who then?"

He turned. Two red hand prints close at his face on the door post stopped him. Sudden despair shuddered and ripped, scalded blades on deep bone, wounds too deep. Unable to gird he grimaced and sagged against the frame guilty, exposed.

Gert recoiled from the door and clutched her neck amulet. "What hunts us so?"

The Innkeeper spread his palsied hand beside the mark. It curled slow, certain, even as his soul pleaded for respite.

"Hands of an angry God."

CHAPTER NINETEEN

Dayne worried.

His father and Gert did too. He saw it.

Breaths ragged and arms tired, he rested the filled water bucket on the floor at the drink room counter. The constant trips to the cellar spring blurred and wore but he sensed their need.

At the hearth his father stared grim and stubborn into the fire. Burdened shoulders angled tense and hands braced against the stone, he stood a man alone against a great falling boulder.

"As many loads as you can carry," his father said. "Here and then upstairs."

Dayne continued across the room. Gert filled kettles and pots from the bucket and her fingers gripped firm on his.

"Stay strong," she said. "Move quick."

Urgency and alarm in her voice unsettled and Dayne kept eyes from the door. He did not want to think of the kind man's dead body so close.

Spectacles neatly wiped and folded, the gentleman rose from his table and approached the hearth.

"We are cornered," he said. "We cannot stay. We cannot leave. A smart man pays the bribe. The cost of survival."

The sad woman collected cider pitchers to a table. "Yes. For all our sakes, Keeper, give up the wagons. They are nothing compared to lives."

"Yield the contraband and you yield the valley. It cannot be done." The sick man looked up from his lonely chair near the wood pile, fevered face stricken and unable to solve its pain.

The cane walker turned from his pace near the window. "My wagons are not contraband, sir."

"Trust not the savages," the sick man said. "They will take the weapons and still kill us. I have heard it done so."

"You say that for purpose." The cane walker rumbled his throat.

The sick man wearily shook his head. "I say it because it is true."

On a stool beside the fire the driver fingered his pipe bowl clean. "Dump the guns and powder outside or in the barn. Give them the damn prize. Be done with it."

Gert nudged Dayne and the bucket toward the cellar. "More water, child."

He crossed among rear tables but looked back. On the blanket by the steps the stranger busied with the squaw strap on his pack, intent and separate.

The cane walker approached Dayne's father. "You decide more than your own fortune, Keeper. You know what must happen. What say you?"

Dayne's father pulled slow on his beard. Eyes still on the fire, he waited. "Cold fate yields no courage, no will."

"We are not in church," said the cripple. "What do you intend?"

Dayne moved aside as his father strode past to the rear corner, ripped open a damaged crate and dropped muskets on the table.

"Each man loads and carries all he can," his father said. "We defend."

The gentleman squinted displeasure. "Unwise."

"Madness." The cane walker stomped again toward the shuttered window.

The driver spit and threw bark into the fire. "You burn us sure."

"I will not forsake my kind." Choice made, Dayne's father turned. Hardened, he wanted no further talk or emotion. Dayne knew the look well.

The stranger cackled. "A fine, bold decision. But grave for all."

"Five here oppose you, Keeper," said the gentleman. "What if we choose other?"

"The freight stays."

The cripple's jowls quivered. "Brute tyranny. Unfit. Unfair. You curry no favor and hazard our lives for your own pride. Admit it."

The gentleman clutched the handle of his satchel beneath his chair. "Come to terms with the marauder. Avoid."

"None here can shun the Beast," said the sick man.

The stranger rose from his blanket and his fingers rippled air, an unseen web. "A hot fire. Boil and bubble. Bubble and boil. Animal grease. Sweet gravy. Needless, dire, true."

The sad woman moaned and sat her chair. "You need not be so vivid."

The driver rose and strode toward the bar counter. "At least open the ale casks. If I face slaughter it shall be bellied full of sot."

Dayne's father stepped between the counter and rear shelves. "No drink."

The driver turned hard. "Poser. Your weakling son was a fool and died a drunk fool. But where did he learn such stench? Tell us. Tell us plain."

The angry words crackled. Dayne shifted the bucket in his hands, upset.

"No drink."

"Be different later when I've a mind." The driver stood defiant.

His father thrust a rifle against the man's chest.

The driver dropped it to the counter. "I'm a free man, not a lackey to be ordered about. Why should I fight for any of you?"

"Pull a trigger for yourself if no other," Dayne's father said.

The driver turned toward the window and outside door. Dayne moved from his path.

"It's quiet out," said the driver. "Maybe the savages have gone, left."

"Would they leave?" The sad woman looked up, hopeful.

"Quiet is the hunter's lure," the stranger said. "Only prey listen for hope. The strong make it."

"Could run for the river," said the driver. "Better that than to wait here, a caught rat, and burn alive."

The sick man shook his head. "Where would you go? The coach cannot take the snow and the nearest settlement is two days distant."

The driver wheeled. "You have no say, wormer. And I need no coach. Only a horse and some rifles."

Spasm pinched the cripple's face. "The weapons are not yours to take."

"Nor the horses," said the gentleman.

The driver sneered scorn. "Who will stop me? Either of you?"

"The freight stays." Dayne's father lowered the rifle across his arm toward the driver.

"We fight needless among each other," said Gert. "It helps none."

The sick man lofted a weak arm. "I know weapons and can shoot."

Dayne's father gathered powder, shot and rifles from the table and crossed to the sick man at the woodpile. He looked back. "Who else?"

None answered.

Returned to the table, Dayne's father retrieved another rifle and tossed it to the cripple. "You served the militia. Or was that just air?"

The cripple pursed and chewed, musket in one hand and cane stiff in the other. "I resent this intrusion, Keeper. Deeply."

"I more."

The gentleman looked dubious at the gun and powder horn extended to him. "I am not a soldier. Yet not a fool."

He held the musket awkward, unconvincing.

Dayne's father turned to the sad woman. "Stay close with Gert when the time comes. She will know best for you."

The sick man folded over with cough. "The Beast will not waste warriors on the lower part of the house. Stone and too easily defended. But the roof is part wood. Mind the top."

Clinks of shackles interrupted. The stranger moved close to the fire and with his hands gathered cold ash near the grate. "Fire, nature's great test. The bane of the besieged."

"You'll burn with us, canter," said the driver. "Chained and trussed like a cur dog."

The wanderer blinked and slow shifted his gaze to the driver. "The agile oft wiggle from the hook. Not so the slug."

The dark man strode forward but the stranger crumbled the ash and blew a rebuke of rude dust. The driver wiped at his coat and retreated.

Finger tapped against the chain lock, the stranger turned to Dayne's father. "Do not parley. An easy ruse. They will fire the barn and take or slaughter the animals. You are wise to bring the cow in."

The owl feather in Dayne's breeches pocket burned his hand, a hot coal, and fresh frights knotted his chest. The bears. The wolf. The owl. All crept closer, bolder, the final darkness of his dreams come real. Death he accepted as he owned no past and no future. Yet destruction of his father, Gert and the house seemed unnatural, unneeded. He wondered if the farm or any part of his being would remain. Lauch and his mother did not. Sadness dried his mouth and he could not swallow.

He looked at the fire. The flames no longer held warmth, only fear. He closed quiet upon himself and the others' voices faded.

Empty bucket carried toward the cellar, Dayne did not know what to fight with or if he would live or die the night.

Until then he would believe in the earth's spring and the hope of water.

◐

Gert cracked open the door to the missionary's room.

Uneasy intruder in her own house, she posed tray and kettle ready in familiar ruse as if he waited alive and aware within. Inside she shut the door, needful of spare solitude to unwind her fears and ponder questions.

The Moravian's restless body on the tavern door brought wicked new reprisal, blunt taunt. Her skills and potions seemed misguided, null. Strange blackness and void blotted her vision forward. Unwelcome unease.

Too much happened. Too much remained.

She opened a book on the quilt. Curious fingers fluttered over strange letters and touched quill marks. How preachers found faith in paper words and not nature always puzzled.

The mule girth lay on the floor beside the pack saddle. Gert traced its re-sewed threads, pleased at her work. She cared not the missionary was false or what his hid papers showed. He was gone. His hand wounds had not lied about Lauch's death. Or perhaps they had and he fell victim to some other, deeper darkness. More questions she could not sort.

Rumbled coughs from the landing, shuffled boots along the hall and ugly retched sounds in the hall closet soiled the silence.

The surveyor. His disease, lies and unclean dangers to her house and Dayne she would no longer abide. He misjudged her and spoke too much of other events, troubles laid elsewhere. The valley would survive the war and the Nations or not. And though Gert lived its soil, she earned her place and owed no loyalty beyond the farm.

The house and boy were all she had, all she could protect. The surveyor carried danger and ill darkness well hid. The typhus was a true sign. She would stop him. The poke weed worked its wrath slow, steady. So more.

Gert waited for his footsteps and shut of a door before she stepped into the hall, moved quiet to his room and knocked.

Feeble on the bare bed of husk sacks, the surveyor's uncovered head beaded sweat and louses. Angry sores and dirtied bandages marred his neck, harsh scratches his hands.

Gert remained distant in the doorway.

"You look hard, grim," the surveyor said. "I make no effort to hide."

He shivered and pulled his blanket close. "There is new chill in the house."

"Fever. Your humors are twisted, unbalanced. Nature gone wrong." She entered and set the tray on the side table.

"You can save me," he said. "Do not yet forsake my soul."

Gert filled a bowl with dark brew from the kettle, set it on the table edge and stepped back. "God punishes all sins, you said."

"Yes, all. And righteous is it."

Scalp scratched, he thumbed lice from his finger and sipped but stopped. "Bitter again, as before."

"Drink."

He looked up, vague concern. "Remember our bargain."

"Nothing changes."

"Now you frighten me."

"Drink more."

The surveyor hesitated. "My fate or yours?"

"Choice is not fate."

He forced more sips and set the bowl aside. "No better. I will stop."

Fitful weak coughs slumped his shoulders. "Distract me. Idle my thoughts. Speak of your garden and plants. In the end we are all creatures of the earth."

Gert paused at the tray. No one ever asked so she told him of colors, smells and favorites. Of seasons, harvests and uses. But not all.

Eyes drifted closed, he gnawed his discolored lemon peel and smiled faint. "One day I should like to see it. In all its glory."

The surveyor struggled up to retrieve the bound journal from his saddlebag draped over the chair. "I show you something. Perhaps you become my final messenger."

He displayed a crowded page of descriptions, numbers and field diagrams.

"Your book of secrets," said Gert.

"Indeed, my Bible. Was always so."

His fingertip ran between lines. "What you do not see is the secret. The juice of lemon writs the paper clear and unseen. But apply heat from even a slim candle and the juice will mark the page. Here, above and below the quill ink."

He chewed his peel and tried to smile. "Hence the gnawed rinds. You and the others think me odd, awkward. A useful guise."

"Uncommon treachery, this."

"I am a surveyor truly. But also a watcher who travels the roads and tracks the woods. I notice what needs notice. Only that."

He closed the journal. "Know you John Burke?"

"I hear the name. By Crowners mostly."

"A rich man, propertied, he lived across down river and is experienced in Indian and militia affairs. He fled to Canada at the war but still visits the valley and meets with the Nations. If I am unable, deliver this journal to Burke for me. He will see it home."

The surveyor offered a small wax sealed envelope. "This letter explains all, even you, with my thanks. Keep it if need. Burn it if not."

"Little good it has. I read nor write no letters."

"Can you not?"

"What use on this farm?"

He removed a small bead and leather cord from a pouch in the saddlebag. "Then have this. Show it and perhaps there will be no harm for you or the boy. Is a token from the Iroquois."

"I hold no stranger's charm or bracelet."

He set the cord and bead on the bed toward her. "Is yours regardless."

Coughs again took him and his eyes narrowed slow. "You are an old tree limb bent and knotted hard around a soft core. Perhaps that is why I chose you."

"I no longer remember soft."

"I think you do. It lives in the boy."

He shuddered and lay back. "I still taste your brew. Maybe I will rest now."

"Drink again when able. As much as you can keep down."

The surveyor gestured at the cord and bead. "For the child. I will feel better of it."

Gert took the token in an apron covered hand and retrieved the tray. Paused at the door, she did not look back and left the room.

Remorse and question briefly trickled her throat. Her choice was made. At the end of the hall she pinched the candle flame into a wisp of trailing smoke.

◐

The wicked glint of the flask fetched the Innkeeper's weary eyes.

In puddled candlelight beside his bed it beguiled, relentless and adept. Sharply real yet imagined rum taste swirled his mouth, clouded his thoughts and twitched his swollen hands. Temptation, surrender, remorse. Each comfort waited.

The nub flickered. Gaze shifted, he escaped chafed and uneasy.

Sudden memories flooded past. Parts of images and bits of sound promised clarity and pried open his soul. Instead, hateful looks and garbled angry words with Lauch on the tavern steps pierced deep. Unforgiving guilt squeezed his heart.

He failed. Himself, his farm, his sons. The storm and gypsy came for him. Reckoning, awful and sure. He no longer doubted it.

Rue and torment galled his throat. A truer past, better choices and different ways danced and teased, vague bitter notions. But no wish would undo his path. Enemies surrounded within and without. He saw no dawn, no tomorrow. Only struggle, end.

Rifle gathered, the Innkeeper left the room and followed his shadow along the hall. Water pots lined the main entrance and powder horns and upright muskets guarded the second floor stairs. He checked flintlocks and loads a final time, made sure, and probed the front door braces for weakness or advantage, aware the lambs were useless. The fight stayed his alone.

His house become a fortress. Low groans leaked walls and floors, old burdens and yokes he could not cast off. The inn rotted like him. He blocked most of the noise, blunt refusal and defiance.

From the common room the Innkeeper dragged benches and the long meal table into the hall as barricades.

Gert emerged from the kitchen doorway and helped angle the table on its edge. "You stay stubborn."

"This house is built to withstand. So are we."

He turned toward the door to the tavern steps. Dayne peeked around the slightly open door.

"Come, Dayne, and bring your bucket. We need the fill."

Both shoulders slumped, Dayne lurched into the hall and sloshed water to the floor.

"I know you tire. Keep at it." Gert cupped the boy's chin, took the bucket and filled pots.

"Upstairs remains," said the Innkeeper. "See you remember it."

Dayne stared forward and shook his head.

The Innkeeper roughly grabbed his son's arm. "Do not shake your head at me. Not now. Not this night."

Gert stepped between but the Innkeeper blocked her.

"Ungrateful spite. Who am I?" He leaned close at Dayne, low voice insistent.

Hasty fear and confusion darted Dayne's eyes. Two fingers placed across his mouth, he extended his fingers in a string of unspoken words and emotions.

The Innkeeper forced his son's chin back. "Who am I? Say it."

Harsh sounds choked Dayne's throat. A dogged tear trickled his cheek and he snorted, a pained plea and angry contort.

Rage clamped the Innkeeper's jaw. "Why are you afraid of me? Say it!"

Dayne shook his head once, wrenched free and picked up the bucket.

The Innkeeper straightened over him. "Be not so proud. You carry my blood, my spoil. My weakness. We are not so different."

Dayne quivered, angry and confused.

Fled with the bucket to the safety of the drink room steps, he stared at a broken pull on the front of his coat. The truth of his father's words scalded his ears. He did not want it to be so.

Breaths slowed, he gathered and closed his eyes. Welcome quiet once more.

The gunshot burst loud, sudden, violent.

Dayne flinched. The sad woman's frightened scream pierced his uneasy cocoon and he turned toward the drink room.

Above, his father flung open the door to the steps and raced past with rifle ready. Dayne followed. Crossed to the outside door, his father stopped and wheeled toward the cellar.

The driver lay on the floor near the bar, an ungraceful mound. Dark face surprised and angry, blood spread beneath his head. The gentleman stood alongside. Smoke wafted from the barrel of his pistol.

"Why this?" Dayne's father approached the bar.

The gentleman lowered the weapon. "The man could not be trusted and made threats. He pried your cabinets to get rum despite my warning. There was no choice."

"Are we attacked again?" The cane walker caned awkward and heavy down the steps, musket clutched ungainly across his girth, and passed Dayne.

Behind him the sick man teetered weak, pistol in one hand and head bandages the other.

"Stand back with your filth, sir." The cane walker moved further from him.

Gert pulled Dayne close against her apron front. He glanced back and forth between the outside door, the driver and the empty step where Lauch once lay. No light lingered for any. Three killings in three days. Sudden losses, ends unexpected and unwanted. Dayne had never seen a dead person before.

The woman slumped at her table. "This was personal. Murder for no cause."

The gentleman minced, hand at his mouth. "The knave knew not his place. He leeched beyond his right."

"Yet did he deserve this?" The woman turned away.

Dayne's father checked shelves behind the counter. "I see no marks toward the ale."

"He was about to proceed so." The gentleman set the pistol on the bar.

Crossed back toward the steps, Dayne's father glanced furious and burdened at Gert but ignored Dayne.

He stood over the stranger in the corner. "What saw or heard you? Tell it true."

The tinker twisted a cord of shells on his pack. It unwound slow. "One killed the other. Fear the Beast."

Near the fireplace the cane walker abandoned the musket to a table and wobbled, fist unsteady over the head of his stick. "Is your fault, Keeper. This inn is an abomination. We are desperate, doomed. All here."

Gert took the bucket from Dayne and knelt. "You have done and seen enough. There need be no more of this."

Nearby, the sick man retched loud and dark dribble cornered his mouth. He looked at the others afraid, unsure. "I regret. Sudden ailment again fills my throat."

Post clutched, he struggled up two steps but lost balance and slumped awkward on his haunches.

"Feel now the burn of your rude righteousness toward me," said the cane walker. "Your foul disease marks you, a leper no longer wanted."

The sick man's bleary, pained eyes searched, pleaded.

Dayne reached to help but Gert lowered his hand and embraced him back to her skirt. "You cannot touch him, son. I know it is hard."

Bounds wrists extended as a brace, the stranger lifted the surveyor upright.

"You show pity," said the sick man. "Kindness."

The stranger's lips puffed. "No. Just a cruel pucker before you go."

Face hardened, the sick man took one step up and turned. "God watches."

The stranger clapped and spread his hands. "And righteous is it."

CHAPTER TWENTY

HIS INN TURNED FORT.

In the dim candlelight of the main hall the Innkeeper set boards and nails beside the door to the tavern steps. A final hindrance to intruders in case the cellar and tavern were taken.

Ramrods pulled from muskets leaned against the second floor stairs for quicker access, he readied extra loads of powder and shot and stared wary at the braced front door for weakness and betrayal, unsure of its will to hold.

Obstacles, weapons and fire buckets crowded his house with cold emptiness. He could do no more yet doubt, misgiving scraped his jaw and he clutched his beard. The storm's final wrath took hold.

Gert carried a tray and kettle down the second floor stairs.

"The end may be the upper hall and rooms," he said. "The beddings and tables will serve to block. I will take guns and powder up."

"You worry it worse now."

"I will not lose this house." He grunted and released his beard.

"Someday you will. Nature will have its way. Regardless."

The Innkeeper nodded and looked away, voice quiet. "The night moves odd, unbrooked. There is purpose, end."

"I have never seen you this troubled."

"No."

"And the tinker?"

"I will not let him win."

Muskets gathered, the Innkeeper started past Gert but stopped. He did not look at her. "What of the surveyor?"

"A bother no more."

The Innkeeper continued up the stairs, footsteps burdened and slow in the silence. He turned the corner.

Gert waited beside the overturned meal table in the main hall. The house ached disarray, confusion, a mirror of herself. Winter's bitter harvest come too soon.

She stared at the kettle. Another dark choice made. Or perhaps no choice and simple fate, hers and others'. She blamed her hands, always her hands. Their gnarled bony fingers twitched too much, pried too much, knew too much. Regrets, evils, secrets. The past and not the future set life. An oddity, an upside down.

Gert stepped into the empty common room. Countless faces and bleats of countless lambs blended in single noise. She stopped at the kitchen doorway, surprised she could not enter. Pots, cuttings and the blackened hearth stood lonely, wistful. Moments and glimpses distinct, blurred. Warmth given and taken. Laughs and touches, angers and festers. Toils, family. Sustenance.

True and untrue, all of it. Part hers, part unwanted. None to be changed.

Galling numbness crept her skin. Slow awareness. Reluctant, she went down the hall to her room. The door candle cast long patient shadows inside and the knob's soft closing click lingered too long.

Her things waited. Simple and unadorned spirits, fallen leaves from the past. Keepsakes and comforts, empty relics of an unstraight life.

Gert's fingers reached to feel, connect. Her hand closed unfilled.

Memories flooded too fast, untold moments gone, lost. Warmth and remembrance faded. Change, rupture drifted the air. She knew why. Eager darkness and spirit marks on the walls told. She sat the edge of the bed.

No future came. No spring promise waited. Her path ended, earned and deserved, chosen many years prior. Yet things undone, garden notions and wishes peppered and teased.

Gert rarely pondered time. Its course ran regardless, like the seasons. Nature's unending, unyielding cycle of life. Some plants seeded and survived, renewed. Others withered and were lost, short glories forgotten. She wondered which she would be.

Dayne's birth rags took her eyes. Eleven years of stolen joy, the price of her life. A brief wrinkle in time, eternal damnation.

The door behind opened slow.

Gert tugged tight her high collar. Dryness refused her swallow. She did not turn.

"Is time," said the Peddler.

Her voice quivered more than she wanted. "I am not ready."

"Matters not." He entered behind and shut the door.

She handled a clout taken from its wall peg. "Dayne came first, born easy, smooth. Then the other, unexpected, unwanted. Grim evil face, wicked shaped head. Old, contorted, cruel. I knew what it was. What I had to do."

"And the Keeper?"

"I never told. Though he saw the smother pillow and second bloody blanket he never asked. He knew in his heart what I did for him."

"And yourself."

Gert nodded. "Aye, that was part."

She fingered the clout. "The past always lurks, never ceases. An ill ghost hid in haunts of the present."

"Choice turned bitter, cruel. Yet the end stays the same."

The Peddler approached the bed. His shadow crossed the wall as he picked up its pillow. "You shiver."

"I am not afraid of you."

Gert kept eyes forward. "Will I remember? Will I feel?"

"No."

A single tear trickled her cheek. "Was not supposed to be me."

"Was always you."

"And if I wish another dawn?"

"Sin must have its blood." His shadow moved closer, larger.

"You will not hurt the boy?"

"That test remains. His enemies grow hungry."

Gert did not resist. She held a long final breath, sad to leave the sweet joys of memory or air. Her life slowly dwindled as her lungs did. A distant glint as of a mirror wavered and ended somewhere within. Her regrets did not.

She emptied, defiant yet burdened, unseeing eyes slit open. Around Dayne's clout in her lap, coarse killing hands flexed in final protest and resignation, quelled at last.

◑

Maybe he dreamed. Maybe he saw.

Dayne could no longer tell which.

Eyes scared wide in night's utter blackness, he crouched bundled in blankets on the floor at the corner of his bed. Angry upheaval came. He wanted to be small.

Eager fears and deep dreads surrounded, hungry for his spirit. Bones rattled by sharp cold, he shivered despite the kitten clutched close. Her ears brushed his neck, an alarmed turn toward the door.

Dayne listened intent, afraid to breathe. Storm sounds, groans from the spines of walls and floor, the quiet shut of Gert's door across the hall. Fretful silence.

He waited. Presence seeped, an unkind lurk. Bare wisp and hint, sensed more than heard. Whether guile or guess, Dayne wondered unsure.

A claw's chill scrape. A marble's purposed, winding roll on the hall floor. The presence lingered and wanted him to know.

Dayne wished for Gert, his brother, his father. He did not want to cease alone, uncertain who and why he was. The confused lure of the stranger wormed his mind, shadow and light together.

Anger welled. Unwilling to wait trapped, he felt for and edged open the door. The candle at the end of the hall burned dim, a faint puddle in thick darkness. Beside him the kitten peeped anxious.

His foot covered a small hard object and he knelt. The colored bead found in the mule's stall quivered his palm, warning and reminder.

Unclear whispers wept from under Gert's door and passed, a slight shift in the air, before unwanted stillness, an end and goodbye.

Dayne crept along the hall past his father's room to the drink room steps.

Ash and smoke taint drifted and he reached for the partly open door. It creaked sudden and Dayne jumped back, bead dropped to the floor and scattered by his foot. He ran beyond the overturned meal table at the second floor stairs, through the common room and into welcome light of the kitchen doorway.

Gert's empty chair stopped him. The crowded work table and hearth filled by pots, bowls and buckets waited her touch. Her footprints still marked the floor ash. Loss feathered his heart and twitched his mouth. Another unexpected parting, another cruel taking. Life changed without reason once more.

He sat his stool facing the door, poker in hand. Red fire glow stained walls and shadows crouched corners. He pretended to be warm, pretended not to be afraid. Neither ruse worked.

Dayne listened. Muffled creaks, perhaps from the hall, more unsettled silence. The kitten peeked unsure behind his breeches leg, ready to flee.

New fears, new sadness and new burdens trembled Dayne. Tense and tight yet weary and confused, he sat alone in fringe firelight until his mind let go and he drifted, aware and not.

Maybe he dreamed. Maybe he saw.

Loud crash behind startled Dayne awake. Rigid, he refused to turn. A soft ruffle and wicked, insistent click nettled the air. The kitten fled behind corner tubs.

Dayne looked back slow. Atop a fallen shelf on Gert's window table the owl ruffled its wings. Merciless, cruel gaze fixed on him, it waited patient and unhurried. One long talon tapped wood unappeased.

Gut fear and dread ripped Dayne's chest His body emptied, numb and unable to move.

The owl jumped closer, bold on the back of Gert's chair and blinked prideful, sure. Its horrid screech of conquest peeled Dayne's skin. Flinched backward, he tipped the stool and dropped to the floor.

Poker lost, he struggled upright and ran through the common room into the main hall. His legs collided with the overturned meal table and he staggered to the drink room door and limped down the steps.

Dayne wheeled at the dwindled hearth. Pain from his bruised knee shortened one leg and he leaned unsteady, hand on the stone. His eyes darted hopeful, frantic, disappointed. A small candle nub burned on his father's empty rear table. Open iron shackles lay alone beside the stranger's pack. Neither grownup would save him. Forsaken once again.

Harsh cold and storm gusts leaked the room and the house groaned deep rents, anguished cries. Collapse came. It and those within could stand no more.

The lower steps shimmered a tease of warmth and memory but sharp pain and loss lurked behind. Regret over the slaughtered pig, his failure to warn Lauch and strangled lost voice, the end of the kind man, Gert and the farm battered Dayne. Shame, weakness, mistake. No different than his father.

He choked on ash withered air. Shadows stirred in corners and flames danced along dark walls, he knew not how or why. The hearth burst sudden alive, flames hungry for his skin, and forced him into dim light across the room near the bar.

Unsure of any path, Dayne stopped. Tables and chairs crowded too close and drifted too far, mute witnesses empty and indifferent. Blackness oozed from the wagon freight and stacked muskets leered triumphant, long barrels eager to gorge their glint. Sadness and angry red stains puddled the floor in front of the counter. The kind man's words mixed with the driver's unkind taunts, confused noises of the dead.

Dayne fingered the paper scrap in his pocket and heard the faint echo of the kind man's voice. Warning, sorrow, truth. All the world, upside down.

Harsh wind gusts rattled the outside door. Angry cold slithered his spine and corded his throat. The storm still hunted him.

Dayne never looked back and fled into the uncertain dark of the cellar.

◗

Total blackness.

By feel Dayne found and dragged heavy sacks of grain and potatoes to block the cellar door shut. He listened, ear close at the wood. Grunts and grumbles, upset voices or perhaps the bear or the wolf from his dreams, teased and blistered his ears then stopped. Prey beast stench seeped the dark and Dayne strained harder to hear.

A claw tapped and scratched the door opposite his face and he pulled back. Whatever waited knew where he was.

Silence drifted uneasy. Unsure what to do, Dayne felt for the door and leaned close once more. Vicious thuds pounded the wood and angry snarls swirled its edges.

Dayne crawled quick along the passage toward the rear cellar. Only the distinct smells of different stored roots, earth grit on his hands and gurgle of the spring ahead guided his path.

Frantic, beside the water he piled loose straw and scraped the flint arrowhead from his pocket against a small stone. He needed light. A few sparks fluttered brief but none took and he tried again and again, fingers more anxious with each failure.

At last fresh sparks flared the straw and he blew careful until it flamed. Candle nub lit, small puddled light wavered dim and uncertain. The kitten peeped, approached from the passage and sat beside the light. Dayne clutched it close to his neck. He missed the soft fur touch, the eager life beat.

Breaths quiet, he listened toward the drink room. Long shadows surrounded. Deep cold settled thick. Expectant stillness resumed, waited.

Buckets, pails and pots crowded the edge of the spring and the ancient rock trickled unmindful as always. Dayne fingered the dark surface of the spring, unsure if it might save him.

A hiding place. He saw no other way.

Odd crates, boards and baskets wedged against the far corner beside the water, Dayne built a small enclosure and placed apples, cured meat and an old blanket in the narrow opening. He crawled inside with the nub and the kitten.

Huddled tight in Lauch's ill fit coat, Dayne tried to gather but flinched at every sound or hint of movement.

No air moved, only the taint of hog tallow from the candle. Restless yet confined, soon he shivered and grim grayness grew as the candle waned.

Sadness stirred. Gert's presence and his father's strength always controlled. Darkness, death and perhaps the stranger took both away. Unsettled loss and uncertain change, the end of what Dayne knew. For the first time he doubted the promise of dawn.

Unwilling to cease, bound and swallowed by fear, Dayne pushed out of the shelter and breathed deep, fitful. Strange new light beckoned from the front passage. Wary, he slid forward.

Three candles marked the ground at the far end of the narrow alcove near the drink room door. The flickered light enticed with presence, perhaps the stranger or his father, or perhaps a trap. Dayne thought to retreat but loneliness and need lured him ahead.

Beyond the candles a large wood object dimmed by shadow blocked the passage. Dayne recognized it too late. Lauch's death box, lid askew across the top.

Dayne stopped. The sacks still blocked the door. He was caught once again.

Chirps. Faint at first then closer and louder, the hopeful sounds of a young bird lonely for its companion, its family, itself.

The calls nestled deep within Dayne and he replied in kind. Not the anguished cries and snorts which sometimes welled his throat but streams of word sounds, deep emotions bright and raw.

The chirps quickened, beckoned, drew. They always did.

Dayne continued, willing and needful of heart. A shape moved and blended blackness at the passage corner. Instinct and memory screamed and warned yet Dayne would not heed. He wanted only to feel and end his quiet, his voice joined with his brother's, life new and changed forever.

The chirps stopped. Dayne's calls dwindled, disappointed. Abandonment reared ugly, sharp. Confusion and failure surged.

He set the carved root and black flint on the ground in offering, equal parts him and his brother. Anxious silence throttled his breaths. Belief faded. Resentment burned.

Eyes and ears strained, in vain Dayne chirped alone. Desperate anguished pleas shouted forward and back across time, ancient and near. No answer except the mock of his mother's cruel cackle from the neck cameo.

The farm boy from the burned cabin stepped into the dim halo of the candles behind the coffin. Sad, lonely eyes spoke inner pain and absence Dayne knew too well.

"One day you will fill a forever box," the boy said. "It takes a long time for the stink to go away."

The words caught Dayne's ear. The sound of his voice unhid and open, unafraid. Before with his father he heard only hints, tastes he could not unravel.

The boy fingered the black arrowhead and shifted it between hands. "Mine. I found it first. You know that."

He pawed the carved root and smiled wicked. "You never see me right. And your hands are poor, can't shape the truth. Will stay undone, like us."

Dayne and the boy briefly touched each other's face. Familiar strangers, brothers. Dayne saw his eyes, his mouth, himself. Wonder. Remembrance. Separation. Loss.

His brother darkened. "I should have been you. Not right. Not fair."

Dayne often wondered why only he survived, continued. Fate, chance, coincidence, choice. None explained it. Or all did. He did not know if his long years of quiet, guilt and silent torment were his own or shared. He groaned for both of them, a strangled awful sound from deep within.

His brother sneered. Snarls and snorts echoed Dayne's pain, his failed voice. "You let me die. You took what was mine. You still do."

Punished, Dayne turned away.

The attack came swift.

His brother pounded Dayne's head with the root and his other hand crushed Dayne's throat. Stunned, Dayne wrenched and twisted until free and tried to breathe.

His brother laughed, jealous fury, and forced him to the ground. Ancient grudge, death and decay, oozed between them.

"Soon you will be like me and wander all alone, forgotten and unwanted. It makes me happy." His brother sat on Dayne's chest and chirped loud, triumphant.

Legs scissored, Dayne pried him backward and climbed upright. He circled taut and wary, chided the foolish notion his brother would ever forgive. Hate and blood emotion girded his muscles. He charged.

They wrestled, grabbed, bit and scraped as so many times before. No escape, no refuge, no quarter. Neither would win yet neither stopped. Ageless adversaries, timeless foes. Twins.

Each used guile, cunning. At times his brother looked wistful, ashamed. At others he spit hate, cruelty and wrath. Dayne replied in kind, the gall of survival.

A prey beast pressing for advantage, his brother edged sly back and forth. He leapt forward, pushed Dayne to the ground and with a fallen candle seared his cheek.

Caught in a stranglehold, Dayne fingered the dirt for the arrowhead and sliced his brother's forehead and nose to break free.

His brother's mouth curled menace as he bled. "Weakling. You cannot rid me. Now or ever."

Dayne shook his head fierce, defiant.

His brother receded into the cellar dark.

Exhausted and heaving, burned flesh harsh in his nose, Dayne waited. He did not trust any longer. Bruised, scratched and battered he dropped slow, knees to the ground, and closed his eyes. For a time he struggled to stay within himself but soon faded and drifted uncaring.

Maybe he would wake up. Maybe he would not.

◑

In forlorn shadows near the tavern bar the Innkeeper listened to the creaks and groans of his house. The end came. Too much weight. Too much burden. Nature at last exacted its toll.

Empty iron leg shackles on the blanket in the corner needled, a wicked taunt. Was the tinker's fault. All of it. Ire and resentment gritted his throat.

He tried to enter the cellar but the door refused despite his shoulder hard against the wood. "Dayne! Dayne! The tinker is loose. Hide yourself. Let not him touch you."

With the rifle butt the Innkeeper pounded the door, mind blurred. Dayne's vacant room upstairs worried and he knew no other place his son would be. Worse, perhaps the tinker blocked the cellar in order to open its rear door for marauders.

He tried the stubborn wood a second time, failed and turned from the bar. At a corner table near the piled freight he filled a bucket with firing hammers removed from muskets stacked alongside. Destruction bettered bare concealment and he would leave no benefit for the Beast.

Stiffened hands trembled and ached regardless of his will and curled into misshapen fists, stricken for unclear reason like his farm and life. Years of toil, plan and careful avoidance and neutrality mattered not.

The weapons decided it. What they carried, what they would cause forced the final choice and molded his fate. The valley would not survive his failure to act. Yet an unfair outcome even if purposed, unquestioned, his reluctant price. He clutched tight, deep in his beard.

The Peddler came down the steps. "You ponder hard. Unhappy."

"It started with you." The Innkeeper carried a small keg of powder past him to the steps for use upstairs.

"No. I only end it." Crossed to the hearth, the Peddler stilled the pendulum on its mantel clock.

"Leave the clock be."

"A reminder. Time stops for all. Nature's curse. Its blessing."

The Innkeeper pried floor boards loose with the scalping knife from his belt. The old wood groaned brittle, mournful in stubborn yield. He dropped the bucket of hammers to exposed ground and emptied kegs of gun powder and casks of rum. Black dust and drink spill stained his breeches, boots and arms. The grim taint rankled.

"Your bitter pus," said the Peddler. "Seize it. Let your spirit bleed."

"I spite you."

"Then finish."

The Innkeeper grumbled. Behind the bar counter he unlocked cabinets, carried tavern casks to the corner hole and violently ruptured each with the rifle butt and knife. Drink and staves spilled into the dark chasm and rum, ale and powder swirled, smothered. His fingers and mouth twitched with familiar temptation and surrender, desire and failure, timeless scar and reminder. Each pour drew him to one knee, rage and fury at his weakness driven by desperate longing for refuge and taste.

Caught between, he paused over the last cask. Mind winced shut, he shuddered defiant and drained the foulness.

Odd quiet, respite followed. Residue dripped his rigid fingers.

He asked reluctant, without looking up. "My older son. Was it I?"

"Late sprouts your heart."

"Tell me."

"Doubt is a wicked thorn. Vexing. Useful."

The Peddler dropped the leg irons into the floor opening. "Bury all your stink."

The Innkeeper toed the last piece of cask into the hole, reset the floor boards and pounded crooked nails. Sudden dismay clutched. His secret filth finally poisoned the land, the best part of him.

Anger, resentment ground tight the Innkeeper's jaw. "You come unneeded, unwanted. An ill summons."

"This earth weeps, bespoiled from choices made, paths followed. Needed cleansing."

"Why hunt the farm?"

"Is not the farm I seek."

The Innkeeper slammed his fist on the table and stared hard. "Then why hunt me?"

Head cocked curious, the Peddler scratched beside his mouth. "Your day is over. Yield."

Rifle raised, the Innkeeper's finger curled the trigger. "Said I would kill you first. We finish my way. No more gypsy guile."

The Peddler stared blunt, almost sad, and angled his forehead flat against the rifle bore. "Our dance continues. Unashamed."

The Peddler kept his head at the barrel. "Fear or flaw? Fate or fortune? Mine or yours?"

His voice quickened. "Pull or not pull. What say you, brother? Speak it. Speak it loud."

Tremors palsied the Innkeeper's grip and the rifle barrel wavered more than he wanted. You bait me."

"No need. Even now, righteous in anger, you shake unsure."

Blackness crowded the Innkeeper's sight. Enraged yet stymied and confused, he blinked and screamed inward at failed hands, failed strength. Deep snarl throttled, scoured his throat and his finger jerked the trigger. The hammer clicked forward, the primer pan flashed and the rifle recoiled hard against his shoulder.

Too late. All of it. The Peddler's arm swept the barrel aside an instant before and the bullet splintered into the steps beyond. Drift of black smoke and burned powder marred the air.

The Peddler clapped once, joyless, and spread rag covered hands. "An untimely sputter."

"Black magic."

Rifle snatched away, the tinker dismissed it to the floor and turned toward his blanket.

The Innkeeper lunged and with both hands drove the scalping knife deep into the angle of the Peddler's neck and shoulder. A second blow sliced the back of the frock coat and the blade glistened black ooze.

The tinker staggered, straightened. Annoyed, he turned slow and rotated his shoulder. "Who is the savage beast now? You wield death too easy."

Fury and hate pinched the Innkeeper's voice. "You will not have my house."

He again sliced ruthless with the knife. The Peddler blocked each blow and forced the angry blade edge tight against the Innkeeper's bearded throat.

Accustomed to physical dominance, the Innkeeper struggled surprised and in vain. He twisted and turned, pushed and pulled but the Peddler held fast. A brief stalemate, an illusion of control, a cruel tease.

The Peddler hissed soft, close. "Where is your strength, Keeper? I thought you more stubborn. Show me your wile."

The Innkeeper growled. "Thief. Taker."

"Of the worst kind." The Peddler released the knife.

Wrenched off balance, the Innkeeper fell backward over a freight box. His head and back cracked hard against the floor and the blade fell useless from numb hands. He arched frantic for breath but the Peddler straddled his chest and pinned his arms.

The Innkeeper strained to reach the pistol butts in his belt but the gypsy threw the guns across the floor toward the steps, grasped the Innkeeper's jaw and forced open his mouth.

"Taste now your bitter rind. Both sons did." The Peddler's nubbed finger smeared spilled ale and gun powder across the Innkeeper's cheek and gums. He gagged and spit.

"Fight," said the Peddler. "Struggle harder. Be worthy."

Tongue curled around the tainted finger, the tinker smeared once more. "Again."

The Innkeeper heaved and arched but did not break free. Awareness blurred and strength waned. Darkness dimmed his sight and crept shadows foretold. He did not know what it would be to cease. Unforgiving oblivion and eternal banishment from his farm made no sense, held no purpose. He refused.

"The lesson of the seasons, Keeper. The harsh truth of the cauldron." The Peddler rose and turned toward the hearth.

Rolled to one side, the Innkeeper coughed blood into his beard and looked for the pistols. Legs unable to push, his arms pulled his misshapen body across the cold scrape of floor to the steps. He reached for the first gun.

Stepped past him, the Peddler clicked his tongue and moved both pistols to the fifth step. "Earn the right to feed."

The Innkeeper groaned ire. Grimaced, he willed himself up the first two steps, gathered pained legs underneath and reached again.

Perched on the fifth step, the Peddler placed a candle nub and three bent nails beside the pistols. "To succor your journey."

The Innkeeper squinted at the evil goads. Guilt, torment and memories, sounds unwanted flooded and choked. His shaking fingers grasped the candle.

"A telling choice," the Peddler said.

The Innkeeper struggled to speak. "My life is my own. All of it. I make no excuse."

The candle fell from his hand, rolled slow across and fell down each step to the floor. He reached but knocked the powder keg off and it cracked on the floor.

The Peddler retrieved the Indian broom from beneath his blanket and set its end into the fire at the hearth.

An unexpected chance. Brief, final hope surged the Innkeeper. He fumbled one pistol to the floor and took the other. Barely able to cock the hammer, he twisted and fired wild. Recoiled off balance, he toppled backward and slid upside down on the lower step into the dark stain of powder.

The Peddler sneered. "You learn nothing."

He approached with the flaming broom. Leaned close, his nose almost touched and his long fingernail flicked the Innkeeper's beard. He dallied two bent nails, ground them in his fist and iron dust fell across the Innkeeper's face.

"Poison seed," the Peddler said. "Choke on it."

Images of Gert, Lauch, Dayne and his nameless son in a bloodied blanket choked the Innkeeper. He squirmed, mouth filled by blood and bile.

Fiery broom whirled in a wide circle overhead, the Peddler confronted and demanded. "Who am I? Who am I?"

The Innkeeper's head shook in final rage, refusal. An apparition at the bar corner, a faint glow of light, sparked hope and belief without reason, the uncertain plea of life's end. Dayne.

Continuance.

The flame came forward, relentless.

Spare the boy. The words burst the Innkeeper's throat, longed for and needed affirmation. Yet he gagged for sound, voice.

The plea strangled on itself, unheard.

CHAPTER TWENTY-ONE

Maybe Dayne dreamed.

Black stillness surrounded. He floated unsure and uncaring where or what he was and gorged needy on the quiet absence of feeling and emotion. Ancient currents of change and renewal, paths old and new, drifted by and through. Peaceful surround filled him all. No time, no memory. No fear, no hurt.

Faint sound gathered, grew deep within. Distant drum beats, life rhythm. Presence, wisps and colored specks came close, curious. Dim awareness nudged patient, stubborn. Dayne paid no heed. He had no hurry, wanted none.

Yet the life rhythms continued, took him. Hints of new warmth and the birth of being formed within. Nature at work.

Eye opened, Dayne lay on one side. Deep earth sound rumbled thick rock close at his face and harsh prods notched his back. Marks on the stone showed the passage of many beings, many lives. Two similar stick figures etched beside each other drew his finger. He traced both shapes and the rough skin of the rock.

Dayne sat up in damp grayness. Animal bones and charred rocks bedded the ground and water rushed down crusted layers of white ice across a narrow cave-like entrance. The insistent flow embraced and soothed, a familiar clutch.

Dayne peeked reluctant around a corner of the ice into the bright glare of sunlight. Snow mounds covered barren woods and a partly frozen stream.

He did not want the outside, did not want to give up the den. Eyes closed, Dayne wished only to again drift free and content in the safety of stillness, unburdened, un-beset. The pretend did not last. His heart pushed stubborn, persistent. He had no choice but to renew.

Crawled from his cocoon, Dayne stretched into his body and stood stiff, open and exposed, unsure of his place. An ill fit hide coat did not dull sharp, intrusive cold and he shivered as he pushed through deep drifts among boulders beside the stream. Overhead loomed a massive high rock ledge, its ancient dents and staggered waterfalls iced veils of solemn tears beneath watchful, sad eyes.

Large animal sign broke snow along the stream bank but no people tracks. At the melted area around a hot spring he lingered in warm, rising vapors. Water sound and the shroud of icy stillness quelled Dayne's unease.

The black arrowhead sat on the snow crust for him to find. Bits of violent images flashed and his hand reached, stopped, reached again. Disturbance and fear bubbled Dayne's throat and piercing, hungry cold crept his spine.

Young bird chirps wafted on the breeze and he turned. Across the stream a large bear watched poised, intent behind purposed hunter's eyes. Despite blunt strength and presence the bear seemed hesitant, burdened and confused, pained by a dark unwanted nature.

The bear growled low and charged forward bold into the stream.

Dayne fled toward the upper bank. Against stubborn drifts and unseen rock barriers he dug and clawed, grabbed a tree limb and pulled himself forward and up. The branch snapped and he fell, scoured by the snow's icy grit. Sight briefly lost, he struggled to his feet and wheeled to defend with the jagged limb.

A young farm boy stood on the near side of the stream but moved no closer, content to frighten and remind.

Lonely, sad eyes beckoned but his sly, mocking mouth betrayed hidden hate, menace. Fresh scars marred his forehead and nose. Hands lifted open in guileful gesture, the farm boy moved closer.

Shadow, uncertainty and a bitter taste of self squeezed Dayne's heart. But weakness gave way to fear and anger. He would run no longer.

Arrowhead clenched between his teeth, he growled defiant and unwilling, the broken limb wielded in a fierce circle above his head.

The farm boy stopped, grinned knowing and backed toward the water.

Flint spit out, Dayne heaved cold air. He wanted an end, knew it would not come. Paths remained with the boy and the bear. Twisted, bound, unchanged.

On the far side of the stream an imposing, bearded man looked back brief and turned among trees and thickets. Unexplained hurt and loss tugged at Dayne.

He threw the black arrowhead high and far and it disappeared into the snow mass. The dark goad would find him again.

Dayne turned and confronted a narrow, crooked valley. No chill wind bothered and sharp open sky dwarfed the bristled gray rise of a mountain opposite. Unsure what awaited, he swam forward into the white pond.

◗

Dayne awoke.

Empty grayness rimmed his sight but faded slow into faint colors. He blinked, gradual and unsure awareness.

On his side on the ground, rough-hewn boards and an overturned milk stool blocked close at his face. Snaps of sharp cornstalks nettled his back and cold breaths rasped his throat. Dirty straw and thick barn smells swirled familiar, surprise comforts, and he recognized the stall of the Welsh Red cow. Dayne reached out to touch, feel and make sure he lived.

Dried blood creased his bruised, scarred hands and swollen fingers. Deep aches stiffened his arms and legs. He did not know why. An owl feather and broken piece of young turtle shell lay together on the ground.

A large animal's low rumble intruded. Fear, dismay and a gut instinct to flee quickened Dayne's heart. He rolled over slow, pushed quick to his knees and wielded the stool as a shield.

Jerusalem's strong neck and head towered above, dark eyes solemn and guarded. The mule sniffed and stepped back from the stall gate.

Dayne rose, limped into the barn corridor on a battered leg and breathed full, grateful, confused. The large freight wagons loomed hushed, empty in gray quiet. Across the corridor the open door on the gentleman's coach waited expectant.

Dayne's hand traced the shattered wheel on the rear wagon and hovered over the dark stain of gun powder on the ground. Blurred wisps of prior events surrounded, needled pain and loss. Dayne refused to look past the coach toward the mule's stall.

No memory told how he came to the barn. He recalled only parts of his flight to the cellar, fearsome struggles against cruel unknown hands, and empty darkness. Later a faint light drew him close and vague feelings and sounds, perhaps words and perhaps not, drifted past and through.

Daylight filtered past planks in the barn wall. Door shouldered open against heavy snow drifts, he winced in bright glare and stepped into the barn yard.

Black smoke wafted from gouged and ruptured earth on the hillside. Spiked timbers collapsed inward like remains of a slaughtered beast, the inn's charred ruins smoldered over strewn foundation rock. Remnants of the drink room hearth and chimney pointed a jagged stone finger angry against the sky. Shattered basement walls resembled sparse, rotten teeth on an old hog jawbone. Scattered broken pieces of the inn and cellar pocked and littered the snow.

Dayne quivered side to side, caught between past and present, stunned by the unexpected destruction of all he knew. Burned powder smell drifted harsh, without pity on his eyes and nose. No light lingered in the ruins and he sifted no presence of his father, Gert or the others.

The sad woman rose from a large building stone thrown beside the fence, injured arm in a makeshift shawl sling and other hand protective across her stomach.

Tattered and torn, face bruised, she peered surprised at Dayne. "Nature is strange. What it takes, what it leaves."

The woman approached. "I am sorry for your family. For you. For all of it."

Dayne's unspoken question answered. His home and family ended, ceased. Life's simple familiar peeled away, replaced for the hurt and chance of continuance. A steep price, lonely and uneven.

He turned. Across the yard the large tree used to hoist the hogs splintered to one side near the toppled, snow buried cauldron. At the smoke house beyond, chickens clucked and searched for feed near dead companions.

Mounted militia approached up the front road and entered the side yard. Stubborn plough blades, the horses' chests pushed aside deep snow.

The militia leader pulled a crusted scarf from his face. "We saw the smoke this morning from the river. What happened?"

"Gun powder and arms were taken into the inn," said the woman. "Contraband wagons full. Rumor held the Beast was come this way for the supply. Disputes arose on what to do. A giant blast decided it."

"The Beast turned east toward Schoharie," the leader said. "The storm stopped him short and he left the valley. A narrow escape."

He surveyed the rubble. "This inn was strong built, sturdy. The Keeper even stronger. How is it you survived?"

The woman blinked slow. "I do not know."

"And the boy?"

"He was spared. Was meant to be so."

The leader turned his horse. "I continue up the mountain road but will leave some men here for comfort and aid."

He stopped and looked back. "We found the prison wagon not far from here. Overturned, cage open, Thaler and his men felled and scalped clean. An ambush, likely. But be aware. War parties may still roam."

He directed three men to stay and returned to the road with the others.

Dayne struggled across yard drifts and from the snow picked up the cow bell on its torn rope collar. Awkward legs upright and underbelly exposed, the body of the Welsh Red lay not far away. There would be no spring calf. His father's great hope and bargain, taken and lost.

Inside the basement walls remnants of the cellar and drink room piled blast ravaged ground. Red inked paper shifted with the breeze and Dayne briefly retrieved the gentleman's cracked spectacles. Nearby he found the cane walker's snapped silver headed stick. Memory of its constant annoyed tap drummed Dayne's ears. He would miss neither man.

Without need to see what his heart knew, he went no further. His father, Gert and the kitten hid somewhere in the rubble and would stay so. Emptiness took his gut. Loss. Regret. Struggle. Survival.

Dayne did not understand life. He only knew that he lived.

Water trickle perked his ears. Among remains of cellar vegetables and crates the spring gurgled from its rock ledge, open to the sun. Dayne knelt and dipped his marred hands in its cold embrace.

Faded white cloth fluttered the ground at his feet and he touched his tattered, bloodied birth clout. Beneath the cloth the black arrowhead gleamed. Frightful images, sounds and sharp emotions crackled and shuddered but vanished as quick, lost in time. He clutched the clout to his hands and rose but reached back for the flint. His renewal, his curse. He would show both to his brother.

Dayne looked across snow mounded farm fields. Bright sunlight sparkled their icy crust, welcome reminder of what often followed a storm's hate and fury. Hid under cold husks nature's secret waited for those who believed, endured.

His fields. His future and past together, separate. Many times. Many lives.

Farther up on the ridgeline the wolf waited patient, ever watchful. Turned among barren trees, it blended back into the forest.

Dayne's voice came clear, strong. Certain.

"Father."

AFTERWORD

DOUGLAS MARTIN was a practicing attorney for twenty-five years, though his passions were writing and history. *Hands of an Angry God* was the melding of both passions.

The author passed away before his dream of publishing this book could be realized. He worked on *Hands of an Angry God* for six years while simultaneously battling cancer. His one unfulfilled dream was that people would read and enjoy his writing. Thank you to the readers who have kept his dream alive.

— *P.E. Nowell*

www.ingramcontent.com/pod-product-compliance
Lightning Source LLC
Chambersburg PA
CBHW030313200626
46816CB00006BA/1766